D1554322

Cooper's Promise

Cooper's Promise

A Novel

Timothy Jay Smith

Owl Canyon Press

First Edition, 2011

All Rights Reserved

Library of Congress Cataloging-in-Publication Data

Smith, Timothy Jay.

Cooper's Promise —1st ed.

p. cm.

ISBN: 780983476436

2012939610

Owl Canyon Press

Boulder, Colorado

For Michael

1

The rain turned to steam as soon as it hit the ground, or so it seemed to Cooper as he ran down the street, stopping only long enough to help a woman load a box onto a pickup truck before dashing off again. He heard a girl shout from a doorway, "You going to see Little Sister, American Cooper?" and he turned around to run backward, water splashing at his heels as he spread his hands, silently asking, *What choice do I have?*

The girl flashed her white teeth in a big smile. A second prostitute, the same young age as the first, cried out, "Why you go all that way, American Cooper, when you got a Little Sister right here?"

Their laughter trailed him all the way to The Mining Pan. When he pushed through the saloon doors, everyone in the bar, by a discreet glance or hiccup in their conversation, took note of his entrance. Staying alert is how you survived in Lalanga, but by the time the doors stopped swinging behind him, Cooper's small ripple effect had already passed through the room, and he made his way to the long bar. The storm had knocked out the power, and water streamed in through the damaged roof where a mortar shell had landed during the last rebel offensive—if one mortar shell and two dead drunks merited being called an offensive—but no one seemed worried about the puddle creeping across the floor, certainly not the men preoccupied with fixing themselves up with a girl. They had more pressing matters than rain puddles and civil wars on their minds.

Cooper brushed water from his buzz cut but didn't have a sleeve to wipe off his face. He'd torn those off his army-issued shirt as soon as he'd arrived in the godforsaken country and felt its waterlogged air. He slid onto a barstool and ordered. "A G and T, Juma, and this time, try to remember the ice."

The barman, his eyes bloodshot from the perfumed smoke perpetually hanging around his head, took a hit off a joint before handing it back to a customer. "Americans always want too much ice," he complained. Juma was tall, with a shaved head and a pirate's gold-loop earring.

Cooper swiveled his head to the left and right. "If you're worried about running short, I don't see a lot of my compatriots around."

Juma scooped some cubes into a glass from the wheezing ice machine. "Too much ice makes the gin no good."

"It's no good anyway."

"It's distilled properly for our weather."

"You got that right; it sucks and leaves you thirsty."

The barman passed him his drink, and Cooper took a long swallow. He knew he'd been in Lalanga too long when the flat tonic and gunpowdery gin had started to taste good. Rolling the cold glass across his forehead, he swung around on his seat to check out the room. The usual hookers and thieves were there, but no Lulay. She called herself Lucy for the johns, but he preferred her real name: Lulay.

When the power flickered back on, Juma plugged a coin into the jukebox so his girls could keep their johns dancing between drinking. Conversations grew brighter. There was raucous laughter from a corner where a couple of sotted Thick Necks, holed up at a table, were pawing two girls and grabbing the asses of any others who came within range. Cooper had seen the oilmen's whole whiskey-and-groping scene so many times it felt exponential. He assumed they were oilmen; as far as he knew, no other white men had remained in the country except for oilmen, and every one of them seemed to have a thick neck.

He swung back around so as not to see them but couldn't help looking in the mirror running the length of the bar when one of the Thick Necks started banging his bottle on the table to order a second. Cooper recognized him from his fancy moustache, twisted at the ends like a dandy's—though as acne-scarred as he was, he was hardly a dandy. Rarely without the stump of a cigar clenched between his teeth, he had a habit of getting very drunk and more than a little rough with the girls.

"Must be payday," Cooper remarked.

Juma pulled a bottle off the shelf. "They're celebrating," he said.

"What's to celebrate?"

"They found oil."

"Sure they did. Just like the last time and the ten times before that."

"This time," Sam Brown said, sliding onto the next barstool, "it's been confirmed by experts." He wasn't brown but black, and not African but American—soul patch included—and he had scars on his cheeks that could have been mistaken for tribal marks if they'd been more symmetrical. He had started showing up at the bar two weeks earlier and had become a regular pain in the ass, acting like they should be friends, both being Americans and all.

Cooper didn't bother to look at him when he asked, "What the fuck do you want?"

"They have nice girls in here, or haven't you noticed?"

At that moment Lulay splashed her way out through the tinkling beaded curtain. Behind it was a labyrinth of rooms that offered mattresses and little privacy. An almond-eyed beauty with skin the color of a dark nut, she had every man's attention as she headed straight for the bar, where Juma held out a glass of ice water for her. She popped her bubblegum as she reached for it, and he nodded discreetly at a fat man sitting alone in a booth. Lulay glanced around at him. Cooper did too. He didn't want to think of Lulay going with the fat man, but he knew she would; he knew they'd be together. It was something he couldn't stop, not every time, not without enough money to buy Lulay a free hour, let alone all her hours.

"She's a pretty one, for instance," Sam Brown commented.

"She's a kid."

"She's still pretty."

Cooper knew if he said anything more, about how it wasn't right to look at kids in that way, they'd probably come to blows, and coming to blows with Sam Brown wouldn't change Lulay's foul circumstances. He'd only manage to get himself exiled from the bar. Juma had strict rules about not causing trouble.

Lulay drank her glass of water slowly, rattling the ice in it, buying herself some time. She touched her hair and straightened her skirt and snuggled her toes in her flip flops to make them fit tighter as she crossed the room. Cooper knew that she knew he was watching her by the way she sashayed her bottom, exaggerating her own pigeon-toed way of walking before sliding onto the bench across from the fat john. He seemed genuinely surprised that she had appeared and quickly called out a drink order. Lulay accepted his offer of a cigarette and lit it with his. Once it caught, she swiveled around and blew smoke directly at Cooper—fiercely, in Lucy's angry way.

Cooper stood to leave, pulling moldy bills from a pocket in his cutoffs and stacking them on the bar. "You leave too much money," the barman said while making no effort to hand it back.

"Buy Lulay some bubblegum, will you?"

He'd stepped away when Sam Brown said behind him, "Aren't you going to say good-bye ... *Sergeant?*"

Cooper stopped, swallowed hard, and turned around slowly. He remembered the first time he'd seen Sam Brown, when he'd caught him staring at him in the long mirror. He had glanced up and Sam Brown hadn't looked away. That's why Cooper had always suspected that he'd come looking for him, and there certainly were enough reasons why someone might. "You got a reason for calling me that?"

"You just look the part, with your half uniform and all."

"I bought it at a half-price shop."

"Sounds like you could use somebody to buy you a whole drink."

"I thought you preferred little girls."

"Maybe we should finally talk business."

"I don't want any business with you."

Cooper turned on his heels to maneuver past sodden dancers before pushing his way out the saloon doors. A cheer went up as he did, and he glanced back to see the Thick Necks boisterously toasting each other. The fat man was disappearing behind the beaded curtain close on Lulay's heels, and where they'd been sitting, another girl and her john now shared the booth.

The monsoon had left behind heavy droplets to ping on Langatown's ubiquitous tin roofs. After such a thorough washing, Cooper almost liked the place. The peeling colors seemed brighter, the streets cleaner, the people cheerier. It was all illusion, of course; like a shower after a long trip, the rains refreshed Langatown without curing its essential exhaustion. When the last rainbow had dissolved, men would still be leaning against their bicycle taxis, hoping for someone to need a ride home, and the maimed—the lucky minority who had survived indecent wounds—would still be waiting patiently next to their almsmen's cups for pity's coins.

Mud had camouflaged the potholes, slowing traffic to more of a crawl than usual, and the rain's lingering freshness soon dissipated in the onslaught of exhaust fumes. Cooper ducked into the side streets, where he came across women slapping laundry on porches or picking through fruits or doing other chores. His presence brought a look of alarm to their faces, and automatically they glanced around for their menfolk and children, making sure none of mining or fighting age could be spotted. That left only the very young and very old, and the women who risked their own forced conscription by staying behind to care for them.

The drainage ditch that coursed the middle of the unpaved lane had overflowed from the rain, and Cooper dodged its effluent until it—and he—spilled onto the wharf and its tangle of vendors and beggars. Women manned most of the stands, and their hawking cries were the stuff of gospel riffs, birdsongs, and fishwives. A ways beyond the hubbub, a yacht Cooper had not seen before was docking. He didn't know yachts from sputniks, but compared to the other hulks floating—or in some cases, sinking—in the bay, this yacht was long, sleek, and low-slung, with a polished black hull, dark-tinted windows, and a sophisticated radar rotating atop the bridge while the throaty chug of the engine hinted at her power. Two crewmen had perched themselves fore and aft waiting for the captain to swing the yacht around, and when he did, Cooper could read her name on the stern.

African Lady.

The crewman in the prow successfully leaped onto the wharf, but lashing the yacht too quickly to the dock, he caused the man aft to stumble and miss his chance to hop ashore. The yacht, suddenly caught by one of the renegade currents that plagued the bay, started to swing away from the dock where she was hooked by her nose. "Hey!" the man aft shouted, and flung his coiled line to Cooper, who caught it and pulled the yacht in. The crewman jumped off, and taking the line from Cooper, gave him a causal high five.

Both crewmen were members of the Cool Tribe, or so Cooper had dubbed the hotshot guys with their mirrored sunglasses and flamboyant shirts, and swaggers that suggested they were immune to the horrors that stalked everyone else. He'd seen their type around, usually buying provisions, sometimes cruising the bars on Cowboy Mile, and wondered where the Cool Tribe came from. Now he knew at least some of them came from the *African Lady*. Wondering where she came from, he examined her flag and didn't recognize whatever obscure country it represented.

COOPER'S PROMISE

Cooper didn't know much about boats. He hadn't seen the ocean until he'd turned eighteen and enlisted and was sent to California for boot camp. So he was curious about boats and hung around the *African Lady* to watch the crewmen retie their lashings, hang rubber bumpers, and secure a gangplank. The captain, another member of the Cool Tribe, eventually appeared on the bridge and climbed a ladder down to the deck. Before ducking into the cabin he upbraided the crewman who had tied off his line too quickly. The crewman shot Cooper a hostile look as if it were his fault and asked, "You want something?"

Walking off, Cooper had to shield his eyes from the hot light reflecting off the water. Wide-beamed fishing boats bobbed offshore, and along a concrete dock, rusty cranes loomed over the hulls of cargo ships swarmed by workers blackened by sun as much as by birth. Some worked for free hauling exhausting freight while praying for someone else to fall victim to malaria so a job would open up. At day's end they'd likely be shooed off, but maybe not all of them, maybe there *would* be a malarial victim; and every man strove to prove he had any job's qualifications: strong back, quick on his feet, a noncomplainer.

The buildings strung along the waterfront dated from an earlier era when commerce was more gracious. An arcaded boardwalk ran for two long blocks, the shops festooned with gingerbread and painted incongruous pastel colors. Cooper mounted its steps and passed storefronts occupied by indolent shipping clerks smoking foul beedies, others by diamond dealers with their weighing scales and iron safes, sipping mint tea and waiting for the infrequent client—buyer or seller, it didn't matter; their business was trade.

In his pocket Cooper rolled together two stones that could have been chunks of driveway gravel. Nothing made them diamonds as he'd grown up thinking diamonds to be—sharp-edged and sparkling—but they were diamonds all right. He survived by buying rough stones sneaked out of the mines by children and reselling them for profits that were good even at the start of a diamond's brilliant journey. Profitable enough for Cooper to rent a lousy room with a torn mosquito net and unreliable overhead fan, which was the best that Langatown had to offer.

As Cooper approached the open door of al-Basma Diamonds, he thought he saw Mazen al-Basma bent over the safe behind a ceiling-high cage that bisected the room, but when he stepped inside, it turned out to be a youth whom Cooper guessed to be Mazen's son. He resembled his father, tall and thin with thick, curly black hair (though his father's had streaks of gray), and the same handsome beaked nose. But the son was a shade darker, a café latte color, and a trim black beard accentuated his angular face whereas his father was clean-shaven. Mazen had spoken proudly of his boy in Beirut, and he *was* a boy if not yet being twenty made him one. Cooper himself wasn't much older.

The youth discreetly slipped a display tray back into the safe and nudged it closed. "May I help you?"

"You must be Sadiq."

"I am."

"Your father said you were coming home."

"He seems to have told everybody." It was only a half-hearted complaint; obviously the boy had been flattered by the attention. He stepped out of the cage to ask, "Do you have business with my father?"

Cooper had never sold diamonds to anyone but Mazen before. He liked the older man, who seemed honest and was certainly affable enough, and his plum-colored shop, with its slowly revolving ceiling fan, was always a welcomed relief from the sun-stricken streets. His son too seemed trustworthy; perhaps it was his faint English accent that contributed to that impression.

"I have these," Cooper said, displaying the two stones in his palm. "Do you know diamonds?"

The boy laughed, and that's when Cooper noticed his eyes. Lapis blue and veined with gray, they might have been precious stones if they were not so alive. "My family only knows diamonds," he replied, and bowing grandiosely added, "I am Sadiq al-Basma, the grandson of many grandsons of diamond dealers."

Cooper stuck out his hand. "I'm Cooper Chance."

When they released their clasp, Sadiq briefly touched his heart. "Will you take a tea?" he asked. "Or no, you're an American, you'll want coffee. I have learned about your national addiction."

"Do you really have coffee?"

"I'm afraid I have become addicted as well." Sadiq held up a small bag. "I have come home prepared, though I have only Arabic coffee, not American."

"As long as it's strong and spells caffeine," Cooper replied.

Sadiq stepped over to a small table holding his father's tea-making equipment and spooned finely ground coffee into a spouted copper pot. He lit a gas burner under it. Again Cooper was reminded of the boy's father who, like the legions of Lebanese middlemen in Lalanga's diamond trade, couldn't conduct business without first serving sugary mint tea in stubby glasses.

"To call me an addict is an understatement," Cooper admitted, "and there is no good coffee in Langatown. Half the time it tastes like ground-up nuts."

"Half the time it *is* ground-up nuts," Sadiq told him.

At that moment Mazen entered, who smiled broadly the instant he saw Cooper. "*Mas salaam*," he greeted him. "I see you have met my son!"

"You must be glad that he's finally home."

"A father is always happy to have his son come home!"

"I'll try to remember to remind my father the next time I see him."

"Will you take a tea?"

"I've already made him coffee, Father," Sadiq said, while pouring it between two demitasses.

Mazen rolled his eyes at Cooper. "I'm afraid my son has come home with some radical ideas."

Sadiq set the cups on a small table that held a jeweler's scale and gooseneck lamp. "Coffee is hardly a radical idea. Besides, Mr. Chance prefers coffee, and the customer is always right."

"You see, you send your son away for some education, and he returns thinking he's smarter than you!"

"Please sit," Sadiq said to Cooper, "and show me your diamonds. Unless, Father, you would you prefer to help Mr. Chance yourself?"

"No, no, he's your customer, and I have other things to do."

What other things Cooper couldn't imagine as he sat opposite Sadiq. There was neither desk, paperwork, nor anything else in the small shop to engage the older man, and of course he hovered over them. Cooper sensed the boy's annoyance, and sipping from the small cup said, "The coffee is very good." He smiled, and hoped the youth understood that he was on his side.

Sadiq didn't say a word, but his bright eyes narrowed with a smile that showed he appreciated Cooper's remark. "So what do you have?" he asked.

Cooper slid the rough stones across the table, and Sadiq flicked on the lamp. After rubbing them hard with a chamois, he gave them a cursory examination to ascertain that Cooper had not, in fact, mistaken driveway gravel for diamonds. He weighed them before slipping on a loupe, and then balancing one of the stones on his fingertips, he nimbly turned it to peer into its heart. Cooper became mesmerized by how he rotated the stone, perched on his long fingers, touching it as little as possible to let more light enter.

"Where did you get these?" he asked, and picked up the second stone.

"They're legal," Cooper assured him.

Sadiq adjusted the lamp. "There are no legal diamonds in Lalanga," he remarked, "not according to the UN."

"The UN's not paying my rent."

Sadiq removed his loupe. "They have impurities," he said, and slid the stones across the table to Cooper.

Cooper slid them right back. "They all have impurities. That's why you have diamond cutters."

Again Sadiq passed back the stones, this time along with his loupe. "There are too many fracture lines. Look for yourself."

Cooper waved away the eyepiece. "I can never see anything with those things except my eyelashes all blown up."

Mazen reached around his son and plucked up the rough diamonds. "Cooper is a good customer."

"But, Father!" Sadiq protested.

"It's a good market for diamonds now, even for small ones." The older man rebuked his son and stepped inside the cage to take the cashbox from the safe. As he measured out money, Cooper tried to catch Sadiq's eye, who merely watched his father's movements with his lips pursed in annoyance.

Mazen returned and handed a wad of bills to Cooper. "Come back when you have more diamonds so Sadiq can practice his English."

"His English is already perfect."

"He can always improve."

Sadiq offered his hand. "Thank you, Mr. Chance."

"We can be friends if you call me Cooper." He held on to the youth's hand an extra moment to convey his hope that they would be.

Walking off, he heard father and son start to argue.

On the horizon, the sun flashed and disappeared. Cooper debated the merits of going home or back to The Mining Pan and decided it was too early for home. He tucked the wads of money deeper into his pockets and patted them flat, keeping enough loose bills handy to buy something to eat. He settled on two cornmeal pasties wrapped in banana leaves, hotly spiced, and was licking up the last of the paprika when he came alongside the *African Lady*. The two crewmen were slouched against her guardrails drinking from longnecks, while from belowdecks came the sounds of a raucous party that reminded Cooper too much of The Mining Pan. He decided he needed a night off from bar life and aimed for home.

Night had fallen fast, and the town's streets, given over to the women during the day, were thick with men and boys who had emerged to conduct affairs too dangerous for the daylight when they risked conscription. Cook fires turned their jaundiced eyes even more yellow as they slipped past Cooper in a steady stream, leaving only glimpses of a bright cap or earring. Soon enough the touts honed in on him, offering to sell everything from their virgin sisters to bootlegged cigarettes. When he first arrived in Lalanga, Cooper had frequently hired one of the boys to show him a new way home, learning shortcuts through the tangled streets that he wouldn't have found on his own. He hadn't experienced a lot of the world, but he knew what a shortcut could be worth: his life.

His room was up a flight of steps in the back of a two-storey stucco building. The landlady lived below and did her best to keep it clean and functioning against the ravages of mold and tropical storms. A large mango tree loomed over the yard, and Cooper searched the ground hoping to find a fallen one. He did, and he pulled his knife from his boot, flicking it open to peel the leathery skin. The power had gone out, but the light from a perfect half-moon was bright enough to guide him up the steps. He realized that he didn't know if it was waxing or waning, when not many months earlier, moonlight had been the only light to spill across the Iraqi desert. Moonlight had factored into every nighttime mission.

From the landing, he tossed the mango pit into the yard. He licked his fingers as he walked inside. The room was stuffy. Cooper hated that. Whether hot or cold outside, he never closed his windows. He liked the air to be moving.

COOPER'S PROMISE

He rinsed his knife at the tap and took a couple of swallows from a beer he pulled from his half-size fridge. He set the bottle next to his bed, slipped his knife under the pillow, and flicked a switch so the ceiling fan would come on when the power returned.

He pissed, took a shower, and without drying off returned to the room dripping a trail of water. He fell back onto the bed and, arms wide open, offered himself to the fan if only it would come on. The Bushmen, he'd read, lie in holes in the desert lined with dried squash husks that they've pissed on, waiting for it to evaporate and cool them off. That night, Cooper would have opted for Bushman air conditioning over the listless heat in his room.

He reached for his beer, glimpsed a corner of money sticking out his shorts, and pulled wads of the filthy, worthless bills from his pockets. Flattening them as best he could, he stacked them in a single pile and estimated how long his stash would last. *Not long* was his prediction.

When the fan powered on Cooper gratefully rolled onto his back, though the hot breeze brought scant relief. The blades wobbled disconcertingly, eventually picking up enough speed to sound like a propeller. The breeze blew the top bills off his stack of money and Cooper only halfheartedly grabbed for them. When more blew off, he let them flutter over him and started to laugh at his ridiculous situation. Trapped in a loony country! Plastered to a bed by sweat! Funny money blowing over him! He started flinging fistfuls of the soggy bills at the fan until the pile was depleted and notes lay scattered all over. Cooper hadn't had so much fun in a long time and fell back against his pillow, his thoughts reverting to Sadiq.

The youth had been behind Cooper's every thought since they met. They could be friends, he was sure of it, and Langatown might be bearable if he had a friend. He wouldn't hound him, though; he wouldn't make that mistake with Sadiq. He closed his eyes, recalling the youth's lapis eyes, black curls, café latte skin … and how his slender fingers had so nimbly balanced the diamonds. Cooper could imagine his fingers as clearly as if he were sitting next to him on the edge of the bed; and with his eyes still closed, he reached for Sadiq's hand, drawing it to him, touching himself with it. He'd hardly been aroused since Iraq. Some memories wouldn't leave him. But that night Cooper had new memories as he slipped into a relieved sleep, his and the café latte boy's fingers entwined.

2

A bell tinkled when Cooper entered the pharmacy. He hadn't had much experience shopping in foreign countries and didn't like doing it. The shops were always small, the owners invariably solicitous when he preferred browsing on his own and not being asked what he wanted in a language he didn't understand or what size he needed in a measurement system he didn't know.

The compact pharmacy's shelves were crammed with everything from hairspray to make-it-yourself prosthesis to dried lion penis (in capsules). A long metal rack was devoted to glass vials holding obscure things in syrupy liquids that reminded Cooper of things he'd seen in horror movies as a kid. A stick of sandalwood incense perpetually burned in the corner, in his opinion polluting the air worse than the cars outside but apparently not in the opinion of the cheerful pharmacist and his wife, the latter's smile always fading when Cooper entered. Almost the only things he ever bought were condoms and apparently she didn't approve. Fortunately that morning she was distracted by another customer.

As he approached the counter, the pharmacist smiled and rocked his head in the pleasant way Indians do. "It's a good morning, Mr. Chance!" he said buoyantly.

"It seems a lot like yesterday," Cooper commented, "hot and miserable."

"It's our weather."

"Like I said."

The pharmacist reached under the counter. "It's the usual dozen rubbers, is it, Mr. Chance?"

His wife, overhearing him, shot them both a withering look.

"Yeah, twelve was always my favorite number in the multiplications tables," Cooper replied.

They sold the condoms singly, which seemed peculiar to Cooper, who imagined most men needing one would soon use up the standard packet of three, but that was one of those local shopping customs he didn't understand. As the pharmacist counted them out, he asked quietly, "Are all Americans so vigorous?" and glanced at his own wife with an expression that suggested he couldn't remember their *ever* needing a dozen condoms.

Cooper scooped up the slippery packets and stuffed them into his pockets. "Yeah, we're a fucking empire." He left some money on the counter and walked out.

He'd crisscrossed that shanty capital more times than a spider building a web. It was his second nature to find escape routes. He'd grown up on perpetual reconnaissance. His father's flashpoint temper, set off by everything from missing trash day to missing curfew, had meant that Cooper—ever-alert to ambushes—never stopped planning a way to get away. His honed reconnaissance skills had come in handy in Iraq where every house, every car, even the enemy was the same color of sand, and he had to find his way in—and hopefully out—of fatal zones. He'd learned every alley, every barricade, every shadow where he could hide or ditch his identity, and when he'd eventually fled that desert, he was still thinking about his survival, not wanting to get his head blown off because his CO couldn't handle the personal situation that'd come up between them. For a split second, when Cooper heard cries of alarm and a burst of gunfire, he thought he was back in one of those sand-colored towns with insurgents around every corner.

Instinctively he pressed himself against a wall just as a band of rebels came scrambling past, dragging two terrified men they had hobbled together. Not much taller than tall midgets, they were easily identifiable as members of the Stubby Tribe, the traditional enemies of the Elongated Tribe, which had seized power a year earlier—or so Cooper had christened them when he'd been unable to discern any other distinguishing characteristic between them—certainly not in their willingness to be cruel—that could otherwise account for their bloody rivalry dating back to the Stone Age. The Longs versus the Shorts. It seemed to come down to that.

When the rebels saw Cooper, they whirled on him with a clatter of weapons and ammunition belts, and he was instantly staring up the barrels of a half dozen assorted firearms. At their best, Lalanga's rebel armies were undisciplined louts who made up their own rogue orders as they went along, and they could as easily have shot him as not. Their mirrored sunglasses made it impossible to read their intention in their drugged eyes. It didn't much matter. There was nothing reliable about the men pointing their weapons at him except their madness.

Only one rebel had not raised his rifle. He was the tallest among their short ranks, and Cooper suspected he was their commander. He tried to make eye contact with him to communicate at some basic level that might stave off his slaughter, but the man's sunglasses merely reflected back a miniature image of himself. The longer they held each other's blind gaze, the more dangerous Cooper's situation became. One trigger-happy rebel would provoke a fusillade, and they had already started glancing between themselves, almost daring one another to take the first shot before their commander barked an order to lower their weapons. As they reluctantly obeyed, he raised his own rifle to point it squarely at Cooper's chest.

There was no chance of escape. He wouldn't make it more than two steps in any direction and steeled himself for the searing bullets that were sure to come. He'd asked men who'd been shot what it had felt like, curious to know what pain he had inflicted on others, expecting someday it would be inflicted on him, and he'd been relieved to learn that shock masked pain so completely that a fast death almost felt like nothing at all. Life simply seeped away, they had reassured him—those, that is, who had tread that closely to death. It was the survivors who suffered the most— those missing limbs, or living with pain, or suffering pitiless guilt for surviving when their buddies had not.

At that moment, what did it matter? Cooper wouldn't survive. A band of rebels itching to shoot a white man would make sure of that. But instead of shooting him, the rebel leader threw back his head and laughed, his mouth flashing lewd and pink between his black sunglasses and blacker beard. His rifle bobbed carelessly in his loose hands. "Today is your lucky day, white man," he finally said, lingering over "white man" to underscore his control of the situation. "Do you know, white man, why this is your lucky day?"

Cooper hadn't a clue, especially since he didn't feel lucky at that particular moment and figured he'd better not venture a wrong guess.

That wasn't the right move.

The rebel leader, annoyed by his silence, asked his men, "What do you think? Maybe this white man is not so lucky today?"

Again every weapon was pointed at Cooper, cocked and ready to fire.

"What if I guess wrong?" Cooper asked.

"You guess!"

"I can go home?"

That made the rebel leader laugh again. "Where is home?"

"America."

"America! Good rifles, America!" He fired his rifle into the air and his men did as well, until shell casings were rolling off the backs of their two prisoners who had collapsed terrified onto the dirt street. "America is a good friend of Josef Nimwe! And I am Josef Nimwe! The future president of Lalanga!" There was another burst of gunfire, and the prisoners jerked spasmodically.

COOPER'S PROMISE

So that's Josef Nimwe, Cooper thought, the man whose ragtag followers he'd skirmished with while serving in Colonel Diamond's private army-for-hire, fending off his rebel bid to seize control of the diamond mines and have a sure shot at toppling the colonel. The country had more tribes, factions, and shifting alliances than a diamond has facets, and precisely because of its diamonds the chronic civil war plodded along. Whoever controlled the diamond mines had the money to buy weapons. When Cooper first arrived in the country, recruited out of Iraq and flown to Lalanga on Blackwing's ticket, Josef Nimwe had been the biggest threat to Colonel Diamond, and apparently he'd become more menacing if he dared to carry out daylight raids in the center of Langatown, expanding his firepower one kidnapping at a time. When Cooper was fighting him, his men weren't carrying American assault weapons but rusting Kalishnikovs, though he was certain Nimwe's strategy had not changed: to terrorize the population into supporting him until the day he could seize power, and then, if history was any precedent, he'd unleash an even more vicious brutality because he wouldn't know how else to govern.

Cooper figured he had nothing to lose when he risked asking, "What about these two guys? Can they have a lucky day too?"

The rebels didn't seem to know what to do. They were used to people begging for their own lives or slobbering over their pardon but never asking their commander a favor. A couple raised their weapons again, and Nimwe, lowering his, gestured for them to do the same. He lifted his mirrored glasses to look Cooper straight in the eye. "Do you want to trade your lucky day for theirs?"

Cooper didn't. As tempted as he was to say yes, prodding Nimwe into being honorable and sparing them all, he knew it wouldn't happen. Wars weren't won honorably. Men like Nimwe didn't step up to the plate. It would be a clean swap, his life in exchange for the prisoners, until they executed him—right there on the spot, Cooper could predict it—and promptly tied up their prisoners again. All this went through his head while getting his first good look at Josef Nimwe and wondering how a man, despite being so height-challenged, could look so determined. His eyes, jaundiced but not drugged, dared Cooper to risk it all.

Ah, what the hell … Cooper was thinking, one syllable away from blurting, *Sure. I'll trade my lucky day. Heck, there's two of them and only one of me!* But he didn't. He didn't incriminate himself further than posing the one question he had already asked, and Nimwe appeared profoundly disappointed. He'd wanted the opportunity to act judicious even when he would not have; not when, in his demented world, killing Cooper would be respected more than acting honorably.

Cooper's silence was nothing more than a wish to live. He hadn't intended to condemn the prisoners. A look of self-loathing must have crossed his face, and Nimwe recognized it for what it was and smirked. He dropped his sunglasses back into place and jerked his head for his men to move on. They prodded the prisoners to get on their feet, who looked woefully at Cooper, realizing it was a world gone mad—and they were lost in it—if a white man could not intervene on their behalf. Nimwe fell in with his men as they disappeared around a corner.

Cooper peered around his own corner where he saw a man's body sprawled in the street. Two scrawny old grannies were tugging at his clothes, barely budging him, and as soon as they saw Cooper they ran off, arms flapping, squawking like geese.

That left him alone with the dead man in his T-shirt and patched jeans. Flies were already buzzing over his wounds when Cooper crouched to ascertain the obvious—that the man was dead—by testing for a pulse in his neck. He stood up, scanning the nearby buildings, ready to do what anybody asked. He saw women skulking in the windows, shadows of themselves they so wanted to disappear, but no one emerged. Unwilling to abandon the body in the street, he took off his shirt and tucked it under his belt, and kneeling, wrapped his hands around the dead man's waist. He paused long enough for someone to protest, and when no one did, he swung the corpse over his shoulder and stood up.

Dead weight is heavy at any weight, and Cooper staggered a couple of steps before gaining his balance. He turned in a circle, one slow step at a time, pointing the body like a needle on a dial. He'd almost come full circle before a woman stepped out a door. She was the murdered man's wife, Cooper felt with certainty. With her hands locked on her elbows, she looked defiant, as if daring him to be the good Samaritan he was trying to be. But once he took a step, two, three toward her, she doubled over in a spasm of grief.

He stepped past her into her spare home, empty of everything but grass mats and two simple chairs. The women who had hidden inside moved out of his way, and he knelt to roll the body onto the floor, careful to catch the man's head so it wouldn't hit too hard. The dead man's wife followed him inside, squeaking as if her cries were too big to come out, and clawing the air with untamed hands. When Cooper slipped back outside and started to walk away, her anguished cries finally escaped her, and he could hear her long after he was gone.

He wound his way through the warren of hovels that stank of too many people living too close together, until he reached the wharf where a fresher breeze blew into his face. By the way people stared at him, he knew he was bloody, and he could feel it thick and sticky on his back. The corpse had leaked. Of course it would; you don't fight wars and not learn that corpses leak. Only in wars, you don't have time to think about your shirt, and Cooper was glad he had thought about his. It was the only passably decent one he owned.

Scaly heads and slimy entrails peppered the paving stones where the morning fish market had been, and he decided that that wasn't the best stretch of the wharf for finding clean water. Not that the water in the bay was ever clean, but there were spots less littered, and he found one a short ways from where the *African Lady* was docked. The friendlier of the two crewmen was on deck smoking a cigarette, and Cooper gave him a short wave. The crewman barely nodded back.

He hung on to a rusting marine ladder imbedded in the wharf and splashed water on his back. Pinkish water trickled down his legs and ran into his boots. He took them off, keeping them in easy reach, and continued his contortions trying to rinse off. There was too much blood, and every time he ran a hand across his shoulders, it came back red. He had the choice of returning home to shower or diving into the bay, and it had to be the bay. He'd come too close to the diamond arcade and Sadiq to turn back. But then the question became how to manage his boots and shirt? He couldn't strip and dive in without the fleet-footed kids stealing everything before he surfaced. He didn't have to see them to know that many pairs of eyes, attached to very sticky fingers, were watching.

Cooper waved to the crewman, and pointing to his boots and shirt, he shouted, "Hey! Watch my stuff, will you?"

The crewman barely nodded again.

That was good enough for Cooper, who wanted to make it a quick bath anyway. He jumped feet first into the water and was enjoying the initial jolt of coolness when suddenly it felt as if someone had grabbed his ankles and started to drag him deeper and deeper. He'd heard about the renegade currents, unpredictable and powerful, that sometimes carried swimmers to the crocodile-infested mangrove swamps at the tip of the bay, and as hard as he tried, he couldn't swim out of it. The current tumbled him over and over again until finally slamming him into the sea wall. He braced his feet against it and shot to the surface.

Cooper heard the first gunshot as he broke out of the water. Gasping for air, he paddled hard to stay afloat to see what was going on. There was a second shot. A boy was running off with his boots, and the *African Lady*'s crewman was shooting at him.

"*Don't shoot him!*" Cooper cried.

The guard took another shot.

COOPER'S PROMISE

BANG!

A puff of dirt exploded between the kid's feet.

He was an easy target, running straight, not zigzagging like he should to dodge bullets. Holding one of Cooper's army boots in each hand, he was barely tall enough to keep from dragging them.

"*No! Don't shoot!*"

BANG!

Again the crewman hit between the kid's feet whose little legs never faltered.

Cooper scrambled up the dock's ladder. "*No! Don't! Don't shoot!*"

BANG!

Again he hit between the kid's feet

The crewman, Cooper realized, was a good shot, and as the kid was honing in on a corner he could duck around, Cooper watched the crewman raise his gun, aiming for the boy's skinny back.

"*He'll hit you this time!*" Cooper shouted, and without missing a step, the kid dropped the boots and spurted around the corner a split second before a bullet blew off a chunk of stucco exactly where he'd been.

Cooper, climbing out of the water grabbed his shirt and ran to retrieve his boots before any of the other children who'd appeared at the sound of gunfire could get there first. He checked to make sure his knife hadn't fallen out of his boots and slipped them on. He was glad his boots had not been stolen but wasn't especially grateful to the crewman. Fortunately, the man wasn't on deck when Cooper walked past the yacht, so there was no need to thank him.

Within sight of the diamond arcade's cheerful pastel colors, Cooper slipped on his shirt and wandered closer, feigning a nonchalance he didn't feel at the prospect of seeing Sadiq again. He stopped where he expected to be able to look into al-Basma Diamonds, though with the sun's glare, he could only make out that someone was inside. With his heart pounding, he stepped closer to the door at the exact moment that Mazen al-Basma stepped outside.

"*Sabah al-khair,*" the older man greeted him.

"*Sabah il-noor,*" Cooper replied, relying on one of the Arabic phrases he'd learned in Iraq, never imagining that they would do him any good anyplace else. He peered around the older man and could see that Sadiq wasn't there.

"Will you smoke?" Mazen asked, offering his pack of cigarettes. "But of course not, you Americans have strange habits. You drink coffee and don't smoke." He lit a cigarette. "Why are your shorts wet?"

"I swam in the bay," Cooper answered casually, as if every day he swam fully clothed in that vile water.

"In your clothes?"

"I was afraid they'd be stolen if I took them off."

"It used to be different here," Mazen remarked.

No doubt Lalanga was a different country before being turned inside-out by sequential insurrections that started anew before the victors of the last rebellion had been sworn into power; still, Cooper couldn't imagine it had ever been safe enough to leave his clothes on the dock.

"Lalanga will see better times soon," Mazen predicted, "now that we have oil."

"That rumor travels fast."

"One of the biggest reserves in the world!" Mazen boasted, as if he, personally, made the discovery.

Cooper figured it might be true. He'd heard rumors of oil ever since he'd landed in the country, and lately there *had* been more Thick Necks around. "If it's true, that should be good for business," he remarked.

Mazen carefully stubbed out his half-smoked cigarette and tucked it back into the pack. "So come inside and show me your diamonds."

Of course the older man would assume that Cooper had brought diamonds; until yesterday it had been his only reason for coming to the shop. "I hope I'll have more tomorrow," he told him.

"Come in the afternoon when Sadiq is here. You can speak English to him, and I'll tell him to give you a good price."

"I'll remind him," Cooper replied agreeably. Reluctant to leave, hoping the boy might return at any moment, he asked, "So will Sadiq work in the shop every day?"

"What else would he do?"

"He won't go back to Beirut?"

"Of course he likes Beirut; he is a young man. But he will stay home now."

"Is that where he is now? At home?"

Beaming, Mazen told him, "Sadiq has returned a true Arab! Now he goes to the hammam every day!"

"The hammam?"

"You don't know our baths?" Mazen launched into a description of the hammam that sounded remarkable for its many pleasurable bathing pools, not to mention their medicinal properties. "Each one so healthful!" he proclaimed, and of the masseurs he said, "They pull you this way, and push you another way, and you come home very relaxed." As Mazen spoke, he adopted postures that looked anything but relaxing. "Why people call them *Turkish* baths, I don't know," he complained, "when our hammam is an *Arab* tradition!"

"I thought diamonds were your tradition," Cooper joked lamely.

"Diamonds are business, our hammam is our tradition, and now Sadiq won't stay away from it!"

"Is that good?"

"Of course it's good! He's a man!"

Sadiq still had not returned, and Cooper, not big on small talk, retreated along the diamond arcade's spongy boardwalk. Its frilly colors reminded him of his childish vision of the Dark Continent, gleaned from television, of happy, robust natives with the biggest, whitest teeth imaginable; a view disconnected from reality, Cooper didn't have to remind himself, as he dodged the vendors and amputees working the wharf.

The wind had kicked up driven by a black monsoon galloping toward them. In the bay, small fishing boats bobbed precariously on the steely sea. Cooper stopped to observe the *African Lady*'s crewmen reset her lines, but their scowls soon sent him along the waterfront where brightly clad women were struggling in the gusting wind to roll up the straw mats that served as their market stalls. He helped one old granny get control of her wildly flapping matt by holding down one end while she rolled it from the other. When their knuckles touched, she smiled, showing teeth stained bright red from the betel nuts she sold. She pressed one into Cooper's hand, already sliced and wrapped in a leaf, and closed his fingers around it.

Holding it tight so it wouldn't fall apart, he ducked into Langatown's twisting lanes to get out of the wind. The tin roofs were flapping so noisily there could have been an army of children running over them. He had never eaten betel nut before and examined it, unrolling the leaf to find bits of nut and crushed red pepper.

When he turned a corner he nearly bumped into Sadiq waiting outside the pharmacy. Wet black curls clung to the youth's forehead. "Sadiq?"

"Coopah?"

"Close enough. Why do you have an English accent?"

"I had an English nanny while growing up."

"That must've been nice. I suppose that explains why your English is perfect."

"I can always improve."

Reminded of Mazen's remark, they exchanged wry smiles, and Cooper commented, "So I hear." He felt certain he had never seen a more handsome man. "You must be coming from the hammam."

"Do you know our hammam?"

"I know it's an Arab tradition, not a Turkish one."

Sadiq laughed outright. "Obviously you have spoken with my father!"

"I have."

"He has a thing about tradition."

"So I gather. I also gather that he's definitely glad you're home."

"So *he* can go to the hammam!"

"He's waiting for you now."

"I know." Suddenly annoyed, Sadiq glanced into the pharmacy. "My friend needed something."

His friend, also wearing a beige caftan, stood at the pharmacy's counter with his back to them. In the same moment that they glanced inside, he happened to look around, and seeing them observing him, frowned and turned furtively away. It could've been a drug deal going down, it looked that suspicious, until the pharmacist set the box of condoms on the counter, and catching Cooper's eye, winked at him. Reminded that his own pockets bulged with the same slippery packets, he checked that no telltale shiny corners were sticking out.

"You should try it," Sadiq suggested.

"What?"

"The hammam. It's a couple of streets over and has a big stone arch. You can't miss it."

Cooper exaggeratedly wiped his brow. "Why bother with a steam bath when we live in one?"

"There *is* the cold pool."

Suddenly Cooper was interested. "The cold pool?"

"You can only stay in it a minute, it's so cold."

"That sounds a lot nicer than sweating."

"If you go, Americans always tip too much," Sadiq cautioned him, "when almost nothing is enough."

"That's never my problem."

"How long have you been here?"

"A few months. Make that six."

"Are you an oilman?"

"No."

"I heard that all the other Americans had left."

"You can't believe rumors. Besides, I can't think of any place I'd rather be."

"Then you haven't been to Beirut, have you?" There was something mischievous in the way Sadiq said it, and Cooper was instantly jealous, imagining the café latte boy in free-and-easy Beirut. Certainly freer and easier than Langatown.

"Unfortunately, no," he answered, "or fortunately—how do I know if I've never been there? I've been here and Iraq and a few airports in between, and nothing I've seen so far makes me want to see much of the rest of the world."

"Beirut would change your mind."

"Will you go back?"

Sadiq's friend interrupted them by stepping out of the pharmacy. He had a pronounced limp, and a ragged scar zigzagged down his left cheek to bury itself in his wiry black beard. An apparently recent wound—bright pink, with coarse stitch marks that ran alongside it like shoelace holes. Cooper could see that he had been handsome; in fact, he still was, only now his scar would forever be the first reason strangers would glance at him.

He looked suspiciously between Cooper and Sadiq, who spoke briefly in Arabic before he said, "This is my friend Munir."

"Cooper Chance." He introduced himself.

They shook hands.

"Tell your friend it's nice to meet him."

"I speak English," Munir said.

"Good, because the extent of my Arabic starts with *aiwa* and ends with *la*. Yes and no, and *shokrun*, thanks."

Sadiq told him, "Munir is visiting from Beirut."

"That's a long way to come for a visit, especially when you end up in Langatown."

"Are you an American?" Munir asked.

"The last time I checked my passport. But I'm thinking of applying for citizenship."

"You live here?"

"I'm surviving here if that counts. How about you? Are you staying a long time?"

"Not so long," Sadiq interjected.

Good, Cooper thought.

"Why do you stay when all the other Americans have left?" Munir asked.

"They did?" Cooper asked facetiously.

Munir's eyes narrowed, wary of being teased. "It is better if they did."

"Better?"

"Safer."

Sadiq spoke sharply to Munir and then said to Cooper, "He means there were threats."

"We're Americans, we expect it."

"Is that betel nut?" Munir demanded. It was clear he didn't approve.

"I think so."

"Do you chew it?"

"Not yet." Cooper offered it to him. "Do you want it?"

"No!" Disgusted, Munir turned abruptly and limped away.

"I guess he doesn't like betel nut."

"It's *haram*," Sadiq said, looking concerned after his friend who jerked so acutely to one side that he risked elbowing everybody he passed.

"Haram?" Cooper asked.

"Forbidden. Munir is very devout," Sadiq explained, "he approves of no drugs."

"It's a drug?" Cooper had assumed betel nut was like gum or candy, and from the way it turned everyone's mouth bright red, it looked as if it should be sweet.

"The natives chew it so they won't feel hungry."

"You're kidding? And nobody's told me about it before?"

"I don't suppose you would like it very much. It tastes rather like peppery soap."

"I'd eat peppery soap if it would keep my stomach from growling so loud that it sounds like snoring!"

At a thunderclap, they both looked up at the approaching storm, and Sadiq remarked, "I suppose I should return to the shop before the rains start."

"I suppose I should get someplace too," Cooper said, without any place in particular to go.

"When you have more diamonds, bring them in the afternoon when my father is at the hammam."

"I'll remember that."

Sadiq touched his heart before hurrying off to catch up with Munir. They could have been brothers in their twin caftans, or best of buddies, a notion seemingly consummated when he placed a hand on Munir's shoulder to steer him around the corner. Cooper touched his own heart as they disappeared.

Despite the rumbling thunder, he wanted to find the hammam, though he knew he wouldn't venture into it despite the temptation of the cold pool. He'd feel too conspicuous in that foreign world.

He easily found its big stone arch dominating a small side street. There was no identifying sign, and nothing about its facade suggested that, behind its thick, stuccoed walls men were stretching out on hot marble slabs or slipping into icy pools. Cooper discovered it was a dead-end street and about the only people on it were men going to or leaving the hammam, so he found a spot on the corner where he could watch them while nibbling away on the betel nut, which indeed tasted like peppery soap. By far, most of the men belonged to the large Lebanese community, distinguishable by their caftans, but many Indians also patronized the place, as did members of the Elongated Tribe who slipped fearlessly inside.

The galloping clouds finally caught up with the sun, blotting it out and turning the sky an ominous yellow. The wind gusted violently, and Cooper was about to move on when a man who was black and tall enough to be a member of the Elongated Tribe emerged, but his movements were all American. When his baseball cap blew off, Cooper recognized Sam Brown. He chased after his cap, and Cooper went in the opposite direction.

The flailing tin roofs sounded like fenders bending, and people were running for shelter, shielding their eyes from the blowing grit. With another enormous thunderclap the roiling sky opened up, pouring down rain in buckets, in cats and dogs, in every quantity imaginable. There was no escaping it, and soon everyone was laughing at the sheer volume of water being dumped on them. Children shrieked in delight and shrieked even louder when Cooper flashed his betel-red teeth at them.

Miraculously, the storm hadn't knocked out the power, and before he arrived at Cowboy Mile he could hear music coming from the bars. Barely noon and the girls were already working; the truckers passing through Langatown had 'round-the-clock needs. As he shouldered his way through The Mining Pan's doors, he attracted a few looks, the regulars recognizing him, the others sizing him up. A trio of girls danced halfheartedly to a scratchy tune on the jukebox while trawling for tricks among the men chugging beers at the bar.

Cooper was stepping over the stream of rainwater running through the room when a lipsticked boy, maybe fifteen like Lulay, maybe younger, tugged at his shirt and asked, "You buy me a beer, mister?"

"No money."

"Juma give you credit."

"I'm already over my limit."

"You want me? Me cheap-cheap."

"Not today."

"Tomorrow?"

"Not ever."

Shrugging him off, Cooper slid onto a barstool.

"You come early today," Juma greeted him.

"Yeah, I love this place. Is your ice machine working?" Cooper knew it was; he could hear its asthmatic wheezing.

The barman shook his head as if dealing with a stubborn child. "It ruins the gin."

"I didn't order gin, I ordered ice, and make that with a large splash of water."

"You pay for water."

"So give me another reason to love this place."

As Juma scooped ice cubes into a glass, Cooper searched the long mirror for Lulay and found her sitting in a booth across from a john. The barman plunked his water in front of Cooper, who rolled the glass slowly across his forehead to appreciate its coolness before pouring it over his head, using his fingers as a sieve to hold back the ice.

It was cold enough that he shivered. That was worth the price of water.

He opened his eyes and in the mirror saw Lulay laughing at him while her john was twisting around, trying to see what was happening.

He handed the glass back to Juma. "Now add the gin."

The barman took it, saying, "I don't know a crazier white man."

"Neither do I," Sam Brown said, sliding onto the next barstool. He'd been drenched too by the torrential rain, and his baseball cap stuck out his back pocket.

Cooper said, "I wasn't saving that seat for you."

"Oh, you weren't?" Sam Brown glanced around the room. "Then where is he?"

Instantly Cooper was on his feet grabbing Sam Brown by his collar. "What are you trying to imply?"

All the conversations in the bar petered out.

Sam Brown dropped his arms limply, daring Cooper to take it further.

"No trouble," Juma warned him.

Cooper pulled Sam Brown half off his seat, not sure how far he was going to take it when he glanced up and saw Lulay looking scared. Cooper screwed up his face as fierce as he could, snarling like a madman ready to rip open Sam Brown's cheek, when he suddenly smiled as big as he could and showed off his bright red teeth. People laughed, conversations restarted, and Cooper set Sam Brown back on the barstool.

He drained his G and T and plopped his glass on the bar. "You said you'd buy me a whole drink."

Sam Brown ordered his refill.

"That's a double," Cooper specified, and Juma ran the bottle over his glass a second time. He couldn't help but see Lulay in the mirror, clenching his jaw every time her john reached across the table to paw her. This one was as ugly as a bulldog trying to pass itself off as human. Sam Brown followed Cooper's gaze, who silently dared him to say something suggestive about the girl.

He wisely said nothing.

Cooper swallowed more of the cheap gin. "What the fuck do you want from me?"

"I hear you're a good shot."

"How would anyone know to tell you that?"

"It's easy to get answers if you know the right people."

"Yeah? And who might those people be?"

"I'm a recruiter," Sam Brown told him. "Let's leave it at that."

Cooper swirled some drink in his mouth, swallowed it, and checked his teeth in the mirror. The red was fading. "You got my name off the wrong mailing list. Are you with Blackwing?"

"A different outfit."

"You all fuck the same."

"We pay well."

"Yeah, until it's *adios, amigo,* and waving bye-bye from an airplane window."

"You could have gone home with them."

"And end up in jail?" Cooper asked. "No thanks. I've been locked up enough times already."

"You'd be fighting for your country this time."

"You make it sound almost patriotic."

"Maybe I can offer you a deal."

"What kind of deal?"

"A ticket home after your service."

"Yeah, right."

Cooper wanted to believe Sam Brown so hard that he almost talked himself into it. He knew back home wasn't exactly the Promised Land, but at least he could ask for his shoe size and talk-talk the language and not hang out in bars where the average age of the working girls was less than driving age. He'd do anything to go home free except sell his soul to the devil. He'd seen that face enough times too. "You guys can all go fuck yourselves," Cooper finally responded. "I'm tired of fighting other people's lousy wars. Uncle Sam's lousy wars. Colonel Diamond's lousy wars. I've got my own lousy war to fight. I've got Cooper's war. Besides, I'm retired."

"You're a little young to retire."

"I invested wisely."

Through the mirror, Cooper saw Lulay's john stumble off to the men's room. He clapped Sam Brown on the back. "So now you have my answer and can stop coming around. Thanks for the drink."

He grabbed his glass, and a dozen steps later slipped into the seat opposite the girl.

"I'm busy," Lulay said petulantly.

"I'll leave when he comes back."

"Why are your teeth red?"

He flashed them. "Do you like them?"

It showed all over her face that Lulay wanted to laugh, and he wanted to hear the girlish laugh that she still had, but she was holding it in, always trying to act grown up. "Why are you all the time bothering me?" she complained. "Juma makes *me* pay if you scare my john-john away."

"I'll pay Juma."

Cooper fished a fistful of condoms from his pocket and thrust them at her. "Take these."

"You crazy, Cooper! Where am I going to put them now?"

"I don't want you running out of them."

"I still got some left."

"You shouldn't."

"I wash them out."

"They're not intended to be recycled. Here, at least take two. If he's drunk, he'll try to do it twice."

Lulay slipped both condoms into her halter. "He's too drunk for twice. Now go away!"

Stuffing the rest of the slippery packets back into his pockets, one shot under the table and Cooper dived for it.

"Hurry, Cooper!" Lulay cried.

Blindly he patted the sticky floor.

"He's coming back!"

There it was!

He poked his head up at the moment her john arrived. "Eureka!"

The john looked even more like a bulldog than at a distance, and Cooper wouldn't have been surprised if the john had barked while glancing fiercely between him and Lulay. Sticking his face into hers, the man said something in a local dialect that Cooper guessed to mean, *Who is this asshole?*

He climbed out of the booth, and when the bulldog john swung around to confront him, he discovered that Cooper was a head taller and backed off. Cooper slapped the condom into his hand, saying, "You make her sick-sick with the skinny-skinny, and I'll find your ugly fucking face and fucking kill-kill you. So use it."

On the street, he allowed himself a big smile. He knew the john wouldn't argue about using protection, at least not that time. His good humor was short-lived, though, as he walked down the mean streets passing girls in garish getups, soldiers pissing against a wall, johns and touts looking to score sex, drugs, an easy make—and they were all watching him. A white man was quickly noticed in that black scene.

Beyond the range of Cowboy Mile's colored lights, walking became more treacherous on the rough streets as he steadily climbed Langatown's highest hill. The roads narrowed to steep tracks that were deserted by sleepers and revelers alike. The few light bulbs, swinging on their cords in the faint breeze, spilled shadows around corners that made Cooper jump more than once thinking someone was coming at him. He'd hear footsteps, only to turn a corner and no one would be there. Dogs growled menacingly in the dark, the thin moonlight revealing their oily coats and yellowy eyes. One dog, pacing, head down watching Cooper approach, lunged at him, snapping its fanged teeth at his throat. He felt the animal's stale breath on his face before a tether yanked it back to the ground.

He rounded a corner, and the church steeple—glittering as brilliantly as the diamonds that had paid for it—soared over the uneven roofs. The shanty houses soon fell away to a green zone encircling the church, though calling that No Man's Land a green zone was a stretch for a patch of picked-over dirt where only sticker weeds could grow. Cooper heard faint *tap-tap tapping* sounds, and through the ghostly mist, he could make out men poking sticks through whatever refuse had been dumped there—or in some cases, squatting to leave their own.

The church kept its distance from the squalid city by rising above it. The early missionaries had appropriated Langatown's only hill for God's house. Cooper wasn't a believer—he felt every religion should be put on trial for crimes against humanity—but churches themselves had been his safe havens when growing up. He had never been hit in one, and if the price of admission was to make the sign of the cross, it was a low price to pay.

He'd first come to Langatown's church the night his Blackwing buddies flew out, abandoning him on the tarmac, an American who couldn't go home. He'd landed in trouble on too many fronts, and the prospect of being thrown in jail was enough to make him break out in a cold, terrified sweat. The deserter had been deserted. Cooper had needed a miracle that night, and he still did.

The church's white picket fence was whiter and brighter than anything else in town, and he entered the churchyard through its simple gate. On both sides of a short, uneven sidewalk, scores of families had taken the notion of church-as-sanctuary to heart and camped out. Smokey tendrils from their grills reminded Cooper that he hadn't eaten since forever. As discreetly as he could, he pulled a few bills from his pocket—they felt about the right number to buy a chicken leg—and offered them to a woman stirring her meager coals. Before she could piece together what Cooper was trying to say, he was accosted on all sides with offers for an assortment of grilled morsels held out in as many greasy fingers. The woman quickly snatched the bills from Cooper's hand, replacing them with a measly chicken wing. He protested, salivating for the leg, and she gave him a second starved wing, leaving only the leg for her and, he saw then, two kids sitting in the dirt watching their dinner being bargained away. Cooper handed back one of the wings.

A few of the would-be-sellers of their own dinners hounded Cooper up the broad, short steps to the church door, where they finally let him alone and drifted away. He crossed himself with the chicken wing and then finished nibbling off every morsel of meat and gristle on its brittle bones. When there was absolutely nothing more to be had, he looked around for a place to discard them and ended up leaving the bones in the dry baptismal fount intending to retrieve them on his way out.

The ends of the pews shined dully from the oil of the many hands that had touched them. He proceeded up the center aisle until he reached the altar. Face-to-face with God, Cooper never had much to say. Whenever he had prayed, he'd not been very impressed with the results, though he *had* been praying for help the night he met Innocence, and he had to admit, that was a small miracle. That night three months earlier he'd bought his first diamonds from the boy and suddenly had a livelihood. That same night, the church had rocked with women dancing and praying and shaking noisy charms, begging for miracles Cooper imagined Jesus would have been hard-pressed to perform: miracles to return a stolen child, or cure a desperately ill spouse—or cure anyone for that matter, since all illness in Lalanga was desperate. Innocence had slipped unnoticed into the pew behind him, as if blindness made him soundless, too, and he was startled when the youngster asked, "Are you American?"

"Yeah, I'm an American," Cooper replied brusquely, not looking at the boy, annoyed by the interruption. Not that his prayers ever had beginnings or ends; they were more like continuous distress signals; but he was tired of being hassled by touts and beggars. It didn't surprise him that they didn't consider the church off-limits—nothing was. "How could you tell? By my lapel pin?" he'd asked.

"By your smell," Innocence told him.

"Yeah?" Cooper hadn't expected the kid's answer. "What do we smell like?"

"Different."

"Different how?"

"Different like Americans."

It was only then that Cooper noticed the boy's opaque eyes.

Now he was looking for the blind boy again, and there he was in the church's doorway, listening, getting his bearings. Cooper could have sworn he actually sniffed the air! As Innocence started up the center aisle, that night there were no women dancing and shaking noisy charms, nothing louder than muffled scraps of prayers. Innocence walked slowly, and upright, giving him an air of naive dignity. He was thirteen, he'd told Cooper, who imagined him growing up to be a wise, lean man.

As quietly as he could, Cooper scooted over to the far end of his pew, holding his breath to make as little noise as possible. The boy drew closer and stopped, concentrating a good few seconds. That time he did sniff the air. "You are here, American Cooper?" he asked.

"Damn! Do I smell *that* bad?"

"I said you smell 'different,' not bad." The boy joined him in the pew. He wore a *Chicago Cubs* T-shirt. "You come back quick-quick this time."

"Market conditions have improved."

"Then my prices go up."

"Don't push your luck. Do you have more stones?"

"You try to become rich-rich, American?"

"Naw, I'm trying to make *you* rich-rich."

"I hope you try very hard!"

"Ha ha ha. Listen, the last stones had lots of impurities, I almost couldn't sell them."

"It's God who puts the diamonds in Janjay's hands," Innocence reminded him. "Maybe if you pray, my sister finds better diamonds."

"I'm praying you have some stones right now."

"Janjay has not come home tonight."

Even Innocence's opaque eyes couldn't hide his distress. Some nights the soldiers let the boys go home, keeping the girls, and sometimes they kept only the boys, and sometimes both or neither. There was no predicting the soldiers' whims, only the sordidness of their pleasures.

"She'll be okay," Cooper offered encouragingly, not believing it himself; it was its own kind of prayer.

He left Innocence in the pew, and passing the baptismal font, noticed that the bones were gone when he heard a distinct *crunch!* and peered toward the sound. A crippled boy propped up on a crutch under one arm was cracking the chicken bones with his teeth. He wore a tattered shirt the color of dirt that hung to his bare knees. He never blinked and never took his sallow eyes off Cooper, who felt them follow him into the muggy night.

3

Cooper slapped himself awake the next morning, aiming for a mosquito and instead hitting his ear so hard that he worried he had ruptured his eardrum. When the mosquito dive-bombed again, its buzzing sounded loud and clear. That time he caught it mid-flight and opened his fist to reveal a bloody patch on his palm. He'd stopped using his mosquito net; it was worthless protection when he was bitten by mosquitoes every day anyway, plus it blocked the breeze from the ceiling fan when the power was on—but not that morning.

He rolled from bed and took a piss and a cold shower, cursing, as he did every morning, that it was only tepid and not really cold. Without drying off, he trailed water back into the main room where he dropped to the floor to do a hundred pushups, a hundred sit-ups, and back into the shower where he brushed his teeth, gargling noisily under the spray, not worrying whether the water was safe to drink or not. Nothing had killed him yet. He'd shaved a couple of days earlier and decided he was good for a couple more in an effort to conserve his razor blade. Tepid or not, the running water felt more refreshing than the sweaty day, and Cooper stayed under it until he heard the predictable loud knock on the ceiling downstairs.

"Too long shower, American!" his landlady shouted.

"Yeah, yeah, yeah," he grumbled, turning off the water, not wanting her to come upstairs and bang on his door, which he knew she would do; or worse, like the first time, when he'd ignored her banging completely and she marched right into his bathroom and turned off the shower with

Cooper still in it.

"Too long shower, American," she had said calmly and walked out.

He dressed without drying off, pulling on the same cutoffs and sleeveless shirt that he'd worn for an endless stretch of days. His only other shirt lay rolled up in a closet corner suffering from end-stage jungle rot. He laced up his army boots before poking around in the kitchen for something to eat, craving fried eggs but not having any, let alone the electricity to cook them. Instead Cooper had to settle for instant coffee made with tap water, a handful of cereal, and whatever he could salvage from fruit bought a couple of days earlier. It wasn't bountiful, but he wouldn't starve. He rinsed out his coffee mug, made his bed, and split his pile of money into two equal wads, which he stuffed into his front pockets. His passport went into a back pocket and his knife into a boot. He looked around to see if he'd forgotten anything. He had—the rest of the condoms. They followed the money into his pockets.

Pulling the door shut, he was reminded of the rooms he'd shared with his father during his unsettled childhood—motel rooms and occasional apartments when his father took a regular job for more than a few weeks that seemed empty even while they were living in them. Sometimes it worried Cooper that the first room he'd ever rented on his own resembled those empty rooms, but that morning little worried him. His outlook had brightened since he met Sadiq. His luck had changed, and as if proof of it, he found a mango in the yard. He let its sticky juice run down his chin as he set off in search of the news.

Cooper's sharp pangs of homesickness were about as brief as bumper stickers, though sometimes they felt as profound, but he suffered thinking his fate was to never return home, that America was forever lost to him. Any scrap of news would do, and if not news about America, he'd settle for news that proved a world existed beyond loony Lalanga's steamy borders. The country had no newspaper independent of the government, and rarely were foreign correspondents permitted in for fear that they would expose Colonel Diamond's "mockracy." It was Cooper's word for the colonel's pretense of elections and buffoonery as president. After shooting his way to power, the colonel had lost his own rigged election, only to be sworn into office by a Supreme Court he had appointed. The judges declared him the winner due to a technicality: the winning opposition candidate had turned up headless. The colonel had proceeded to run the country into the same ground from which he stole its wealth.

Colonel Diamond was the only name Cooper knew for the president-"unelect," and he guessed, it's how the majority of the nonelectorate knew him too. He'd been nicknamed by a French journalist who also turned up headless after exposing the Colonel's ballooning bank accounts; and whose head, when it finally arrived at the newspaper's Paris headquarters, had the article stuck in its mouth. The colonel eventually embraced his nickname, turning a state stigma into a state joke at which everyone dutifully chuckled whenever invoked.

It had become a game for Cooper to find a shred of credible news when typically so little was reported. That morning, though, its easiness proved unprecedented. Overnight, tabloid sheets had been pasted indiscriminately on walls touting the country's recent oil discovery. "Vast Reserves" one claimed, while others boasted Lalanga to "Rule OPEC!" and "Celebrate! We're Rich!"

Reaching the port, Cooper made his way to a kiosk selling newspapers and was reading the lead article—Intl Experts Confirm Huge Reserves—when a piece of cardboard was slipped over the top of the stack of papers to block his view.

"You pay for look-look," said the vendor.

Cooper didn't bother to buy it; he already knew the gist of the story. Geologists confirmed as long-rumored that Lalanga had oil and lots of it; her vast oilfields likely surpassed Iraq's. So it was probably true too that

Blackwing had been there to protect America's access to the oil, not to protect Colonel Diamond, who ultimately proved to be a fickle ally. When, in a schizophrenic effort to recast himself as a populist, the colonel announced his intention to nationalize the country's nascent oil industry, America's aid pipeline seized up faster than a new inmate's asshole. Blackwing recalled its contract soldiers before Uncle Sam's last check could bounce.

Cooper had his dose of news. Now he had a second mission: to see Sadiq.

Strolling the length of the diamond arcade, Cooper noticed only a couple of old grannies in the shops, no doubt selling their precious stones for pittance. He wondered what Mazen had meant when he said business was good. The international traders, the real wheeler dealers of the diamond business, had disappeared when the UN, citing the role of diamonds in the country's self-perpetuating civil war, had embargoed them long before Cooper had shown up and heard stories about how the dealers used to dart between the shops, briefcases chained to their wrists, a small army of bodyguards waiting on the boardwalk while inside they did million-dollar deals.

Mazen always left his door ajar to catch the scant breeze, and as Cooper walked past it, he saw the older man crouched at the safe. He could see Sadiq wasn't there, so Cooper continued the short distance to the wharf where fishermen were tossing glassy-eyed fish into wooden bins, hacking the larger species into filets and wrapping them in whatever scraps of paper or plastic they had scrounged. Ever-watchful for Sadiq, Cooper kept his eye on the diamond arcade where every few minutes Mazen stepped outside for one of his half-smokes. When the older man noticed Cooper, he waved him over, but as soon as he had he became distracted wooing a granny into his shop.

It was just as well. Cooper only wanted to see Sadiq, and he headed in the direction of the hammam hoping to cross paths with him. He'd act nonchalant if he did. He didn't want Sadiq to think he'd come looking for him. He didn't want to risk choking off their friendship before it had time to grow, not like he'd done with the others he'd been smitten with through his growing-up years, mooning about outside their classes or homes, and finding any excuse to cross their paths. They would start out liking him, relishing the attention, until they sensed he needed something more profound than the other friendships they had known, though they could no more have articulated that than Cooper could have articulated his own smoldering emotions. Eventually they all shunned him. The only silver lining to his father relocating them so frequently was that Cooper escaped those boyhood friends who, once objects of his affection, had become sources of wretched loss and bewilderment. His relationship with Rick—Captain Richard Morrow, his CO in Iraq—had been equally bewildering, but it *had* become something more than simple friendship, and by the time it ended, Cooper considered himself wised up enough to be less needy.

He thought he had conquered his innate loneliness until he met Sadiq, and all his longings returned. He almost felt lonelier for knowing him.

Disappointed to reach the hammam without running into him, Cooper returned to the corner where he could watch the mixture of men coming and going. What was it like inside? What took them there so habitually? He tried to imagine the many pools, the men lounging around them or stretching like athletes because Cooper imagined the hammam to be like an ancient Greek gymnasium—it was the only notion he had of such a place. The men would be naked, of course, and moving among them would be Sadiq. Imagining his lean body in that setting, with the pools' dappled light reflecting off his café latte skin, Cooper became aroused and knew he could never go inside and risk that happening in front of others.

He decided to leave yet lingered on, giving himself five more minutes to catch a glimpse of the boy. Sweating in the relentless sun, he daydreamed about the hammam's cold pool as he had daydreamed about cold showers in Iraq, and they had been cold during the months when the nighttime temperatures dropped low enough to chill the base's water tanks. He thought of Rick again, and how he had started to show up behind Cooper in line for the makeshift showers too often to be coincidental, casually letting his towel flap open or tossing it aside altogether. Cooper could guess what he wanted, and he wanted it too; though for him it truly was more guesswork than not. He had only known about sex in terms of denial. He could express his desires only in terms that embarrassed him, and for a long time, he believed they were his desires uniquely. Until the day Rick, slipping out of the shower, said, "I want to see you in my tent, Sergeant Chance." Cooper had been relieved that it had sounded like an order, otherwise he might have talked himself out of going to Rick's tent, like he was talking himself out of going to the hammam.

An old man came up and stood beside Cooper, his gnarled fist clutching a walking stick, looking apprehensively at the road and its mix of cars and carts bouncing over treacherous potholes. He waited for a safe opening that never came. He looked older than God, and Cooper couldn't believe he was out and about on his own. Offering to help him cross the street, the old man gratefully clasped his arm, and they set off. He seemed to have no weight at all, and a couple of times Cooper, whose attention was on the traffic, had to glance at him to make sure he hadn't let go. When they safely made it across, the man waved his walking stick to indicate that he wanted Cooper's help to the hammam's entrance, and once there, through its arched entrance that led into a modest courtyard. In one corner, a fountain splashed pleasantly, and the walls were entirely covered in tiles the cool colors of water: aquamarine, emerald, turquoise blue. Cooper couldn't imagine how he had missed such a delightful spot and would have stayed planted right there beside the fountain if the old man hadn't managed to pull him a few steps further to the raised platform that functioned as a ticket booth. Atop it sat a turbaned and cross-legged man whose frizzy gray beard draped over his knees. The old man indicated he was paying for Cooper as well, who protested that he wasn't going in, but the old man paid anyway. What choice did he have but to try it?

The turbaned ticket-taker waved them through a door, where they were greeted by a youthful attendant wearing a crisp vanilla-colored shirt and matching linen shorts. The old man said a quick good-bye, and more spryly than Cooper could have imagined possible darted off and left him alone with the attendant, who led him through a warren of dressing cubicles separated by gauzy curtains the same vanilla color as his clothes. Ceiling fans rippled the curtains to reveal men stretched out on cots, some chatting with their neighbors, others watching who went by. At a vacant cubicle, the attendant handed Cooper a long triangular loincloth with long strings dangling from each of its three points.

"Put this on," he said, and indicating an upright locker added, "Your clothes go in here."

Cooper looked inside it. "There's no towel?"

"No towel."

"I only wear this?" He held up the loincloth.

"Nothing is necessary," the attendant told him, and stepped out to let Cooper undress.

He did quickly, and picking up the loincloth by one of its long strings, puzzled over how to wear it. As men walked past, he tried to glimpse how they had fixed theirs, but only one man still had his, and he carried it in his hand. He supposed that's what the boy had meant when he said nothing is necessary—it didn't need to be worn at all. Cooper couldn't imagine himself walking around naked, so he covered what needed to be covered, pulled the strings around his thighs, and tied them with multiple bows. He imagined that he looked like he was wearing a diaper, which is exactly how the attendant grinned at him when he stepped out.

"It's not right, is it?" he asked.

"No problem," the boy told him. "Inside it is finished."

"Inside" meant through a door that, when the attendant opened it, released a cloud of steam that rolled over Cooper like a monsoon from hell. He broke into a sweat before his eyes had time to adjust to the wet twilight. Men lay sprawled across the tiled benches that crawled up three walls like seats in an amphitheater. Where the stage would have been, an energetic few exercised or twisted themselves into positions worthy of mad yogis, but most lolled about in the torpid heat, enjoying a nonchalance that Cooper had never contemplated between men with their backs resting against another's bent leg, hands easily touching, scrotums drooping over thighs like heavy fruits.

"You take massage, Mistuh?" he heard, and turned to see a man so black he was blue. The scalding rain dripping off the ceiling ran down his oiled chest in rivulets. Wearing only a loincloth, he carried two full buckets of water that barely flexed his veined arms. Massage! Cooper had never had one, and the idea made him nervous.

He was about to decline when the man poured out one of his buckets to flush the floor clean. "Here," the masseur said, "face down."

Cooper complied, pressing his nose to the floor. The marble felt cool from the water.

The African asked, "You like hard or soft massage?"

"How about medium?"

"No medium." With that, he plucked at the strings of Cooper's loincloth, roughly pulling it off him and tossing it onto a pile of other discarded ones.

Then he started.

Wherever the African had learned his craft of touch and pressure, he had perfected it. At first he played Cooper like a musical instrument— testing him, tuning him, warming him up—before pressing more decisively, prodding huffs and puffs and occasional groans out of him. Cooper's forehead bounced remorselessly on the marble floor in time with the pounding his back received. Whether he grunted in pleasure or pain, the masseur took it as cue to prod or twist or pull harder. When he finally stopped, Cooper lay there motionless, as exhausted as if he'd had a good workout, hoping he didn't have to move.

Apparently he did.

The African tapped his shoulder, indicating that he should roll onto his back. He did, in the same movement tucking his cock between his legs. Kneeling at his head, the masseur pressed his knees against Cooper's shoulders and drizzled oil on his chest. He ran his hands down Cooper's body, spreading the oil with outstretched fingers, spreading the oil that felt cool and peppery at the same time, reaching to his knees before folding himself back up. He spread the tingling oil a second time, reaching past his knees until the screw curls on his belly tickled Cooper's nose.

And then, without warning, he swooped his body down at an alarming speed, extending himself to his ankles, his loincloth in Cooper's face. As the African repeatedly swept down his body, he jarred loose Cooper's cock from its tucked away place, grazing it every time his hands slid past, and Cooper couldn't help but become aroused. The more he tried not to think of his embarrassment, the more aroused he became, until his rigid cock was soon knocking the man on his chest each time he swooped down him. The masseur appeared oblivious to it, and Cooper, peering into the steam and unable to make out anyone, realized that no one could see him either. So he stopped fretting and succumbed to the African's pleasures who, when he had finished, retrieved a loincloth from the discard pile and draped it over him.

Floating blissfully in that warm, wet world, Cooper didn't want to move and only did when he remembered that Sadiq or Sam Brown might be there. He shot to his feet and looked around, relieved he didn't see them. By then he was ready to move and again considered how to secure the loincloth. He decided not to; only a handful of men wore theirs, and he was feeling easier with his nakedness. He dropped it back on the discard pile and followed other men into a corridor lined with hot jets that rinsed off the steam bath's sweat and oil as he passed through. At the far end, another door led into the grand pavilion with its many sapphire pools, graduating from warm to icy cold, though not, as Mazen had pointed out, laid out in any particular order. The pools sparkled, and daylight streamed in through circular holes in the massive dome, crisscrossing the pavilion with laser beams of golden light.

The largest and most popular pool was in the center, ringed with idle bathers whose muted voices echoed off the tiled walls. Men had draped themselves everywhere and were straddling marble benches, dangling their feet in water, stretching like the Greek athletes in Cooper's imagination.

A lobster-red man appeared to be boiling in one pool, and Cooper confirmed it was scalding hot by dipping his toe into it. He was the whitest of the bathers, but that wasn't why he received looks that were more than curious; he was a handsome man, in better shape than most. He returned their glances, taking in the lithe and fat, handsome and not, and more than once he thought he saw Sadiq, black-haired and eagle-beaked, but the olive-skinned youth always turned out to be another.

He moved around the pavilion testing the pools and observing nothing more exotic than men enjoying a chat in a bath, eventually coming to a pool tucked away with many men gathered around it. Like a tribe, they exchanged nuanced glances as soon as Cooper entered their territory. Their complicity followed him to the pool's edge, where a youth, dark and bronzed-skin like so many of them—like Sadiq—was dangling his legs in the water. In fact, it *was* Sadiq, and Cooper stepped closer.

"Sadiq?"

It was then that he saw the other boy bobbing between the youth's legs. At first Cooper couldn't make out what was happening; the glint off the water was more concealing than revealing. Then he guessed their obscene act.

"Sadiq!"

The boy at the pool's edge languidly peered around so as not to interrupt his essential pleasure. So certain that it was Sadiq, that's who Cooper saw at first; it took him a moment to realize that it was another young man altogether.

To the amusement of the men around him, Cooper fled that indecent pool, back through the steam room and its orgy of sweat to the maze of curtained cubicles. The vanilla-clad attendant, surprised to see him, asked, "Mister is finished already?"

"Mister is finished and outta here."

"I show you the way."

He pushed past the boy. "I know my way."

Cooper didn't, and he finally had to be shown his cubicle among all the curtains waving lazily in the breeze of the overhead fans. "Okay, scram," he told the attendant, who stayed put smiling broadly, visible every time the curtain to Cooper's cubicle fell open. Cooper got dressed in double time, scowling at any man who dared glance at him while walking past. He was embarrassed by what he'd seen, embarrassed that these men might have seen him watching, embarrassed that they might think him willing to make the same public display. In his experience sex had always been so furtive—the manner of the act itself the revelation of deepest secrets—that he couldn't imagine making such a casual display of it. How could Sadiq?

Cooper had to remind himself that it hadn't been Sadiq in the pool; he'd been mistaken. At first the light had played a trick on him. *Or perhaps*, he suddenly worried, *the light had played the opposite trick, morphing Sadiq into someone else when it really* was *him all along?* The possibility of it made Cooper heartsick. If it was true, they couldn't be friends. He knew enough about sordid love. He wanted something else. He'd read enough books to imagine romantic love and convinced himself that it was attainable.

He had to know if it had been Sadiq in that pool. He broke into a trot, taking every shortcut he knew, sprinting down the last stretch of wharf realizing he was on a crazy mission that revealed more about himself than anything he might find out about the boy. For all Cooper knew, Sadiq could have returned to Beirut! Crazy mission or not, as he came into sight of the first pink fringe of the gingerbread arcade, with all his heart he wished Sadiq to be there. He could not have beaten Cooper back from the hammam, so if he was there, he was innocent.

Cooper ducked behind cargo stacked on the wharf, where he could observe al-Basma Diamonds. The shop's door was ajar, but the sun flashed so brilliantly off the windows that it blinded him. The sweat streaming into his eyes didn't help either. He seemed to wait a long time and had begun to feel conspicuous when Mazen stepped outside. Cooper was crestfallen. He watched the older man retrieve a half cigarette, light it, and blow out smoke while thoughtfully gazing over the bay. His beloved son was home, his business was good, but Mazen moved with the heaviness of a troubled man. Cooper felt like he was prying on private matters by watching him, and he was about to leave when Sadiq stepped outside to hand his father an ashtray. The older man examined it as if he held a foreign object before tossing his cigarette into the street and following his son back inside.

Cooper almost yelped with happiness! Sadiq hadn't been at the hammam! He wanted to celebrate the boy's innocence. His heart overflowing, he wanted to share his joy, tell somebody he had a worthy friend, but he only had his acquaintances at The Mining Pan, and that was bar talk if anyone was sober enough to talk at all. Besides, how could they understand what he felt for Sadiq when they'd be thinking in terms of lipsticked boys?

He decided to write his sister a postcard; that's what he would do. His news would cheer Becky up. Deciding to write a postcard, though, was easier said than done in Langatown, which was about as far off the tourist route as any destination could be, so postcards weren't plentiful.

He stopped at *Auntie's Junk-it*, a shop that sold nautical paraphernalia, antiques, gimcrack African crafts, and a jumble of everybody else's discards, which occasionally included postcards. Auntie was seated in her raised chair behind the counter, high enough that she could see every nook and cranny in the overstuffed shop. She was an ample woman fond of the loose-fitting floral prints favored by the local women and wore a flamboyant headdress crafted from stiff red material shaped into a flying saucer that towered three feet over her head and was just as wide. Single-handedly she filled one end of her shop. Popeye, her one-eyed parrot with an eye patch, sat perched on her shoulder, and the only time she stopped fanning both of them with a cheap Japanese fan was when she collected money from a customer. Cooper couldn't remember ever seeing Auntie off her throne or without her parrot.

Squaaaawk! The bird greeted Cooper when he entered.

"Squaaaawk, Popeye," he replied. "How are you, Auntie?"

"Suffering this life," she complained, which was her usual complaint. "You take your time to look-look. Auntie will be right here. Or is it only a postcard that you want today?"

"Unless you have books?" he asked hopefully. Cooper had bought other things there—a towel, fork, plate, the only ice cube tray he'd seen in the sweaty country—minimal necessities that he'd discovered amid the shop's jumble. Books were even rarer than postcards.

"I'm running a business, not a library," she quipped.

"Then only a postcard," he told her.

Lines of twine, decorated with small colored flags, led to color-coded drawers that Auntie could open without moving. She pulled on her blue line, and with a lumbered effort reached into the drawer as her parrot—*Squaaawk*—walked down her other arm as if it were a counterweight, quickly climbing back to her shoulder—*Squaaawk!*—when she grunted and sat upright again.

When she spread out four postcards like a winning poker hand, he exclaimed, "Wow! How did you get so many at one time?"

"A man died."

"What was he, a collector?" Cooper studied their pictures depicting different exotic places. Shimmering rice terraces. Snow-capped peaks. A grassy plain filled with wildebeest. An Arab riding a camel in the desert. Perhaps the deceased man *had* been a collector, and in diminished Lalanga, his collection had probably been considered grand; certainly unique, a notion which was reinforced when Cooper flipped them over and discovered that none had writing on them! Their glossy white flipsides had yellowed and spotted with age, but they'd been neither addressed nor messaged, and for the first time in Lalanga, he wouldn't have to squeeze in his own words between someone else's lines. He wished he could buy all four.

Holding up the one with the Arab on a camel, he asked, "Where's this?"

Auntie studied the picture. "Somewhere else," she said definitively.

"I'll take it." Cooper handed her some grubby bills and slipped the postcard into his shirt pocket. "I'll be back for the others," he said.

"You make a deposit?"

"How many buyers you got?"

"Not every collector is died."

"I'll take my chances."

Squaaawk! Popeye sounded off as Cooper walked out.

When Cooper wasn't doused by rain in Langatown, sweat soaked him, and he entered The Mining Pan dripping wet, parched, and thinking of nothing but a beer. Chugging one as soon as Juma popped its top, he ordered a second before he'd finished the first. Juma slid it to him in a puddle of condensation.

Two girls Cooper had never seen before were sitting opposite each other in a booth, huddled in its corners, watching the goings-on in the bar. Still kids, they hadn't yet mastered the skills of makeup and tease. Still kids like his kid sis.

"Hey, Juma, let me borrow your pen," Cooper said.

Juma looked at him as if he were demanding all his money.

"Don't worry, I'll pay for the ink."

"You give it back," the barman said, making it sound like a warning, and set aside the pistol he kept on top of his cashbox to rummage in it. He made a point of keeping the weapon in plain sight as a deterrent to trouble.

"When was the last time you used that?" Cooper asked.

Juma slapped a pen down in front of him. "The last time I had to."

A couple of Thick Necks came in and scanned the room to assess the stock of available girls. "Looks like we got ourselves a couple of pretty *stukkies* here!" one of them said in an accent Cooper had learned to recognize as South African. They squeezed into the booth with the new girls, and one of them shouted for a bottle of Juma's best rot gut. He carried it to their table along with four glasses.

Cooper pulled out his postcard and was examining its picture when the barman passed behind him.

"You planning to go there?" he asked.

"Not unless it snows."

"Why is it that you like the cold so much?"

"It probably has something to do with being locked up as a kid in hot little spaces."

"Locked up?"

"Yeah, like in closets."

"It sounds like your parents didn't treat you very good."

"I didn't have parents, only a dad."

"You had a mother once," Juma reminded him, and went back to tending bar.

Cooper flipped the postcard over, staring at the yellowy white space, thinking through what to say. *Hey there, kid sis* is how he started every postcard to her. Becky liked his nickname for her. He knew she'd smile when she read it, so he wrote:

> *Hey there, kid sis, That's not me on the camel! No deserts or camels here. I've made a friend, an Arab—NOT the man on the camel! Still fighting the bad guys down here. But I'm booking myself on the first flight home after Mission Accomplished. C.*

When he finished, he looked up, and there was Lulay in the mirror, fixing her hair and popping her bubblegum. She reminded him of Becky the way she touched her hair, always trying to look older than she was, when in the next instant she'd blow a big bubblegum bubble and be a kid again. Becky! It tore him apart, not knowing what was happening to her, not home to protect her, and when he next looked down to reread what he'd written, a tear blurred a word. He quickly wiped his eyes and put the postcard away.

Across the room, a glass was knocked over and Cooper turned to see a Thick Neck grab hold of one of the girls. "What's the matter, honey, you never touch a man down there before?" he asked, forcing her hand to his crotch. "You better learn to get friendlier real fast!"

Instantly Cooper was on his feet and crossing to the booth.

Lulay intercepted him. "You stop here, Cooper."

"He's going to hurt that girl."

"That's Juma's trouble, and Juma don't want your trouble, too."

Cooper glanced at the barman, who was watching him warily. He glanced back at the Thick Necks, who were getting out of the booth and pulling the girls after them.

"Juma will send you away, Cooper. How can you help me then?"

The oilmen slung their arms over the girls' shoulders, and the louder one plopped the whiskey bottle on the bar and instructed Juma, "Don't let anyone steal that." He shot a look at Cooper that asked *What the fuck are you staring at?,* and Lulay had to grab his hand to keep him from answering with his fist.

Juma spoke sharply to the girls, and they plodded on, resigned to their duties behind the beaded curtain. Cooper wondered where they came from and how they had gotten there, to that bar in Langatown. He didn't even know Lulay's story except that she was poor, had a mother, came from a village, and wanted to go home. She claimed to be seventeen but he guessed fifteen, like his kid sis the last time he saw her. Girl enough to still be sweet. Girl enough to have breasts only starting to bud. Girl enough not to be slipping behind a beaded curtain to service thick-necked johns.

Reluctantly he let Lulay drag him back to the bar, and Juma slid him another beer. "Looks like Lulay's doubling as your bouncer," Cooper said to him.

"I don't need a bouncer when I don't allow trouble in the first place," the barman replied.

"I don't recall passing an admissions test."

"The test is if I let you stay."

Cooper looked around the room. At the mortar hole in the roof giving way to the night sky. At Juma's collection of beer signs blurred by the hovering cloud of cigarette smoke. At the girls and johns cha-cha-chaing. "You can send me anyplace, if it means leaving this dump," he offered.

"Take me with you," Lulay said. "I go anyplace with you."

"I would, if I had anyplace place to go except back to my room. It's not exactly a honeymoon suite."

"You take me there?"

"My room? No. But away from here, I would if I could. I promise you that."

"Men promise lies."

"When have I lied to you?"

"You will."

"I won't, and that's a Cooper promise."

She pressed herself seductively against his knees. "You buy Lulay, Cooper."

He grabbed her wrists to stop her hands from sliding up his thighs. "You know I don't want that."

"You buy me from Juma."

"No can do. We had a Civil War to abolish slavery."

"You in Africa, Cooper. I am Juma's now."

Cooper waved an arm at the barman. "Hey Juma, how much you want for Lulay? She says she's for sale!"

The barman, rinsing out glasses, shot Lulay a warning look.

"You buy me, Cooper," the girl pleaded.

"What's it look like I'm trying to do? Hey Juma, name your price!"

Juma looked unamused.

Cooper could see the urgency in the girl's face. She wanted him to keep his promise to take her away, and she had no doubt that he could—a white man in her world owned more than everything. She lunged at him, groping him, her hand landing on the wad of bills in his pocket, and she mistook him for being aroused. "Why you always say no when I know you want Lucy?"

"Stop it!" he said, and knocked her hand away.

With only herself to barter, Lulay was right back on him, struggling to anchor a hand in one of his pockets. "You buy me!"

"You're acting crazy!" he cried, and jumped off the barstool, yanking out her hand and bringing with it a couple of the slippery condoms that fell to the floor.

Other customers stared.

"Please, Cooper! They making Lulay disappear!"

"Stop it!"

Again she was on him, again clinging to him, again drilling a hand into his pocket to attach herself to him. Another slippery packet popped out, and that time Cooper caught it. He pushed her away and threw it at her. "Stop it!"

But she wouldn't stop and came at him again, trying to touch him, trying to make him want her.

"Stop it! Stop it! Stop it!" he cried, pelting her with condoms until all the slippery packets lay scattered at her feet, and he fled the bar.

4

Cooper woke the next morning sensing something was amiss and slipped his hand under his pillow for his knife. Before he'd rolled back over, he already knew nobody was in the room. It was he who was amiss. Ashamed of himself for humiliating Lulay by throwing condoms at her. She shouldn't have tried to seduce him, but blaming her didn't ease his own misery.

He rolled off the bed and put water on to boil, hoping the power would stay on long enough that he could have a hot cup of coffee. He suspected that his father had mixed coffee with his baby formula (his mother had died at childbirth), which is why he was addicted to it, as well as having been plied with it by the many pseudo-mother waitresses who'd often watched over him.

He finished his essential coffee, set the chipped cup in the sink, and opened the door to leave. From the doorway he glanced back around to make sure he'd left nothing important behind.

It's how Coops—his father's name for him—had grown up. Leaving empty rooms. Learning to take with him anything he didn't want to lose. They might not return to the room they'd left that same morning, though his father never said anything at the time. He'd pick Coops up after school like normal—if normal were the days his father hadn't forgotten him or had "an engagement," as he liked to call them, which young Coops thought meant a job and older Cooper figured out meant otherwise—and off they'd go, their little green trailer swerving behind them. Next address: down the road.

COOPER'S PROMISE

Cooper didn't care too much. Usually by the time they left a town, he'd already burned through his possible friendships and was glad to go. Off they'd ride, leaving behind another rundown apartment in a string of rundown apartments rented when his father had a more promising job than occasional handyman—ahead of them the perpetually elusive promise of better times, a better job, a better apartment. Between times they flopped out in cheap motels. When his father finally bought a little green trailer, at least Cooper had a sense of home, though it was on wheels. He'd almost never had an address until he went to boot camp: c/o Camp Pendleton, California. Becky had sent him his first letter there.

A sense of home by no means translated into a more sedentary lifestyle. If anything, having a trailer encouraged their nomadic tendencies. No leases, no security deposits, no one asking questions. They could pull into any trailer park, hook up the water and toilet lines, and nothing more was wanted from them than a day's rent paid in advance. Cooper figured his father had managed to avoid the authorities over the gaps in his schooling by confining their meanderings to the macho Southwest, where you risked a bullet between the eyes by asking somebody else their business. Foster care was the great maw that threatened to swallow him, and Cooper wasn't going to let it. To keep his grades up, he had become a voracious reader and made a point of studying on the road trips between their itinerant destinations. Wherever he had enrolled in school, he was usually head of his class.

The mysterious *African Lady* had hoisted anchor and sailed off, and Cooper scanned the horizon trying to make out her black hull. He thought he could, heading straight for the open sea, but the sun's intense reflection off the water made it impossible to be certain. Where she had been docked several smaller boats were now tied up.

The cargo pier was busier than usual with a large freighter being offloaded by a crane that picked up containers, and, swinging them precariously, dropped them onto the open backs of flatbed trucks that roared off as soon as they'd been loaded. Some Thick Necks stood nearby, carrying weapons openly for the first time that Cooper had seen. He wondered what cargo they were protecting, and by the sturdy crates guessed it to be oil rig equipment. Nobody was wasting any time to suck up Lalanga's black gold.

Butterflies filled his stomach when approaching the diamond arcade. To glimpse the café latte boy would give his day a purpose. It wasn't yet noon, and Cooper hoped Sadiq would be back from the hammam. He didn't like to think of him in that place, not after what he had witnessed. The boy could have seen it too, and probably had on other days.

In the shipping offices along the boardwalk, the beedi-smoking clerks lounged around, stretching little work into long hours, but all of the diamond shops were closed. Cooper couldn't imagine what had happened. Had there been a raid? A crackdown? A strike? Had the UN sanctions on Lalanga's diamonds finally closed them down?

He picked up his pace, hoping al-Basma Diamonds had been immune to whatever had happened, but he could see the shop's door was closed.

Cooper tried the knob.

Locked! He pressed his face against the window to peer into the plum-colored shop.

Empty. And the ceiling fan wasn't rotating.

He stepped back to gaze at the empty window as if it might disclose the secret of Sadiq's whereabouts.

He'd been hearing in the background the mullah's tinny call to prayer broadcast from the town's only mosque; a sound that, in Iraq, Cooper had heard as a call to war. Its purpose seemed to be to remind him that there were people who wanted to kill him for no other reason than the fact that he existed, and something represented by that sound made them want to do it. It also reminded him that it was Friday, the Muslim holy day, and he guessed that the Lebanese merchants had gone to the mosque to pray. That's where he would find Sadiq.

As well as Cooper knew Langatown, he didn't know well the Arab quarter that fanned out behind the diamond arcade. He'd avoided that knot of dune-colored streets that were far too reminiscent of Fallujah, of Kirkuk, of souks with unpronounceable names that he had gladly forgotten. The mosque lay in the center of Little Baghdad—his name for the district—and he plunged into it, dropping himself back into a territory of eyes secretly watching him, revealed by the slightest movements of a drape or door. Unlike the African neighborhoods, these streets seemed deserted even when not, their loud silence broken only by the melancholy call to prayer that lured Cooper around a corner to discover the pink minaret piercing the cloudless blue sky.

Women had gathered, their somber robes tucked around them, in the mosque's hard-packed yard, chatting amiably while the men prayed inside. Cooper approached its open entrance, not intending to enter, only wanting to peek inside. He drew curious stares from the women, and a couple of them waved him forward, assuming that, though a stranger and inappropriately attired in cutoffs, he'd come to pray.

The mullah had started his sermon, and when cued the many men resting on their haunches in neat rows repeatedly rolled forward in unison to touch their foreheads to the ground, murmuring, "*Allah akbar!*" Cooper was fascinated by it. He'd served in Iraq more than a year and had never witnessed Friday prayers. Of course he had seen men praying almost everywhere when called to prayer—in their shops, beside their parked vehicles, on sidewalks, and in garden patches—but never in a proper mosque. How could he possibly have approached one while dressed in army issue?

An old granny fell upon him, cackling and pointing to his boots and then pointing to a rack chockfull of every kind of shoe and sandal. With his best sign language Cooper tried to explain that he wasn't intending to go inside, but the woman's cackling grew louder, attracting the attention of some of the men at prayer. Rather than cause more stir, he slipped off his boots, discreetly wedging his knife tighter into one boot's toe. The old granny took them with a victorious smile, slapped a paper prayer cap on his head, and gave him a push that sent him across the mosque's threshold.

Cooper wasn't a fish out of water but a man drowning. He had never felt so out of place as he hovered over the backsides of men rhythmically touching their foreheads to the ground. They all wore caftans or baggy pants and white pillbox caps, reminding Cooper how foolishly dressed he was in cutoffs, as if he were out for a jog and not Friday prayers. The old granny, still in the doorway, waved him along to the end of the row, where he knelt and imitated the men around him, trying to follow their movements as he used to do in churches if he didn't know the liturgy. He didn't manage to imitate them very well, but no one seemed to mind, and minutes later they were finished. There was a general shuffle as the men unbent their stiff knees and rolled up their prayer rugs.

Cooper, ready to get out of there, was headed for the entrance when he heard, "Coopah!"

He turned to see Sadiq weaving through the men to reach him. "What are you doing here?" Sadiq asked.

"I—" Cooper didn't know what to say. He could hardly confess that he'd come searching for the youth. "I heard the call to prayer," he finally said lamely.

Puzzled, Sadiq asked, "Did you come to pray?"

"No. It's kinda crazy, huh?"

"Why not?" Sadiq said pleasantly, trying to make heads or tails of him. "Maybe you'll convert. Or maybe you already have!"

"I don't expect that will happen."

"Then you shouldn't be here," said Munir, coming up to stand next to Sadiq. His face was so hard-set that his welted scar pulsed. "It's an offense to mock Allah!" Sadiq tried to placate Munir, who cut him short, saying, "We can speak English for your American friend."

"I wasn't trying to offend anyone," Cooper said.

"You didn't," Sadiq assured him.

"You are wearing a soldier's shirt in this holy place!"

"It *was* a soldier's shirt. Now it's only half a shirt, and it's all mine."

"And what is the business of American soldiers?"

"Please, Munir, not in here."

"To destroy mosques!"

"Munir, really! Coopah is not about to destroy the mosque."

"Destroy the mosque?" Mazen said roundly, coming up to the three young men and clapping Cooper on the shoulder. "Salaam malekum, Cooper. I see you have found our mosque. Is it by coincidence, or did you come to pray? But what does it matter when Allah listens to all prayers, and you see, he has listened to mine." Mazen beamed at Sadiq. "My son is home! Now what is this about destroying the mosque? I should hope that is not something we have to worry about in Lalanga. We may be a poor country, but we are a peaceful one, praise Allah."

"*Humdililah*," Sadiq and Munir replied in unison.

"We were only talking politics, Father," Sadiq added.

"Of course you were talking politics," the older man replied, and to Cooper he directed, "That's all he's talked about since returning home, while ignoring his mother's suggestions for a wife."

"Father!"

"I'm only saying you're old enough to marry, and if you don't soon your urges will get the better of you. It's true for all young men. It's not healthy not to be married."

"A mosque is not a place to speak of urges!" Munir upbraided the older man. "It is a sin to think about them!"

"When you are older," Mazen replied evenly, "you will realize that this is the only place where you *can* speak of urges, freely that is, without fear of some woman eavesdropping on your man's business."

Munir, growing increasingly vexed as the older man spoke, could no longer restrain his fury and stormed off. His crooked limp seemed more pronounced for his agitation.

"You didn't have to provoke him," Sadiq complained.

"Your friend has no sense of humor."

"He's been injured."

"He may use his injury to excuse many things, including his own shortcomings, but it is not excusable to tell me what I can say—or think—inside my own mosque."

"He was only trying to remind you where you are."

"I don't need to be reminded where I am. And I certainly don't need him to be put in my place!"

"Oh, Father, really!"

Sadiq looked disbelievingly at Cooper. *Could he believe how stubborn his father could be!* "I should go," he finally said when Munir had almost reached the door. "He gets lost easily." Sadiq caught up with his friend and put a hand on his shoulder as they stepped outside.

The mosque had emptied except for a couple of sweepers whisking their brooms over the marble floors, and their soft, scratching sound filled the silence until Mazen remarked, "Sometimes I wonder if we should have let him go."

"To Beirut?" Cooper asked.

"It is our tradition for our young men to go away to see something of the world before settling down. But now, the world is so changed, I wonder if we should have let Sadiq go. He's always been so impressionable." Mazen gazed thoughtfully at the mosque's entrance. "His friend has come to Lalanga for a visit. Who comes to Lalanga for a visit?"

"A close friend?" Cooper suggested.

"Some friends should not be brought home." The older man sighed, clearly troubled. "My son has come home with some foolish ideas. Perhaps you could talk to him. He thinks he understands the world when in truth he knows very little."

"I may know even less."

"You will be a good influence on him, I am sure. Do you pray?"

"Pretty much nonstop," Cooper answered honestly.

"Yes, yes, we all pray nonstop, it is our human condition, which is why you must make it a habit to come for Friday prayers. It is a wonderful thing to pray with others. Our voices come together and we feel them in here"—he rapped his chest—"as if the voice of God has come inside us."

"You mean Allah?" Cooper jested.

"The important thing is His voice, not His name."

"I hope He has a better voice than mine."

Mazen smiled indulgently. "Shall we go?"

As they walked out, Cooper mulled over Mazen's speaking to him as an adult, not as a child, which was how he obviously still viewed his son, though Sadiq and he were nearly the same age. He'd given him an adult task—to be a good influence—when Cooper wondered if he himself wasn't the one who needed a good role model. Suddenly he found himself straddling youth and adulthood, with neither foot planted very firmly.

People had lingered after prayers in the sunny yard, the men and women chatting in separate groups, laughing brightly, and enjoying a casualness that was unusual in strife-ridden Langatown. The Arab merchants were endangered only by the risk of being caught in the crossfire, not the risk of conscription. Their function was too important. Everyone counted on selling diamonds to make ends meet or balance the national budget, and the Lebanese were the middlemen for every transaction.

The old granny, waiting for Cooper to come outside, delivered his boots while plucking the paper prayer cap from his head. After checking that his knife was still there, Cooper was putting on his boots when Mazen handed the woman a crumpled bill. "I'll pay," Cooper protested, pulling out his own money.

Mazen restrained him. "It's nothing."

"Thanks."

"You must remember to bring more diamonds soon," Mazen reminded him.

"I'm working on it."

They shook hands, and Mazen walked off to join some friends.

5

Cooper *was* working on getting more diamonds, though he couldn't do much until nightfall when he'd try to find Innocence at the church. He didn't know where the blind boy spent his days, but it wasn't at church, he knew that much. Spotting a couple of the lipsticked boys in the crowded bar, Cooper hoped Innocence didn't spend his days like they did. He couldn't imagine he did; but then, he couldn't imagine most of what went on in that bereft country even when it was happening right before his eyes.

He drained his G and T, signaling to Juma that he wanted another, and telling himself it would be his last that afternoon; he'd better save the rest of his money to bankroll diamonds in case Janjay had found any. He hoped she had, and prayed they were big, wanting to impress Sadiq with more than the gravelly bits she usually managed to sneak out of the mines. He'd also spent the afternoon praying for the ice machine to hold up while dousing himself with ice-water showers. He'd easily spent more on water than cheap gin. Every time he recalled Mazen's encouragement to become friends with his son, Cooper felt like celebrating, and that called for another dousing. He'd started to believe prayers *do* come true when the ice machine shuddered to a stop.

Juma looked at him unhappily. "You make it work too hard," he complained.

"I'm outta here." Cooper pushed his way through the crowd without giving Lulay a glance. All afternoon he'd watched her ply trade on both sides of the beaded curtain. Each time she did, it tore him up inside—and she knew it did—but she never looked at him once, not even when he poured water over his head, which usually made her laugh. She hadn't forgiven him for throwing the condoms at her, and he couldn't blame her.

Some nights in the tropics fall faster than an executioner's ax, and that night was one of them. Cooper hadn't expected it to be dark when he went outside, the saloon doors flapping behind him, and it took him a moment to adjust, like coming out the movies and having it still be daylight. Bar-goers and drunks, and the girls working them, lurched down Cowboy Mile in a hazy neon cloud. Cooper took his own first unsteady steps, feeling wooziness from an afternoon filled with G and Ts. *No doubt about it, there are more Thick Necks around*, he was thinking, when "Hello, American Cooper!" interrupted his thoughts. "What's wrong with Little Sister that she send you home-home so early-early?"

He gestured that he was going home to sleep, and another girl offered, "I got a bed here, American Cooper! You don't have to go all the way home-home!" He spread his hands the way he always did—*I'm helpless, what can I do?*—and they howled with laughter. They all wanted to be his Little Sister.

He couldn't know all the girls working Cowboy Mile, that would be impossible, and a lot more of them recognized him than vice versa. He'd gained a reputation for helping Lulay, bigger than he deserved when he hadn't done much more than to stare down a john or two who'd started getting out of hand, and to buy her condoms. A couple of times he'd bought her time, too, using most of it to lecture her on using protection, like he'd lectured Becky before he deployed to Iraq. There was nothing about Lulay that reminded him of Becky apart from being too much a kid to have had her adult experiences, and that didn't set Lulay apart from any of the other girls working Cowboy Mile. She had simply found Cooper first, sipping his first gunpowdery G and T at The Mining Pan and asking for more ice. He thought she was playacting, a kid who'd walked in off the street to hustle him. She was seventeen, she lied, though even at that false age she still would have been too young to be turning tricks at a bar.

The first time he'd ever paid for a girl's time was that night, and all night he kept her seated right there at the bar, buying her drinks that he drank along with his own, keeping the barman happy and getting very drunk. He couldn't remember how he got home, but he did recall the girl the instant he woke up the next morning. Lulay. Lucy to her johns. What little he knew broke his heart.

At last he cleared the shanty houses and entered No Man's Land. The church steeple's bluish light made the shadows even blacker, and Cooper felt the presence of people around him more than saw them. He caught a whiff of marijuana and glimpsed the red ember pass from hand to hand. From every direction, he heard the relentless *tap-tap tapping* of sticks used to scour the rocky hillock for some overlooked treasure.

He pushed through the white picket fence into the safety of the families huddled around their cookfires. The boy with the crutch who'd eaten his discarded chicken bones gave Cooper a hungry look, and he decided to buy him something to eat on his way back out. He smiled at the boy, gestured he should stay put, and hoped he understood he should stick around.

A dozen truly crazed worshipers had congregated on the steps, rocking and jerking and throwing their hands in the air. Cooper had to run a gauntlet of pointy elbows and knees before literally stumbling across the threshold into the church's hushed interior where candles flickered beckoningly in front of the icons. In reality it was a humble church, not the cathedral Cooper sometimes conjured it to be, and the icons might well have been pagan idols for all their garish imagery.

Churches always seemed like big places to Cooper. They'd been his sanctuaries as a kid. He'd found allies there who didn't pry. When he memorized, in one week, his Sunday school class's memory work for the entire year, they offered him a scholarship to church camp, which they didn't need to do, it wasn't on the list of Memory Work Achievement Awards tacked to the bulletin board. Later, when he was older, he could imagine how the priest and his Sunday school teacher had probably colluded, knowing nothing more than sensing his need to get away from home, and they'd come up with sending him to camp as a solution at least for the week that it lasted. And it had been a solution. It had been a sanctuary in the woods. There had been no brass-latched cupboards in the tents. No father's temper or whipping belt. Churches had been his hideaway places until he was old enough to hang out on his own in roadside diners reading more than prayer books. Instead of Sunday school teachers reciting the lessons, he got a hard-knocks education from sailor-mouthed waitresses and tattooed cooks. There wasn't much in his childhood that hadn't made him grow up fast.

Though he never became a believer, Cooper remained thankful for every safe day a church had given him, and he walked respectfully up the center aisle. He crossed himself, not from faith but superstition, believing they were distinguishable. Once he had dodged a black cat, unexpectedly missing a bullet in the same instant, and from then on he had taken every opportunity to improve his odds. So he was crossing himself a second time when he heard, "You come back fast-fast this time, American."

Innocence had spoken from a couple of pews back, and Cooper turned, only barely able to make out the boy. "How did you let me get past you?"

"Maybe you're not the only white man who comes to pray."

"I didn't know you were running a racket."

"What is a racket?"

"Never mind." He slid onto the pew next to Innocence. "So do we all stink different? I know, I know, you said we smell different, 'stink' is my word for it. But is that what you were doing, trying to figure out if it was me or another white guy by the way I smell?"

"Yes."

"So what do I smell like?"

"Your clothes."

"My clothes?" Cooper sniffed his fraying shirt. "You told me I don't stink."

"Your clothes stink."

"Now you tell me. How do you know I wear clothes?"

Innocence clearly hadn't expected the question, and he smiled bigger than Cooper had ever seen him smile. "Janjay sees for me," he said. "She would tell me if she sees you naked."

"The all-seeing Janjay!" Cooper said grandly. "Speaking of whom, did she bring anything home?"

"Did you pray like I say?"

"Does praying for the Hope Diamond count?"

"Everybody prays for hope."

"I was talking about Hope of a different kind, something more tangible, as in diamonds bigger than watermelons."

Grinning, Innocence displayed two stones nestled in his palm. "Are these big enough watermelons?"

Cooper took them. They *were* big. "Janjay found these?"

"She trades for them."

"What the hell did she trade for rough like this?"

Innocence shrugged, only willing to say, "It's the business-business."

"Yeah, yeah, everything is the business-business around here." Cooper handed the stones back to Innocence. "How much?" The boy answered by spreading his thumb and index finger to indicate a sizable stack of bills. "Are you crazy!" Cooper exclaimed, and squeezing the blind boy's fingers, considerably narrowed the gap.

"You said market conditions have improved," Innocence reminded him, and again increased the gap, though not back to where he'd started.

"I said improved, not gone haywire!" Cooper narrowed the gap again, also less severely.

The boy moved his fingers sideways, measuring the heft of Cooper's offer.

"Don't friggin' try to cheat me," he warned Innocence. "I got it exactly eyeballed."

"Okay." Innocence accepted the offer, and Cooper began to layer the bills between his fingers, wedging in most of his remaining money.

For those stones he was getting a deal, and Sadiq was definitely going to be impressed. "There better not be a lot of impurities," he warned as an afterthought.

"I don't see impurities," Innocence claimed, holding the stones close to his cloudy eyes.

"Very funny. Now give me those."

Innocence handed them to him and quickly tucked the money out of sight. "You are a rich man, American."

Cooper checked to make sure his pockets didn't have holes before dropping a stone into each of them. "It looks like you're the one with all the money now."

"You stay in Lalanga, you get very rich. That's why the white man always comes back."

Cooper briefly wondered what the blind boy's image of a white man could be. "For now," he said, "this white man is outta here." He took Innocence's hand and shook it; it was so tiny in his own big paw. "Thanks, buddy, and thanks to Janjay."

He paused at the baptismal font, thinking the kid with the crutch might have followed him in. He hadn't, and next Cooper had to confront the overzealous worshipers crowding the entrance, oblivious to his desire to pass through them. Innocence joined him, and taking his hand, effortlessly cut a path for them out the door to the top of the steps where the boy let him go, waving blindly as Cooper navigated between the people encroaching on the sidewalk.

That's when the crippled boy suddenly reappeared, slipping inside the gate and wildly waving his crutch in the direction of the church. Cooper glanced back at Innocence, who, sensing something was amiss, stopped waving and slowly dropped his hand.

An enormously fat policeman in a starched white uniform and wearing dark sunglasses followed the boy through the gate. Everything about him said he was the chief of police. The lively chatter subsided in a wave that rippled through the churchyard, and people scrambled to clear the sidewalk for him.

What business could he have with Innocence? Cooper wondered, and glanced back. The boy had disappeared, and he considered retreating into the church himself when a second policeman, as skinny as the police chief was fat, stepped from behind his boss holding a gun pointed at him.

"ID," the chief of police demanded, and held out his hand, his fingers like bloated sausages.

From his back pocket, Cooper pulled out his passport and flattened it some before handing it over.

The chief struggled to read his name through his dark glasses. "You are Mr. Cooper?"

"The name's Chance. Cooper Chance."

The policeman slipped the passport into his breast pocket.

"Hey! That's mine!"

"You come with me."

"I'm not going anywhere until you give back my passport."

"What were you doing inside the church?"

"Praying. What do *you* do inside a church?"

"Empty your pockets."

"Empty my what? Why? I have a right to pray without being hassled; it's in the Geneva Accords." Cooper patted himself down. "Besides, you can see that there's nothing in my pockets."

The police chief signaled his sidekick, a nervous fellow with the nubbiest little ears Cooper had ever seen, to search his pockets. Little Ears frisked him with one hand while keeping the gun pointed loosely at his chin with the other and announced finding the diamonds in Cooper's pockets with a harsh staccato laugh. When he turned to his boss for orders, Cooper used the moment to knock the gun out of his hand, kneeing him in the same movement. The skinny cop went sprawling on the sidewalk.

By then, the chief of police held a gun on Cooper. "Take them out," he said, meaning the diamonds.

Cooper dug into his pockets and displayed them. "Are these what you want to see?"

Little Ears snatched them from Cooper's palms before scooting back to a safe distance, retrieving his gun on the way.

"You are under arrest, Mr. Cooper," the chief of police informed him.

"The name's Chance, and what the fuck for?"

"Stealing."

"Who did I supposedly steal from?"

"Colonel Diamond."

6

Cooper believed in his rights. He believed in his right to give only his serial number, the right to waive Miranda or not, the right to remain silent. That last right was intended for him, the detainee, not for those detaining him, and certainly not the two cops who sat silently in the front seat of a broken-down sedan that passed for a police cruiser in Lalanga.

"Where the fuck are you taking me?" he had asked in as many ways as he could without sounding scared. But he was scared. If he was accused of stealing from Colonel Diamond, he was in trouble. They might chop off his hand before he could sign his confession. He would have jumped out of the car every time they slowed for a pothole, which was often, but the door handles and window cranks had been removed, and despite how far his long fingers could reach into the door's recesses, he couldn't quite spring the lock. A cage separated Cooper from the front seat, trapping him, and he had to fight back his mounting panic.

"I've got rights," he insisted again, and each time he did, Little Ears snickered, revealing his mouth full of decapitated teeth stained betel-red. "I'm invoking my rights under the Geneva Accords," Cooper added, remembering something he'd been instructed at boot camp to say if captured by the enemy.

The police chief grunted and hit a pothole dead center. No doubt they were hard to see through his black sunglasses at night.

"You're required to call the American Embassy," Cooper persisted, "and tell them where you're taking me."

Little Ears's whole body shook with his venomous laughter. "A-bu

Ghra-ib!" he barely managed to spit out. "We take you to Abu Ghraib!"

Cooper struggled to keep his voice calm. "I have a right to a telephone call."

"No telephones work now!"

What had the skinny cop meant by 'now'? A temporary service outage, or the general state of affairs? Or had they driven beyond the telephone service's range? Where *were* they taking him? Then it dawned on him— they were taking him to some killing field to be executed! After stealing his diamonds, now they planned to murder him! He jammed his fingers deeper into the door, working the lock mechanism more urgently, ready to beg for mercy. But he wouldn't beg. He couldn't. In a jungle, the weak are eaten first.

Suddenly the car lurched over a curb to stop in front of a rundown building so riddled with bullet holes that Cooper instantly recalled the Alamo. Somebody had fought hard for it, and then he realized why. A sign identified it as a police station, always a desirable target for replenishing rebel arsenals. It was unclear if his personal situation had improved, but he wasn't going to be nose-deep in some field—at least not yet.

Little Ears let him out of the backseat, and, waving his gun, indicated that he should follow the chief into the crumbling building. In its shabby waiting room a handful of women looked as if they had indeed been waiting for a very long time. The night-duty officer dropped his feet to the floor when the chief entered, and the women quieted and sat up straighter, sternly accusing him with their bodies. They were there for information on missing loved ones, and the chief was implicated in every disappearance. They didn't expect justice, they were simply putting in a customary appearance to honor those they assumed were already dead. Then they noticed Cooper, a white man nudged along by a black one, and that got their attention but not their sympathy. Cooper didn't detect a sympathetic twitch among them. They'd lost too much themselves to care for strangers.

Little Ears steered him into an office with a sign on the door reading *District Chief of Police*. The fat man dropped his sunglasses on the desk, revealing watery, pink eyes above flabby cheeks. With his sunglasses on, he had looked like a menacing man in a uniform; with them off, he was a fat nasty rat and even his teeth appeared to protrude more. A perfect match for his ferrety deputy. He took a moment to check his appearance in a mirror and pick lint off his collar before indicating that they should all sit around a coffee table.

"We shall have a supper," he said graciously, and whisked the top off a deep dish filled with yellowy rice stewed with something Cooper couldn't quite make out. Then he could. They were birds so small he guessed them to be unhatched fetuses.

Little Ears, drooling at the prospect of eating, wiped his mouth with the back of his hand.

"Eat! Eat!" the policeman invited them, scooping up a tiny carcass and licking the rice off it—

Slurp!

—to reveal its feathery black down. Then, with an audible—

Crunch!

—he bit into the skull to suck out its morsel of brain.

Slurp!

He tossed the unhatched bird at a wastebasket, missing it, and the frail gluey body stuck briefly to its side before dropping to the floor.

"Eat! Eat!" the Police Chief exhorted them, and picked up a second tiny bird.

Slurp!

Little Ears hungrily dived in.

Slurp!

Crunch!

Crunch!

They both flung the corpses at the wastebasket and missed.

"Eat! Eat!" the police chief coaxed him, but Cooper decided to forego the delicacy. He had never been very experimental with food, and no matter how hungry he was, bird fetuses would forever remain on his pass list.

"Looks good, but no thanks," he said. "I'm allergic to birds and preemies. Any size, any species, it doesn't matter."

"You are not hungry?" asked the chief.

"I had a late lunch."

Crunch!

Another gooey carcass fell atop the mounting pile.

"Americans are never hungry," the chief observed.

"Some are."

"Americans don't know hungry like a rock."

"You're right about that," Cooper replied agreeably. He hadn't a clue what the police chief meant.

"Why are you here, American—"

Slurp!

"—in Lalanga?"

"I'd always heard that it was a nice place to visit."

That made the fat policeman laugh. "Americans know how to lie like a rock. You too, you American, you lie like a rock. You are hungry. Why don't you eat?" He licked a speck of brain offal from his fingers before plunging them back into the rice and kneading a ball. When he finished, he offered it to Cooper on an open palm. "Because my hand is black, that is why. You don't want food touched by a black man's hand."

Cooper looked at that outstretched hand knowing that he could not even imagine its depraved history. There was no way he could eat from it. "I didn't see you wash your hands first," he replied.

It took the police chief a moment to understand him, and when he did, he popped the rice ball into his mouth, watching Cooper as if to say,

I'll be eating you next—and he was big enough that he could. "Are your hands so clean, American?"

"It's how I was raised."

"To steal?"

"I didn't steal those diamonds, I bought them."

"From the children?"

"What children?"

The police chief pulled out a crisp white handkerchief and wiped his oily fingers, careful not to miss under the nails. "We know the children steal from the mines."

"Yeah, but *I* didn't steal from anybody. I bought those diamonds."

"All diamonds belong to Colonel Diamond."

"He has to sell them sometime, or what good are they? So he sold them to somebody, and I bought them from somebody."

"Who?"

"I don't remember. Besides, under Colonel Diamond's Diamond Law, I don't have to know how they got acquired."

"Is that also in your Geneva Accords, Mr. Cooper?" The chief folded his handkerchief and tucked it away. "You have strange laws, you Americans with clean hands. You come to Lalanga rich and you go home richer."

"Not me. I come to Lalanga poor, I go home poorer. Cross my heart."

"Nobody goes home rich in Lalanga," the chief said, making it sound like an accusation.

"I knew there was a reason I love this place," Cooper replied. "I've gone native."

Little Ears, who'd been busy scarfing down food, exploded in laughter, expelling a grain of rice that shot straight out of his ruinous mouth to land on the chief's white coat. He instantly froze and looked horrified as the fat man retrieved his handkerchief, carefully unfolded it, and gently removed the rice. He held it out for Little Ears to take back, who did, instantly popping it into his mouth. With a kingly nod, the chief indicated that his deputy could keep eating, and Little Ears didn't hesitate to continue, devouring the rice before barely taking the time to roll it into polite balls. That's when Cooper realized that the ferrety cop wasn't just skinny, he was starving. It didn't make him like the man any more.

"Listen, keep the diamonds," he offered, "and we'll call it square on the Colonel Diamond thing." Cooper had gulped hard as he said it. Those rough stones represented his entire bankroll, which he could ill afford to lose if he didn't want to starve too, but better to try and barter the stones for a free walk out the station's door before the policemen simply declared that they were confiscating them. "I'm glad you guys set me straight," he went on, conjuring a believably sincere smile. "If there's one law I know, you don't fuck with the colonel, no way, José. So no more diamonds for this soldier, cross my heart."

Little Ears stopped eating to sniff in Cooper's direction. No more diamonds?

"*Finito la musica*. Finished. On my mother's grave, I promise." Cooper crossed his heart again.

The two policemen glanced at each other. They weren't buying something.

Finally the chief said, "These are good diamonds, American."

Cooper shrugged it off. "What do I know about diamonds?"

"How do you find such good diamonds?"

"Business secrets. You know how that is."

"If your business is finished, you do not need your secrets."

"Sorry, no can do. You keep your secrets secret and your confidences confidential, that's the first rule of business."

"You need protection, American."

"Protection? Whoa, whoa, wait a minute, you're not understanding me. I'm out of the business. O U T. Out. No more diamonds."

"No, American," the police chief told him firmly.

COOPER'S PROMISE

"*No, American?* What is it about 'no more diamonds' that you don't understand?" Then Cooper understood. "Protection from *you?*"

The policemen broke into broad smiles.

"You want a cut from my diamonds?"

The chief drew a triangle between them. "Three ways," he said, as if it needed explaining, and Little Ears starting heehawing.

"Whoa, whoa, whoa …" Cooper held up a hand to slow down his wannabe partners. He didn't have to think about that one; they'd let him live only until they decided to kill him. Saying no outright, though, might be equally dangerous, so he tried to make a joke of it. "Dividing zero three ways doesn't give much to anyone."

Little Ears stopped laughing. "We have no pay for three months," he complained.

"I know, bad economy and all that," Cooper replied, trying to sound sympathetic, "and it's not like I'm not inclined to help you guys. But like I said, Law Number One, you don't fuck with the colonel. I shouldn't have to lecture *you* on that."

"Sixty percent," the chief begrudgingly offered, indicating the two cops would share it.

"Look, guys—"

"Fifty percent," Little Ears countered.

"Is fifty percent of nothing really worth the trouble for you guys?"

The skinny cop thrust his hands in Cooper's face. "I have more wives than hands and more children than fingers. Always they have hungry mouths. How can I feed them?"

Cooper didn't know, and said so.

The chief grunted. "Now you know hungry like a rock, American."

Glancing between the two men, Cooper saw their worries for their destitute families on their unfriendly faces, and for a moment he almost felt sorry for them. He didn't need to know the details of their lives. He had never imagined desperation quite like Lalanga's. Iraq's nightmare had been different—imposed, nonnative, a foreigner's grievance—whereas Lalanga's horror was native-born. When foreigners can be blamed, people still trust their gods and respect their politicians; it's when the chaos is self-wrought that they lose faith in everything, and hopelessness, desperation's sidekick, reigns. That was Lalanga's desperation, the desperation of hopelessness, that had driven the two policemen along a brutal path, for Cooper had no doubt that they had performed despicable acts. That same desperation drove them now to double-cross the colonel by trying to horn in on Cooper's business, and in doing so, risking their own foul deaths when instead they could be home screwing their many wives.

"You tell us the names of the children, American," the chief bluntly ordered. "You tell us your business secrets."

"The children come up to me. I don't know their names."

The chief shook his head as if confronted with a stubborn child. "Americans are too good liars."

"Not this one."

"Why do you want to protect the children, American?"

Why wouldn't you want to protect children? Cooper thought, and answered, "They're only hungry kids trying to survive. Like your kids," he aimed at Little Ears.

His effort to create an ally failed. Instead, Little Ears jumped up madly waggling his fingers. "Look how many hungry children I have. Look!"

"You will help us, American," the chief said in a way that left no room for negotiation. "Do you understand me?"

"I understand that if I break the law, I'm in trouble, and if I don't, I'm also in trouble. Do you see my dilemma?"

"You know why you don't want to understand me, American? Because I am black and you are white, that is why."

"Catch 22," replied Cooper.

Narrowing his ratty eyes, the policeman asked suspiciously, "What is

Catch 22?"

Cooper stared right back at him. "It means that I'll always be white."

The policeman didn't know what to make of his remark, but when it registered that Cooper was mocking him, his anger welled up, and he got to his feet with all the authority that his massive girth inspired. "You American!" he denounced him.

Cooper shot to his feet as well. "I get a phone call!"

"You are under arrest!"

"It's in the Geneva Accords!"

Little Ears fumbled for his gun, which Cooper kicked out of his hand. It hit the wall and fired, and the women in the waiting room screamed. Diving for his ankles, Little Ears managed to entangle Cooper's feet long enough for the chief to use his body as a battering ram to send him crashing to the floor, spilling the remains of the fetus-laden rice over him. Vainly he squirmed to get out from under the chief's colossal weight, but the night-duty officer joined the scrimmage, and grabbing Cooper's legs, started pulling him out of the office.

Cooper managed to latch on to the doorframe, and cried, "Please help me!" to the women in the waiting room, who watched unflinching. "I'm an American! My name is Cooper Chance! Please contact the American Embassy!"

Not one woman stirred. She'd be the next to disappear.

"I'm an American! My name is Cooper Chance! Please contact my Embassy! Cooper Chance! American Embassy!" he kept shouting until the chief's meaty fist slammed into his jaw.

7

Cooper came to sprawled out on a concrete floor. Everything ached. He was afraid to move for fear of causing himself further bodily harm, but gradually he tested his fingers and toes, wiggling them and relieved that he could. Nothing appeared broken, but that didn't make him hurt any less. Touching a scalp wound, he winced; in the thin light he could see blood on his fingers. "Fuck," he muttered, and found himself cradling his jaw throbbing from the exertion of saying a single word. With a yeoman's effort, he scraped himself together and pushed himself upright.

He was staring at a wall.

That's when he twisted around and saw the bars.

Cooper hadn't contemplated confinement. For all the talk of arrest, he had only considered the possibilities of his torture, mutilation, or death, never confinement, and for him it was a worse fate. He tried to fight off the familiar panic, wanting to keep that black curtain from closing, for that's how he thought of his claustrophobia, as a curtain in his brain separating him from everything except his fear.

He lunged at the bars, his fingers frantically assessing the keyhole, hoping to find a forgotten key or an easily triggered latch. He tried to spread two bars wide enough to escape, bellowing as he made a Herculean effort, until his strength gave way and his bellows turned into sobs. His hands slipped down the bars, dragged by his body puddling on the floor.

Count, Coops, to a thousand. Whisper it aloud so you don't make a mistake.

Can't you leave the door open, Daddy? Please, Daddy.

COOPER'S PROMISE

Then you'd see me fixing your surprise.

The cupboard closed.

A bathroom. A closet. The trailer's cupboards with their brass latches.
They had all been his prisons.

Why can't I watch, Daddy?

It wouldn't be a surprise then, would it?

Why can she watch?

She's my little helper—aren't you, sweetheart?

Cooper and his vagabond dad. Dad always talking up the women and
teasing their daughters, too, flirting with them right in front of their
mothers, convincing everyone to call him uncle. Uncle Roy. Raising a boy
on his own was tough, good times or bad, and every mother could
empathize with Uncle Roy's plight, coming up with odd jobs that didn't
need doing simply to give him something to do, until the town ran out of
odd jobs and good will and they moved on. Moving for better work for
which his father always seemed to arrive a day too late. Moving for better
schools for Cooper, which always seemed a lame excuse. Mostly moving
to flee, he would later realize, and it was made easy by hauling a trailer
around, sometimes splurging on flea-bitten motels if they offered a free
breakfast.

You can give her my surprise.

Why would I do that?

To make her stop crying.

Don't worry, Coops. I have a surprise for her.

He did, too, and Cooper later had a good idea what the surprise was,
but for a long time he didn't, he thought it was only a scary game, and his
father always did have a surprise for him like he'd promised. They were
nothing, really, a bird's feather or beaded bracelet or smooth pebble from
a magic creek, mobile bribes for a childhood on-the-run.

No, Daddy, please don't lock me up!

Count to a thousand, Coops, and I'll be finished by then.

Coops squatted in the closet and wrapped his arms around his knees. One ...
two ... three ...

That's good, Coops.

The cupboard door closed.

"NO!" Cooper shouted, remembering.

Count, Coops ...

... four ... five ... six ...

Coops heard a girl crying.

... seven ... eight ...

Cooper supposed later that he'd always heard them crying; only that time, he had listened. He couldn't imagine what would make a girl whimper so sadly, so shamefully.

... NINE ... TEN ... ELEVEN ...

And still he heard her!

STOP IT! STOP IT! STOP IT!

"Mistuh!"

One ... two ... three ... four ... he started over.

Again he heard a girl cry.

"STOP IT!"

"MISTUH!"

"Wha-a-at?" Cooper wasn't sure who was speaking, if anyone.

"You scaring the girl, Mistuh. You yelling at her makes her scared."

Cooper listened and heard a girl sniffling. "I wasn't yelling at her," he said.

"Then you must be yelling at ghosts."

"Who are you?"

"I'm no ghost yet!"

"Where are you, Ghost? Put out your arm." Straining to see through the bars, Cooper peered down the bleak hall, and in the twilight of a single dim bulb, the man's pale palm indeed looked ghostly.

"Where's the girl?"

Ghost pointed to the cell between them.

"Anyone else in here?"

"Only us, Mistuh. They finished with the others already."

"Finished?"

"They take them away."

"Where did they take them?"

"Where we will go."

The girl's sobs erupted.

"You scaring her with your questions," Ghost scolded him.

Cooper considered pointing out that it wasn't his questions but their answers that were scaring the unseen girl—and him too, if the truth be known. "Don't cry … don't cry …" He tried to calm her down. "I'll bet your mother is one of the women in the waiting room and you'll be going home any minute. Do you know her name, Ghost?""

"Ayana."

"What a pretty name, Ayana. I bet you're a pretty girl. Is she pretty, Ghost?"

"She is like the prettiest flower."

That made Ayana cry harder.

"With all those tears, I bet you'll grow into a big flower. Is that what you're doing, Ayana? Are you growing yourself into a big beautiful flower?"

A sniffle.

"Or maybe a whole garden full of pretty flowers? You're sure crying enough to water them all!"

The girl made a funny, squeaky noise.

"I heard that! I heard that smile! Did you hear that smile, Ghost?"

"I heard it." Ghost, it appeared, understood complicity.

Barely audible, the girl murmured, "You can't hear a smile."

"What's that? What did she say, Ghost?"

"I couldn't make it out myself."

"You can't hear a smile!" the girl repeated louder.

A door opened at the end of the hall, and Little Ears staggered into its patch of light. His long silhouette cut through the gloom like a rapier. Cooper didn't need to smell his breath to know he was drunk or take his pulse to know he was dangerous. He'd never met a drunk man in uniform who wasn't, and that included himself.

The door scuffed closed behind him, and Cooper pressed his face to the bars to watch the cop's unsteady progress. He ran a large key over the bars, passing Ghost, until he reached Ayana's cell and stopped, jingling his keys and pressing himself against her keyhole, threatening to enter. The girl wailed, too young for such misery.

"Stop it!" Cooper shouted.

Little Ears shook his keys again, and the girl cried louder.

"Stop it!"

The cop backed off, not angrily, he was having too much fun; besides, inevitably she would be his if she hadn't been already. With what swagger he could muster, he stepped down to Cooper's cell, and in a couple of tries managed to find the right key to open it. "You come with me, American."

Alcohol hadn't distilled his viral breath.

Cooper held back. "Come with you where?"

"With me."

"You have to report my whereabouts to the American Embassy."

"Geneva Accords!" Little Ears guffawed, spewing betel-red spittle. Then he aimed a gun at Cooper, notched the trigger, and fired a shot. He clearly hadn't intended to miss, he was simply too inebriated to hit a target standing in front of him.

"Okay, I go with you," Cooper agreed.

He stepped out of the cell, and from habit glanced back to make sure he'd left nothing behind. He hadn't, except a bit of sanity, and walked toward the door at the end of the corridor with Little Ears jabbing him in the back with his gun, snickering, "Geneva Accords" each time he did.

As they passed Ayana's cell, the girl scrambled as close to the bars as she dared, keeping enough distance that nobody could grab her. She was nothing but fear, her eyes big whiter saucers in her small face. "You sure *are* a pretty flower," he said, and kissing two fingers, pressed them to the bars of her cell. "You're going to be okay."

Ghost had retreated to a dark corner where he could have been overlooked except for his giveaway salt-and-pepper hair. He was thinner than sticks and leaned forward enough that Cooper could see his scarecrow face. "The girl is no more afraid," he reported. Their collusion had paid off.

Then Cooper was at the door, pushing through it and blinking at the unaccustomed bright light.

8

"How did you know to come and find me?"

"Even in this shithole of a country, sometimes somebody does a good deed," Sam Brown admitted, "especially if there's a reward for it."

Cooper flicked away some rice stuck in his boot laces. "What the fuck are you talking about?"

"Apparently you put out an SOS, and someone came running to the Embassy."

So his display in the police station had worked. "Who the fuck are you?"

Sam Brown ignored him, instead holding out his hand and saying, "You owe me twenty bucks."

"Twenty?"

"I didn't think your ass was worth it either."

"You didn't answer my question."

"Which one?"

"Who the fuck are you?"

"CIA." Sam Brown said it like it was yesterday's news.

"That's what I figured."

"Your file says you're smart."

"Fuck you. What did you do, follow me to Lalanga?"

"You might as well have left a forwarding address, it would've been that easy. We just got lucky when you dropped into our laps."

"Why haven't you arrested me?"

"No extradition treaty."

They left the station.

In the glare of the occasional streetlight, people drawn to their shiny fenders like moths to a flame loomed in the car's windows, pressing their hands to the glass and leaving smudgy streaks. "White man! White man!" someone would occasionally cry out, drawing small crowds that Sam Brown had trouble outrunning on the potholed streets without risking serious damage to the car.

"They stole my knife," Cooper complained, feeling vulnerable without it.

"You're lucky they didn't use it on you."

Remembering something else, Cooper patted down all his pockets. "Ah fuck, they stole my passport too!"

A desperate urban landscape slid by outside their windows. Shanty houses were interspersed with two- and three-storey concrete buildings, many unfinished; cookfires indicated where squatters had moved in. Clusters of pushcarts and three-wheelers were chained to every pole or rod available. Night owls prowled the uneven sidewalks for whatever flesh and fun they could find.

"There's a girl back there who needs help," Cooper said.

Sam Brown snorted. "There's a girl back everywhere who needs help," he replied.

"Yeah? Well I want to help *her*." It was clear the CIA had no intention of turning around, and Cooper asked, "So what the fuck do you want from me?"

"Me personally? Nothing. But Langley thinks you can shoot straight."

"What's Langley want me to shoot?"

"Colonel Diamond."

Cooper conjured up an image of the tall colonel in a rifle's crosshairs. "There are lots of guys who can shoot straight," he replied.

"You've never missed a target."

"What makes you think I would do it?"

"An honorable discharge."

"So I shoot the colonel and get to go home?"

"That's the offer."

"But not tonight, okay?" Cooper said. "Because I'm not in a shooting mood tonight."

"It's not often that deserters are given a second chance, Sergeant."

"Well, this Chance didn't ask for one."

"You've been trained for it. We trained you," Sam Brown reminded him.

"I trained myself by shooting rattlesnakes. The army trained me for war, and as far as I know, we aren't at war with Lalanga. And no way are you going to convince me that Colonel Diamond has managed to stockpile weapons of mass destruction when he can't even collect the garbage."

"That doesn't make him any less of a security risk."

"His policemen carry machetes because they don't have bullets for their guns. What's he threatening to do," Cooper asked, "cut the White House lawn?"

"It's not his soldiers or their machetes that we're worried about," the CIA man replied, "but his diamonds and who he's selling them to. They're the most portable money around. Stick them up your asshole and you can take them anywhere you want, buy anything or anyone you want, and a lot of assholes wearing turbans are doing just that. No bank accounts, no transfer slips, no money trails, and their value is terrorist-proof. Every time a terrorist act drives the value of everything else down, diamond prices go up, making it easier for them to do it all over again."

"You guys will use terrorism as an excuse for anything," Cooper said scornfully. "Iraq, Israel, Gitmo, everything."

"When the Twin Towers went down," Sam Brown replied, "some of that falling glass might as well have been the colonel's diamonds."

"How do you figure that, when he's only been in power a year?"

"It's the same diamonds. The same megalomaniac in power. Colonel Diamond is like every other hack dictator who preceded him. We're simply trying to make sure the next guy is better."

"How? By setting an example using Colonel Diamond's hack tactics?"

"We don't want this country's resources falling into enemy hands, it's as simple as that."

"I'm a sharpshooter," Cooper reminded the CIA man, "not a murderer. The army trained me to know the difference. Or are those the kind of laws that the CIA likes to conveniently ignore?"

"Laws? You forget, Sergeant Chance, that you're the deserter."

Cooper's anger flared. "I opted for a different war, okay? In Fallujah I was raiding houses side-by-side with some of the same Blackwing guys who showed up here. If they weren't fighting for America, whose side was *I* fighting on?"

"They were fighting for a paycheck," Sam Brown told him.

"Yeah, well, I didn't enlist to set myself up as a bull's-eye. If I took a fair hit, okay, but the orders I got weren't fair."

"They were your orders."

"I'm a sniper, not a rat, and my CO had me crawling through fucking tunnels."

"They were your orders," Sam Brown repeated.

"Yeah? Did *his* orders include giving me gonorrhea?"

"That's in your record."

"Well then you know."

But Sam Brown couldn't know how it had come about that he had first gone to Rick's tent. How he'd said, "I want to see you in my tent, Sergeant Chance," as if an order. How the tent's flap hung at half-mast, ostensibly to keep the sun out but as well to foil prying eyes. Rick, seated at a desk going through papers, appeared immune to the churning passions that roiled Cooper's gut as he saluted him from the doorway.

"Come inside, soldier," his CO said, and when Cooper had, he added,

"I was going through some paperwork. We'd win this war in one battle if we simply airdropped all our reports on top of the Iraqis. They'd drown alive in bullshit."

"I take it there are a lot of reports, sir."

"A 'lot' doesn't come close. Drop that flap a little, willya, Chance? Damn it, would be nice to have one day that doesn't feel like a heat wave."

Cooper plucked at the knotted cord on the flap, momentarily puzzled why his CO hadn't tied slip knots, when the next thing he knew Rick was standing next to him. "Here, let me help," he said, and Cooper could smell the mint toothpaste on his breath. They were about the same build, but Rick, a couple years older, was darker, an accountant's son from New Jersey who'd watched the Towers burning from his backyard, knowing that his dad worked in the left one. Like Cooper, he'd enlisted on his eighteenth birthday.

"It says in your file that you're smart. Does that mean you can write?"

"You mean reports, sir?" Suddenly Cooper wondered if Rick was recruiting him for work.

"Forget the 'sir' inside here," Rick replied. "We can be friends in my tent."

"Yes, sir."

"You're smart but not a fast learner, is that it?"

"I try."

Rick laughed. "You try at what, not being a fast learner?"

"I try—"

"That's okay, I got what you meant." Rick fiddled with the cord to drop the tent's flap a little lower. "I'm surprised we aren't all slow learners in this heat. It's enough to melt your brains. There, that should keep out more of the sun out. You don't like the heat, do you, Sergeant?"

"No, sir."

"There you are with that 'sir' again."

"I'll try to remember."

"I hate the fucking heat," Rick went on. "Take out Hussein and go home, thirty days max, that's what this war was supposed to be about. What is it, ten years later and we're still fighting it?"

"You've been here since the beginning?" Cooper asked.

"Fuck no. I'm only on my second tour."

"You seem older."

"Yeah, older, wiser … and horny most of the time too. How about you, Sergeant?"

Just hearing the question made Cooper's blood pump harder. "Yeah, of course, who isn't out here?"

Neither young man wanted to make the first move, fearing they might have misread the other's signals, and knowing the repercussions could be serious and certainly humiliating.

"Not that I could do anything about it even if I had the chance," Rick elaborated. "What kind of privacy is there in a tent?"

"At least you bunk alone," Cooper remarked.

"It's not like I can hang a *Do Not Disturb* sign and expect it to be honored, especially if someone thinks they smell a woman in here."

"That's a good one, a *Do Not Disturb* sign on a tent. Like that would matter!"

"Most guys respect it, though, when I close the flap this far."

"We figure you're sleeping."

"Or jerking off?"

"That's been suggested too," Cooper admitted.

"They'd be right, whoever said it. What the fuck are you supposed to do when all the pussy in a country is off-limits?" Rick checked out the sandy alley between the rows of tents to see if anyone was there. No one was. "Do you know why I wanted to see you in my tent, Sergeant?"

Cooper swallowed hard. "I think so."

Rick took a step closer. "Touch it."

Unsure that he could control his trembling legs, Cooper reached out a hand to cup Rick's cock, and when he did, it was apparent that he hadn't misread any signals. He nearly exploded when Rick reciprocated by touching him.

"Take it out," Rick ordered, and when Cooper mistakenly thought he meant himself, his CO took his hand and brought it back to his own crotch. "I meant me."

So began their affair. Quick hand jobs, fast blow jobs, Cooper usually doing Rick, sometimes Rick doing him. It was never exactly making love, but it was Cooper's first sexual experience, and it felt like love to him. Enough like love that he experienced its lightheadedness, its longing, its lust. Merely thinking about Rick would arouse him, and in line for the showers he frequently had to disguise his condition with a strategically placed knot in his towel. Rick never acknowledged that they had a friendly relationship; in fact, in public he grew colder to Cooper, completely ignoring him, no longer subtly flirtatious. He always found excuses, though, for Cooper to come to his tent—to run an errand or write a report or plan his own next mission. At first Rick protested that he was only doing it with Cooper because there were no women to be had, but that pretense soon faded, and he began to enjoy it enough that he confessed to Cooper about having fantasies about him, confessed he wanted to do it for real with him, going so far as to suggest an R&R trip where they could hole up in a hotel and not worry about who might walk by.

But before that trip could be made, Rick turned on him. He blamed Cooper for turning him into a queer and hating himself for it, though that didn't stop him from ordering Cooper to blow him. His needs hadn't changed even if his attitude had. He took Cooper off his sharp-shooting rooftops and ordered him to ferret out insurgents in claustrophobic tunnels and booby-trapped souks. Each mission became more reckless, more suicidal as Rick sought to kill the devil who was tempting him.

"He was sure pissed off when I went to the medic," Cooper admitted to Sam Brown.

"You could have blamed it on a prostitute."

"In my throat? I don't think so. What the fuck do you know anyway? When was the last time you were dodging bullets in a war zone?"

"You don't need a war zone to be dodging bullets."

"I'm impressed," Cooper answered sarcastically. "Do you eat IEDs for breakfast too?"

"You enlisted, Sergeant."

"I enlisted because I thought I could kill two birds at one time, helping my country and getting away from some personal problems. I wasn't expecting to be killing a third bird, namely myself, and that's what my orders amounted to. Go every fucking night on a suicide mission until you finally get whacked."

"In a war, that's every soldier's orders," Sam Brown told him.

"Rick was actually disappointed every time I survived."

"He was still your CO."

"I'm a sniper, not a rat, and he put me in those fucking tunnels knowing it made me crazy."

"How does desertion help your country?" Sam Brown asked.

"What?"

"You said you enlisted because you wanted to help our country. So how does desertion help your country?"

"I'll still be around to pay taxes eventually, which wouldn't be the case if I'm pushing up daisies."

"Did you at least manage to solve your personal problems?"

"I said get away from them, not solve them," Cooper corrected the CIA man, "and you know something funny about personal problems? They're kinda personal."

"At first Becky didn't want to talk about them, either." Sam Brown paused, waiting for Cooper's reaction. When there was none, he pressed on, asking, "Those are the personal problems you're talking about, right?"

Cooper had to force himself to remain calm. "You talked to her?"

"Not me personally."

"Then who personally?"

"Army psychs updating your profile. You made some intelligence hits in Iraq, and they like to make sure you can still keep a secret."

"Just in case I take you up on your offer?"

"That's right."

"You don't have a right to include Becky in any discussions about me," Cooper told him. "She's underage, and —"

"She's eighteen."

"She's seventeen! Until her birthday she's seventeen!"

"She misses you. She told us what happened when we said knowing about extenuating circumstances, might mean you could come home. Your dad added some details."

"He was there?"

"Under eighteen, she's underage. There had to be a guardian present."

"A *guardian*? My *father*? Now that's a fucking joke!"

"Apparently he had a lot to say."

"In a little high-pitched voice, I hope. A fucking little high-pitched voice. Did he show you his balls?"

"He was ready to."

"Right there in front of Becky. I bet right in front of her! You sonofabitch for putting her through that."

"I wasn't there."

"You all have the same fucking DNA! Fucking spook DNA! Who are you to be talking to my sister about that stuff? You should be helping her to forget what happened, not asking her to remember it. You think she's ever going to forget what happened?"

"I doubt it," Sam Brown agreed.

Cooper tried his door handle. It was locked. "Let me out."

"Take it easy, soldier. I'm driving you home."

"I want to get out here! Here!"

"It's not safe—"

"*Here!*"

Sam Brown braked. "Think about what's been offered, Sergeant Chance. Desertion begins to sound a lot like treason when you have an opportunity to prove your patriotism and don't take it."

"Unlock my fucking door."

"You might need this." Sam Brown tossed Cooper's passport into his lap and released the locks.

He got out, slammed the door, and stormed off. He had no idea where he was. His reconnaissance walks had never brought him to those particular mean streets. Sam Brown stayed put, giving him a chance to reconsider and come back, but Cooper disappeared without giving him the satisfaction of looking back. He strode ahead with a sense of purpose he didn't feel. Anger drove his pace. He had put his life on the line dozens of times. Who was that CIA asshole to call him a traitor?

An old granny came around a corner, grumbling what Cooper interpreted to be a serious prayer by how many times she made the sign of the cross. He ducked into the street she'd come from and soon found himself walking alongside a chain-link fence. It took him a minute to see the children stepping up to it as he passed; not begging but silently witnessing. In the light of a prison yard lamp, Cooper could see the flies clotted on their wounds. A little girl showed him her doll whose hand had been cut off too. The woeful, silent children seemed to accuse Cooper of another type of desertion, and he *had* deserted them, ignoring their certain fate when he bought their filched diamonds, knowing the savage justice the colonel would exact if they were caught. For a brief period he'd even served in the colonel's army-for-hire, shamefully protecting his barbaric rule. As he peered into each child's face, he understood that every machete cut they had suffered—every missing finger or hand or foot—was his responsibility. Coming to the end of the fence, he staggered into the street, barely avoiding being hit by an army truck running without lights.

The soldiers in the back laughed as it sped away.

Cooper picked himself up and started to run.

9

He didn't stop running until the derelict town gave way to the breeze-ridden shore at the far end of the sweeping bay. Dawn had broken, and the stretch of sand gleamed mercifully white and inviting. He looked around. There seemed to be no one for miles, and he sprinted to the waterline, where he pulled off his boots and dropped all his clothes next to them. With sea foam draining through his toes, he plunged into the most needed bath he'd ever had, not caring that his scrapes and cuts stung. Nothing mattered at that moment except the water. Cooper had grown up crisscrossing deserts, never seeing an ocean until he went to boot camp, and the first time he had dived into the sea it might as well have been his natal bath, he had felt such a sense of rebirth. He felt that same sense again, and with long strokes he swam deeper, kicking fiercely before turning abruptly to shoot to the surface.

When he did, he saw a girl rummaging through his clothes.

"Hey! Hey stop!" Cooper shouted.

She found his passport, grabbed his boots, and fled as soon as Cooper started swimming furiously back to shore. She was no more than a paperclip with little wiry shoulders and skinny legs that moved faster than a sandpiper's. His boots seemed half her size and nearly tripped her as she scurried off.

"*Hey, stop!*"

She did, flashing a victorious smile and brandishing his passport like a trophy.

"Ah, come on …" he pleaded.

But she was off.

Cooper started swimming to shore but not fast enough. Two boys dashed for his clothes, and grabbing them, ran off. He crawled out of the surf and fell onto his elbows, stripped of everything except for the sand plastered to his groin. He wanted to laugh and cry at the same time.

The boy thieves—both skinnier than starvation—held up in the shade of a coconut grove to examine their booty, and Cooper, realizing they hadn't disappeared, stood up shouting, "Hey! Hey!" They seemed certain to bolt, so he raised his hands in surrender and took a step backward. "*No problem!* Only I can't go walk-walk like this." He indicated his nakedness. "Leave me something to wear, huh?"

The boys weren't convinced, so he tried, "What if your mother sees me?" That made the boys smile ashamedly, and Cooper smiled as coaxingly as he could while thinking he'd like to rip off their fucking heads.

Motherhood worked. One boy plucked Cooper's boxers from their meager loot and guardedly dropped them at a point roughly halfway between them. When he ran off, Cooper raced for his shorts before another ragamuffin could shoot out of nowhere and steal them. He held up *his* trophy, a pair of boxers with a torn fly, and slipped them on.

Standing with his back to the water, Cooper considered the sprawling town, sorting out where his room was in its miasmic haze, and debating the best way to get there protected only by boxer shorts when full body armor had been deemed necessary in his mercenary days. He backtracked a short distance along the beach before ducking into a neighborhood of high walls with broken glass embedded in their masonry crowns. Guards stood sentry at barricaded driveways where fancy cars sat in front of unremarkable homes that passed for luxury in that rundown country. Cooper realized that he had entered the dangerous land of the skittish elite and tried to gauge the threat level behind the guards' suspicious stares at a white man in his skivvies. When one guard unshouldered his

AK-47, Cooper hammed it up acting half-demented.

"Swim-swim good-good here," he said, spastically flailing his arms to imitate the breast stroke, "good swim-swim here." He made the guard laugh, and that bought him enough time to turn a corner and hoof it, as best as he could barefooted, until he felt safely away.

The finer houses soon gave way to rougher neighborhoods, and Cooper didn't pass unnoticed, drawing both dark stares and giggles as he hurried past shacks sagging under the weight of washed laundry. He kept up his madman act, causing a group of schoolgirls to shriek and scurry off clutching their book bags and scaring more than one baby into crying. Cooper was crossing zones where no rules applied, where loyalties shifted as often as the sun rose, but if there was one thing every side agreed upon, it was that the white man had screwed them all. The white man was responsible for their country's faulty borders, for the perpetual war between the supposedly united tribes, for their crushing poverty and shitty lives. More than once he rounded a corner to find a youth or rebel group instantly ready to take on a white man, so Cooper perfected the art of drooling, letting strings of saliva swing from his chin, wanting to appear not only mad but so sick no one would want to touch him.

His antics worked. He made it to Cowboy Mile unscathed, and that's where the real gauntlet started. "Hey, American Cooper," he heard, "did you get dressed up special for Little Sister? You dressed fine enough for me, American Cooper, why don't you stop in here? Little Sister sure going to laugh at your skinny-skinny legs! That's not all she going to laugh at!" Cowboy Mile had probably never seen anyone blush as much as Cooper did that morning.

Juma was first to see him enter and went wide-eyed. Lulay, seated at the bar dabbing her toast into an egg yolk, burst into laughter. Their eyes were squarely focused on Cooper's waist, who'd become more exposed than he realized, and he quickly adjusted his gaping fly. The small crowd of sleepy-eyed customers perked up too, and more than one might have propositioned Cooper if he hadn't headed straight for the bar with an unamused expression.

The barman went back to wiping down the bar. Lulay ignored him too.

"Make that black and steaming hot," Cooper said, "and good morning to you too."

"You can't drink with no clothes on," the barman said.

"I've managed it before."

Juma rinsed out his rag. "The ice machine is broken."

"I didn't ask for ice. I asked for a cup of java."

The barman leaned over the bar to look at Cooper's bare knees. "I don't see where you have any money."

"My credit's good."

"Nobody's credit is good."

"Then take it out of my tip from last night."

"You weren't here last night."

"You're right, and that makes me really appreciate being here this morning. Now how about that java?"

The barman begrudgingly reached for the pot and poured him a cup. No matter how much Juma's coffee normally tasted like battery acid, that morning it was pure nectar and Cooper gratefully sipped it.

"Isn't anybody going to ask me why I'm so well-dressed this morning?"

Lulay said sourly, "The police was here."

"What police?"

"Your friend the police," Juma answered for her.

Cooper instantly wondered which past deed had finally caught up with him. "My 'friend the police' doesn't exist," he said with more bravado than he felt. "What police?"

Lulay screwed her fingers at her ears.

Stunned, Cooper asked, "Little Ears?" How did Little Ears know to look for him at The Mining Pan?

"I don't want white man trouble," the barman warned.

"Two nights ago you were glad to take my white man money."

"I'll still take your money."

"I'll bet you will. Did Little Ears say what he wanted?"

"He says his wives are hungry," Lulay reported.

"Yeah? Well, I'm hungry too. They didn't exactly offer a full menu in the lock-up."

"How did he know you and me are friends?"

That stopped Cooper short. "I never mentioned you."

"He asked for 'Lucy.'"

"I've never used that name for you," Cooper told her honestly, "not since you told me your real name."

Lulay realized that she had been tricked. "Then he's a lying man."

"I'm sure lying's not his worst sin."

"He's too angry at you, Cooper."

"I've got a few bones to pick with him myself."

"How can you help me when the police are too angry at you?"

Cooper didn't want to think about it. He didn't want to think about his hellish night, his calamitous swim, his completely undone situation. He didn't want to think about the problems of the girl who'd forgotten her toast and egg and was about ready to burst into tears.

Then it dawned on him. "You didn't johnny-johnny with him, did you?" he asked.

"He's too angry with you!" Lulay bawled.

Cooper, sickened by the thought of the policeman's rancid mouth panting over her, shouted, "You didn't have to johnny-johnny with him!"

The girl pushed herself off the barstool and ran behind the beaded curtain. Cooper jumped up to follow her, on his way splashing more coffee into his cup under Juma's disapproving gaze. He'd been in the back rooms before, egged on by his Blackwing buddies, when he would pay for a girl's time and ask her to do nothing more than wait out the twenty minutes with him. He didn't do it often and couldn't always pick Lulay; that wouldn't have been fair. To his Blackwing buddies' astonishment, Cooper became the most popular guy in the bar, and they teased him mercilessly about the equipment he must have to please those experienced girls so much. He hadn't been behind the beaded curtain since Blackwing shipped out, but he remembered the warren of hallways, filled with smoke and funky cheap perfume, and lined with doors sawed from plywood that sagged perilously on their hinges. Cooper had stolen enough glimpses into those tossed rooms to learn that everybody squirmed in their lovemaking in about the same way, and for all the passion he'd observed, the mechanically rising and falling bums might as well have been pumping money into slot machines.

Each girl had her own cubicle. That was Juma's rule so they would have a sense of home. He followed Lulay to hers, and she held the door against him.

"Hey, don't make me spill this!" he complained, and cradling his coffee, forced his way in.

She plopped herself on the narrow bed and pretended to ignore him, so he pretended to ignore her as well, and looked around as if seeing her room for the first time. It held no more hint of her than his room did of him, and Cooper wondered if she was a runaway too.

He looked at himself in her small mirror. Cracked down the middle, it split his face into unaligned halves. He spit on his finger to dab at some dried blood on his lip when he noticed, tucked out of sight where only Lulay would know to look, an old Polaroid picture, he guessed taken by a tourist and given to the obliging tribeswoman.

"Is this your mother?"

Lulay was instantly on her feet and snatched it from his hand. "Don't you look at her! It's bad luck, you looking at her!"

"I thought I brought you good luck."

"You brought Little Ears."

"Little Ears brought himself."

Suddenly Lulay was on him, clinging to him, and begging, "You buy me, Cooper! You buy me before Juma sells me!"

He wrestled with her, trying to pry her hands off him, but no sooner would he wrest one free than she would latch onto him somewhere else. "Buy me with your diamonds!"

Groping for diamonds in pants pockets that weren't there, she snagged his boxers' elastic band and slipped them to his knees, slipping down with them and trying to take him in her mouth. "I give you Lucy, I give you Lucy every day …" she blubbered, until he caught her arms and dragged her upright like a marionette on strings, still pantomiming her coarse love. He brought her wrists together over her head and clasped them in one hand and with the other pulled up his shorts.

She squirmed in his fierce grip until she realized struggling was useless, and she went slack, crying like the little girl she was, scared of the world. Cooper let her go, and she dried her wet cheeks with her hands.

"Why would Juma sell you?"

"Before Little Ears can steal me."

"What do you mean, steal you?"

"Everybody feeds the police."

Now Cooper understood. Protection money, only in this case humans were the currency. Juma was running more than a whorehouse. He was trafficking. "You're serious about this slave stuff, aren't you? Did Juma really buy you?"

"The *maribout* told my mother I must go with Juma."

Cooper had seen the eccentric shamans on the streets, sometimes clad in nothing more than ashes, and more often than not they were mad, which quixotically rendered them holy in the local culture. Their ramblings were more riddled than the Delphic oracles', but Cooper also knew (from Blackwing's four hours of cross-cultural training) that the maribouts were regarded as intermediaries to a pantheon of local gods, and thus not to be fucked with.

"Why would the maribout tell your mother that?"

"To pay Juma for his gift."

"His gift?"

"His money."

"Why did she take Juma's money?"

"He promised me a job."

"What job?"

"Not this job!" Lulay answered defiantly.

Cooper glanced out her door to make sure no one was listening when he asked, "Juma doesn't keep you locked up, so why don't you run away and go back home?"

Lulay, suddenly frightened, exclaimed, "The maribout has pieces of me!"

"Pieces of you? Like your toenail or hair or something?"

"It's bad luck to talk about it!" She'd said all she was going to say and turned away.

"Okay, I'll take my chances, and this is *me* talking about it, not *you* talking about it, so it's only *my* luck at risk. So besides your toenail, what did you give him?"

"It was a fingernail," she corrected him.

"Okay, good, a fingernail, it's cleaner anyway. And hair, right?" Cooper had heard that they always took hair, and Lulay grimly nodded. "So let me ask, how often do you cut your fingernails?"

When she looked at him puzzled, he said, "You know, nails clip-clip"—he pretended to be cutting his own—"and hair clip-clip? How long between times? Because that's only how long the maribout has power over you. It doesn't last forever. Do you understand?"

She did.

"Do you believe me?"

She didn't.

"Okay. How much to buy you from Juma?"

"Juma doesn't tell me."

"Sounds like Juma's got himself a sweet deal for the price of a fingernail. Can he *really* sell you?" Cooper wished he hadn't asked when he saw the fear that gripped Lulay's body. She had no one to save her if he didn't come to her rescue, and the way she interpreted his question, he was suggesting that he might not.

"It won't happen," Cooper reassured her. "I won't let Juma sell you."

"Maybe Little Ears will steal me first!"

"Little Ears isn't going to steal you. I won't let him."

"They only want Lucy! They want to make Lulay disappear!"

"I promise, you're not going to disappear! Cross my heart."

Still, the girl looked doubtfully at him, until he added, "That's a Cooper promise."

Her sudden big smile said she trusted him, and in a flash she was out of there, banging the flimsy door behind her.

"Where are you going?" he called after her, but she disappeared too quickly. He stood there impatiently, feeling absurd stranded in a brothel wearing only underpants, hearing the doors to other cubicles open and close and the grunts of hurried coupling. He was relieved when Lulay finally reappeared, and complained, "Where the frig did you go?"

She unrolled a bundle of clothes for him, revealing a safari vest and denim jeans. "You can't help me with no clothes to wear," she said.

"What's with all the rules about clothes all of a sudden?" Cooper asked. "Did Juma turn Christian?" He held up the pants. They were way too long for him. "Where did you get these?"

"I take them from Juma."

Cooper started to slip them on. "Won't he be mad?"

"He steals them first."

"Oh good, now I'm wearing second-generation stolen clothes!" The pants fit at the waist, and Cooper squatted to roll up the long cuffs that extended past his feet. "At least we can deduce that the original owner was a member of the Elongated Tribe."

"The what?" Lulay asked.

"Nothing, it's only my name for them."

Next he examined the safari vest, beleaguered by pockets and well-worn as evidenced by the sweat stains under the armholes. He slipped it on and patted himself down. "Ah, my country for a camera!" he said, feigning confidence he didn't feel. In fact, Cooper felt less confident than when he'd been undressed. He hadn't made so many promises then.

"He hurt me, Cooper," Lulay confided.

"Who hurt you?"

"Little Ears."

"How did he hurt you?"

"Maybe he makes me sick-sick with the skinny-skinny."

"Did you ask him to use protection?"

She nodded, uncomfortable with the subject. She had so many taboos working against her.

"A *cop*? You asked a *cop* to use a rubber?"

"It's not okay?"

"Yes it's okay! It's more than okay, it's great okay! And I'm going to tell him that he should have used one right before I kill him."

Lulay's eyes widened. "You will kill Little Ears?"

"The first chance I get." Cooper kissed two fingers and pressed them to her forehead. "You're not going to disappear."

He was pushing his way out her flimsy door when he remembered, "Make sure Juma fixes the ice machine, will you?"

10

Cooper dashed out of The Mining Pan like a man in a hurry to get someplace when in fact he had nowhere particular to go, no plan of action, nothing except a promise to save Lulay. But how, with his limited resources of twice-pilfered clothes and zero money? No shoes, either, he remembered as soon as his bare feet hit the sunstricken street. He cursed every step and for a while tried darting between weedy patches, which contained their own dangers. Eventually he alighted on a shady corner to rest his feet while he watched the barefoot Natives slip past him, probably one pair of shoes for every four of them. "Native" meant many things in Langatown: Indians with their holiness to bear, blacks with their subjugation excuses, Arabs with their general antipathies, and handsome boys, many of whom resembled Sadiq with their dark beards and blue eyes and café latte skin.

Sadiq! Suddenly Cooper felt an overwhelming need to see him. It seemed that he must have earned the right by enduring such a hellish night, and he set off for the diamond arcade, navigating Langatown's tangled streets as fast as he could and sprinting the last stretch when he reached the waterfront.

With his heart pounding and sweat trickling down his sides, as casually as he could Cooper sauntered past al-Basma Diamonds. Mazen was opening the safe inside the shop. Sadiq was nowhere to be seen. Then it dawned on him. It was morning and Sadiq was probably at the hammam. Annoyed at himself for not remembering, Cooper wandered along the waterfront until he found a shady spot where he could pass the time watching cargo be unloaded while waiting for the boy to return.

A white jeep came bouncing out of the bowels of a ship and down a ramp to fall in line with a short convoy of jeeps displaying GlobOil's distinctive logo: an oil-drenched Earth as sinister as a skull-and-crossbones. A moment later they started to roll forward, two Thick Necks in each jeep, all wearing their uniform sunglasses and khakis and carrying rifles. In the lead vehicle was the oilman with the dandy's moustache who was giving everything a menacing look. He tossed out the stub of his cigar, which rolled to Cooper's feet looking like a dog turd, and then they were gone.

His fingers had been absently exploring his vest's many pockets when they hit a jackpot and unearthed some bank bills secreted away. Amounting to merely pennies, he wondered if the original owner had hidden them there and decided it wasn't likely. That safari vest would have been picked clean many times over. Lulay had hidden them for him, he was sure of it, and he realized that those filthy notes probably represented most of her savings. What little bit of herself she could buy back from Juma! The pittance would barely buy a snack, which Cooper's stomach growled for, but he needed to see Sadiq more than he needed to eat and decided to blow his tiny bankroll on the hammam. The closer he got to it, the more eager he was to arrive, and soon broke into another run, not stopping until he stood panting across from its arched entrance. He waited to catch his breath before approaching the ticket booth.

Considering his hasty departure only a couple of days earlier, the vanilla-attired attendant had reason to be surprised to see Cooper, and he looked curiously at his trousers that were clearly too long. Again he led Cooper through the maze of curtained dressing cubicles, many of their narrow cots occupied by men cruising as a pastime. Where Rick had introduced him to sex's basest satisfactions, these men, in their frankness, hinted at the possibility of a sexuality that both excited and confused him.

The attendant waited outside his cubicle while Cooper undressed and stuffed his purloined clothes into the metal locker. He held up the triangular loincloth by its strings, trying to recall how other men had fixed theirs, and did his best to lasso his legs with a couple of well-secured bows. The attendant gave him a thumbs-up when he reappeared, so he felt more confident when he entered the steam room.

The scalding clouds had drifted lower than last time and Cooper had to duck to breathe as he waddled forward on the slick tiles, almost knocking over an Indian yogi on one leg whose head had totally disappeared in the volcanic-hot vapor. He stumbled across his masseur bouncing someone else's nose on the floor, who gestured that he should wait, he would be next, and Cooper quickly disappeared into the hot showers where he lingered, giving the jets all the time they needed to wash away the grime embedded in his skin. He entered the grand pavilion feeling cleaner than ever before.

In the shimmering light of the sapphire pools, the men lounging around them appeared liquid themselves. When he'd determined that Sadiq wasn't in the main pool, he reluctantly started to explore the satellite pools, ever wary of witnessing something crude and untoward, but he saw nothing queerer than men in assorted ages, sizes, and shapes enjoying their conversations or a moment of quiet. The same beet-red man floated happily alone in his boiling pool. Cooper avoided the blasphemous pool where he thought he had seen Sadiq engaged in a vulgar act, but when the boy wasn't to be found anywhere, he had no choice but to look for him there. He started for it, and twice turned back, not wanting to risk finding Sadiq. He didn't want to ruin him with discovery. But Cooper couldn't keep away for long and again found himself approaching the pool.

That morning, no tribal nuances swept him forward, and no one appeared to pay particular attention to the young men, intent in conversation, stretched along the pool's edge. Yet their collective beauty seemed almost indecent. All were darkly handsome and silhouetted by the blue sparkling water. Their casual behavior made it evident that they were close friends, and at one boy's joke another fell off his elbow onto a third's ankles, who glanced up and saw Cooper.

It was Sadiq.

It took the two young men a moment to put themselves together in the hammam. When they had, Sadiq's surprised expression turned to curiosity, and he looked Cooper over as Cooper had looked over his army buddies in the showers: he was assessing his wounds. Somehow Sadiq knew Cooper had been arrested. The boy's friends, noticing his gaze, glanced at Cooper as well, who started to walk away, though not before recognizing Munir's ragged wound. He'd been the youth who'd fallen across Sadiq's ankles and whom Sadiq was now trying to rouse off him.

Cooper hadn't counted on Sadiq being there with friends, and certainly he didn't want to join them. He hoped Sadiq would follow him, and his heart leapt when he heard "Coopah" behind him and turned around. In his daydreams he had not imagined him to be so beautiful. The reflected pools made his eyes bluer still, if that were possible, and the pavilion's shadows blackened the scruff of his beard. A shaft of sunlight coming through the dome landed on his chest, revealing a body so finely chiseled it could have been a work of Michelangelo.

Sadiq touched his heart. "Salaam aleikum," he said.

"Aleikum salaam," Cooper replied, also touching his heart.

"I see you have learned some Arabic."

"Only that much."

"It's enough to praise Allah. So you have found our hammam."

"It was easy with your directions."

"Is it like I described?"

"It's better."

"Americans always seem to like it."

"I can't imagine anything like this in America. I mean, the building itself is older than the whole country!'"

Sadiq laughed. "I had never thought it like that. Did you have a massage?"

"Not today."

"Then you've come before?" the youth asked, puzzled.

"When you told me about the cold pool, I confess I was too curious not to come."

"It's cold, am I right?"

"My second confession," Cooper said, grimacing at how foolish he was going to sound, "is that I never found it."

"It's right over there." Sadiq indicated the far corner of the pavilion. "You could have asked anyone."

Cooper didn't want to admit that he had fled or why; it seemed his own shame for having witnessed it—not the act itself but the public display of it. "I had no idea there were so many pools," he replied.

"But only one cold pool," Sadiq assured him. "Come join my friends, will you?"

Cooper glanced around and saw that Sadiq's friends had started to drift off. Only Munir held back, waiting for Sadiq to return. For the first time Cooper could see the gash, as fiery and ragged as the scar on his face, that ran the length of his game leg. "I guess I've kept you from them," Cooper apologized half-heartedly.

Sadiq said, "They have to go to work."

"And you don't?"

"My father is a patient man."

Munir, realizing that Sadiq was not rejoining him, walked away. His injured leg gave him trouble on the slippery tiles, and Cooper felt a momentary pang of guilt for his country's culpability in the handsome young man's ruinous injuries.

"And *his* father?" Cooper asked.

"His father is in Iraq."

"I thought you met in Beirut."

"We did." Sadiq touched Cooper's shoulder. "You've been hurt."

"Yeah, thanks to a couple of local thugs who call themselves cops. You know I was arrested, don't you?"

"Yes," Sadiq admitted.

"What is there, some kind of diamond grapevine?"

"You don't know much about diamonds, do you?"

"People pay big bucks for them; what more do I need to know?"

"It's a dangerous business, that's what you need to know." Sadiq traced a bruise stretching from Cooper's shoulder to his back. "You're very blue here, and cut here."

Cooper twisted around, trying to see his own shoulder. "I was knocked unconscious. The SOBs must've dragged me by my arm. Does it look infected?"

"It looks clean."

"I goddamn don't need jungle-itis."

"But here ..."

"Where?"

The boy ran a finger along Cooper's ticklish side. "It's very blue. Does it hurt?"

"No!" Cooper exclaimed, and stopped the boy's hand.

"Have you passed blood?"

"What? Did those SOBs kick me that hard?"

"It's not good if you pass blood for more than twenty-four hours."

"Twenty-four hours? I don't want to be pissing blood for twenty-four *seconds!* Especially in this bastion of health care. Jesus, pissing blood!"

"I think you'll be okay, it doesn't look so bad," Sadiq reassured him, "and the cold water will help your blueses."

"My blueses?"

"Bruises," Sadiq translated. "When I was growing up, 'blueses' is what I thought you called them in English because they are blue."

"We say black-and-blue. Didn't your nanny teach you?"

"It's black too," the boy said, again touching Cooper's side.

It was a tender touch, and Cooper, succumbing to it, felt the hint of arousal. "Maybe I should find the cold pool," he suggested.

"I'll show you where it is."

"What about your friend?"

Across the pavilion they could see Munir arriving at the shower room door where the others had waited for him. "He won't care," Sadiq said.

The hammam had cleared of most younger men, the merchants' sons who now ran the shops, leaving behind their fathers' generation to enjoy their memories. They floated belly-up in the pools or hung on to their tiled sides chatting in low voices as watery *drip-drip-drips* pinged in the cavernous dome. Another working crowd started to trickle in, groomed and oily-haired, the same mixture of Arabs, Indians, and Elongated Blacks twitching their asses like the hot guys they no longer were. Cooper didn't have to be told they came looking to make some old guy happy for a coin. They electrified the atmosphere with a blatant sexuality that was at once forbidden and subscribed.

As he followed Sadiq to the pavilion's far corner, the muggy air became threaded with chilly ribbons licking Cooper seductively. He couldn't determine their origin. Then Sadiq appeared to step through a stone wall before Cooper saw the narrow opening, and he tagged after the boy's smooth shoulders through a river of frigid air until they emerged in a square room. In its center a perfectly square pool emitted a dazzling blue light that disappeared in the soot-covered ceiling.

"It's cold in here, yes?" Sadiq inquired.

"It's cold in here, yes," Cooper confirmed.

They stepped to the edge of the pool. Both their bodies tingled with goose bumps. "There's only one way to go in," Sadiq remarked.

"I know, jump in. Will you?"

Sadiq made the mistake of letting his body language confess his hesitation, and without another thought, Cooper embraced him and took the single step that plunged them into the frigid water. He managed to keep hold of Sadiq until their feet touched the bottom, both with their eyes open and looking wildly shocked by the cold. They exploded with bubbles from laughter and shot their way to the surface.

"Ya Allah!" Sadiq cried, sucking in air like a fish out of water.

"You'll get used to it!"

"Never!"

Cooper's scrappy loincloth bobbed to the surface between them, fueling their enthusiasm. They grabbed for it, and Sadiq flung it away. Trying to scramble from the pool, he lost his grip on the slick tiles and fell back into Cooper's arms. They wrestled, using the cover of playfulness to touch where they willed, and when they finally did climb out, despite the frigid water both young men had some retreating to do.

They flopped down on the pool's edge, face down and breathing hard, embracing themselves for warmth. The water, choppy from their swim, sparkled like glitter on their skin.

Resting his chin on the tiles, Cooper looked down the boy's body, or rather his man's body, for there was nothing boyish about him, not his firm shoulders or trim legs or dark downy hair in the small of his back. Cooper wanted to touch him but didn't dare. Any move seemed too brazen until Sadiq's whole body shuddered and gave Cooper an excuse to place a hand on his shoulder. "Are you cold?" he asked.

Sadiq looked into Cooper's eyes. "It was only a shiver. How are your blueses now?"

"You tell me."

The boy scooted around to examine him. "Where do you hurt?"

"Nowhere," Cooper replied honestly. The cold water numbed him.

Sadiq poked him. "Not here?"

"No."

"Here?"

"Yes there! Jesus! How many places did they kick me?"

"Let me see …" Sadiq said, and touched Cooper in a couple of spots, assessing his condition. "Now turn over."

Cooper flipped, unmindful of embarrassing himself. That's when he saw the concern in Sadiq's blue eyes, and Cooper knew with certainty that he loved the boy. He placed a hand on his chest, where Sadiq let it stay while floating his own hand toward Cooper to land a finger on his nipple. It was that simple gesture that consummated something extraordinary between them. Something profound. There was no room for faulty translation or misinterpretation. What had been said was clear.

After a moment Sadiq removed his finger and remarked, "My father can also be an *im*patient man."

They returned through the hidden passage in the wall, back into the muggier pavilion where they swerved around the pools to reach a door that led them directly to the dressing cubicles. The vanilla-clad lad greeted them with his easy grin and shepherded them to their cubicles. The two young men didn't say good-bye, each presuming they would walk out together.

Cooper examined his limited wardrobe and wished he had said good-bye to Sadiq. He would've preferred that the youth not see him dressed in those ridiculous pants suitable for the world's tallest man, a pitted-out vest, and no shoes. Slipping on the vest, he caught a whiff of his benefactor's old sweat. He rolled up his cuffs as many times as the thick material would allow until it looked as if he had pom-poms gathered at his ankles. He left his cubicle only to realize once again how his sense of direction, so acute in the streets, inexplicably failed him in that curtained labyrinth. Fortunately, the attendant had kept an eye out for him and delivered him straightaway to Sadiq waiting by the door.

He looked at Cooper's strange attire. "You don't have any shoes," he noticed.

"Everything was stolen, all my clothes, including my boots."

"By the police?"

"They started the ball rolling. Some kids took the rest." He indicated his pants and vest. "Even these are stolen. Seems to be a trend."

Sadiq spoke briefly to the attendant, and the attendant ran off. "I've asked Ahmed to bring you some sandals."

"That wasn't necessary."

"Our streets are not so clean."

"You're telling me?"

They both glanced at Cooper's feet to see the nicks he'd already suffered.

Ahmed returned, carrying a pair of flip-flops.

"I don't have any money," Cooper said. "All that was stolen too."

"No charge," Ahmed replied, "you bring back tomorrow."

He slipped them on as Sadiq, contrary to his own advice, tipped the boy handsomely.

Outside on the street, an awkwardness returned to the young men. They didn't want to part, yet neither knew what to suggest—there were so many taboos and restrictions they had to consider. There weren't cafes or other places where they could casually meet, and to meet any other place seemed too much like a date—not to mention too open to public scrutiny. That's when Cooper remembered Mazen's remarks, and said, "Your father wants us to become friends."

"But aren't we friends already?"

"Of course!"

"Then for once I have satisfied one of my father's wishes," Sadiq mused. "Will you come by the shop tomorrow?"

"That's affirmative. What time?"

"Any time. I am never busy."

"I thought market conditions had improved."

"Even so, it is not a busy business."

"Only a dangerous one?"

"Wouldn't it seem so?"

"That's affirmative," Cooper repeated. "I'll see you tomorrow. Malekum salaam."

"Salaam malekum," Sadiq replied.

They parted, and Cooper watched Sadiq walk off, hoping he might turn back to wave. He didn't, and soon the youth's beige caftan disappeared on the busy African street.

"Good morning, Sergeant," he heard over his shoulder.

Cooper whirled around to see Sam Brown. "What the fuck!"

"I said, 'Good morning, Sergeant.'"

"I know what you said. Are you following me?"

"It seems that we naturally cross paths."

"I'm uncrossing them," Cooper said, and turned away.

The CIA man caught his arm. "Calm down, soldier. I only want to have a little chat."

He lifted Sam Brown's hand off his arm. "You don't want to go mano a mano with me."

"Yeah, I forgot. Besides being smart, it says in your file you can squeeze a guy's balls pretty hard."

Cooper balled up his fist and swung a punch, something he'd only done a couple of times in his life, and connected with Sam Brown's square jaw. The CIA man hit the ground, where he stayed. He clearly didn't intend to keep fighting; it was in his job description to be discreet. Cooper had surprised himself by knocking him down with a single punch, and when it was obvious Sam Brown wasn't punching back, he held out a hand to help him up. The onlookers moved on as he brushed himself off.

"I saw you coming out of here the other day," Cooper told him.

"I know. I saw you seeing me."

"Do you like it in there?"

"We come here for different reasons," Sam Brown answered.

"What's that supposed to mean?"

"Your boyfriend is a person-of-interest to us."

"My boyfriend?"

"Sadiq al-Basma, and his friends, too."

"You follow them to the hammam?"

"They like to meet there, and they tend to talk more than they should."

"And you go to listen to them?"

"That's right."

"You speak Arabic?"

"That's right."

"How do you know Arabic?

The CIA man wouldn't say.

"Oh I get it," Cooper said. "This is more of your Colonel Diamond terrorist bullshit, and because they're Arabs, they're suspicious."

"The threat is bigger than anything you could guess."

"I'm supposed to trust you, as simple as that?"

"I'm your only ticket home," the CIA man reminded him.

"What's Sadiq got to do with this?"

"I can't tell you."

Cooper had heard enough. He was ready to be rid of this guy. "You are such a bullshitter. Can you hear yourself? Every time the answer isn't 'shoot Colonel Diamond' you don't have an answer."

"You're not exactly a prime candidate for top-secret clearance," Sam Brown replied evenly.

"How many excuses do you have before you run out? Because I'm going to ask my question that many times until I get an answer out of you. What does Sadiq have to do with anything?" Cooper was worked up, there was no doubting it; no doubting, too, that after his last twenty-four hours, he was running on empty. Sam Brown would have had to be blind not to notice.

"He's got nothing to do with anything tonight," he said, "and soldier, I think you should call it a night too. You look hungry and in need of a bed."

"You're changing the subject." It wasn't a complaint; Cooper was glad he had. He didn't need an argument, he needed that bed, and he'd detected the CIA man's sincerity.

"When did you eat last?"

"Like I was supposed to eat those fucking preemie birds?" Cooper couldn't remember the last time he'd had a real meal, or eaten anything for that matter.

"Soldier to soldier, you gotta eat. Take this." Sam Brown held out a wad of bills.

Not taking the money, Cooper asked, "Soldier to soldier?"

"Twenty-Fourth Amphibious Unit out of Camp Lejeune, North Carolina. It was our barracks that took the direct hit in Beirut in '83."

"Is that what made hash out of your face?"

"I was shaving when the mirror exploded. I was nineteen. Most of my buddies never saw twenty."

"Now I get it," Cooper said, nodding, "you have a legitimate excuse for hating Arabs, not just some general racist thing going on."

"It's when I decided to learn Arabic, to try to keep something like that from happening to my country again."

Cooper heard the implication, and replied, "I signed up to fight for America too."

"You still can." The CIA man held out the money again. "Take this."

"You can't bribe me."

"I'm not trying to bribe you, I'm trying to feed you."

When Cooper still refused the money, Sam Brown stuffed it into one his vest's many pockets. "That's almost an inch of money; you should get at least four squares out of it. Now go home, soldier. You look like you need a good week's sleep."

11

Cooper might have slept a month of Tuesdays for all he knew when he finally woke up the next day. The wet heat seemed to glue him to the bed, and he would have stayed there enjoying the bit of relief provided by the intermittent fan, except his bladder was screaming for relief after how many hours of neglect? He took care of that need, happily noting that he wasn't passing blood while he groggily tried to recall all the details of the day before. Looking in the mirror reminded him that he'd rather not. Except for a split lip, they'd thankfully left his face alone for the most part, though he had bruises and scratches everywhere.

Still wet from the shower, he dropped to the floor to do his pushups and sit-ups, daydreaming the whole time about caffeine. Daydreaming about the cup of coffee he knew didn't exist in Langatown: a good one. Not that Cooper had grown up enjoying fine brews, but he had grown up on coffee. From the time Coops was too big to be locked up in a cupboard, his father, while doing his miserable deeds, had sent the boy off to wait in diners and greasy spoon cafes, places with names like Pete's Sit-Down and Prickly Pastard's, where the waitresses felt sorry for him, a kid trying to do his homework, figuring something was wrong at home if he had to do it there; so they gave him what they had to offer: coffee and lots of it. Cooper credited it with making him a speed reader. Once he finished his homework, he'd sit there devouring books, usually bringing two or three with him at a time. He'd ask everyone, If you had to pick one book to read, what would it be?' and religiously checked out every recommendation, eventually reading everything from the *Odyssey* to *The*

Golden Notebook to every Perry Mason mystery (pressed onto him by a favorite waitresses), letting as many hours go by as he could before returning to his father's trailer.

"One hundred," Cooper said aloud, finishing his sit-ups. He snatched his boxers from the floor and stepped back into the shower, slipping them on and soaping them up. It was his favorite way for doing laundry because he could stay cool in the process. Besides, he had no change of clothes, so he ended up wearing everything wet anyway. He had just turned off the shower when his landlady started banging on his ceiling, shouting, "Too long shower, American!"

He scrounged for anything for breakfast, knowing it would be more meager than most mornings. There was barely enough instant coffee to make a cup, and he ate the last handful of cereal dry since everything else had spoiled, the milk first. Then he considered how to shorten the giraffe -length legs on his purloined pants. When he held them to his waist, they rolled onto the floor. He went to the drawer where he kept his postcards and took out a pen to mark where to cut them. Then he remembered that he had nothing sharp to cut them with. His knife had been stolen, and what else was there? A dull table knife, fork, and a bottle- and can-opener—nothing sharp enough for the task. But he was undaunted. There was no way he was taking another step in those sweltering jeans, and he attacked them with his fork, bending its tongs and destroying it while managing to poke a hole in the pants. Using the dull knife, he enlarged the hole enough to work a couple of fingers into it, and then enlarged it further until he could grasp the denim firmly and rip the pant leg around to its thick seam. That challenged even Cooper's strength until he managed to fray it enough on the pointy corner of his metal kitchen counter to sever it.

By the time he'd completed surgery on the second pant leg, sweat was pouring off him. He slipped on his new cutoffs. They were uneven and rode too high on his thighs, but at least they'd be cool.

Returning the pen to its drawer, Cooper picked up the top postcard on his stack of postcards, all addressed to his kid sis. He glanced at the man on the camel and then turned it over to where he had written *I've made a friend* and inserted the word *good*. He'd been thinking about making the change since he woke up. Becky would be happy that he had a good friend. Cooper wished he could send the postcard right away. He hadn't mailed any of his postcards to her, not wanting anyone to know where he was, and he worried they would track him to Lalanga by the stamp. All his precautions ultimately didn't amount to much. They had tracked him down, even offered him a job he didn't want.

He supposed he could send his postcards now, and wouldn't Becky be surprised to receive so many all at once! He imagined her sitting on her bed, the postcards stacked beside her, reading them from beginning to end like the abbreviated journal they were. Cooper in Iraq. Cooper in Africa. Not exactly a diary, though he thought of them to be like Anne Frank's diary when he felt lost to all else and had to rely on manufactured optimism—aided by G and Ts at The Mining Pan—to carry him through the day. He didn't write a postcard every day like a real diary; of course not, he couldn't afford it, and what would he say? *I sweated today? I sweated more today than yesterday?*

During his mercenary days Cooper never had a permanent camp, or for that matter a camp at all, his nightly home usually the next muddy rut in a jungle full of leeches, and he'd lugged those postcards in his rucksack from rut to rut, having no place safer to keep them than moldering on his back. He'd promised Becky that he'd write her, and right through starting in Iraq he had, though he'd never sent most of them from there, either. He couldn't, but he had faith that whatever ultimately befell him, someone would find his postcards and mail them to her, and she'd realize, if she'd had any doubts, that Cooper had never broken his promise.

He checked his vest pocket. Sam Brown's inch of money was still there. He left his room and locked the door. His borrowed sandals slapped at his heels going down the steps, reminding him how naked he felt without his boots and knife. He scoured the ground looking for a mango, and gave the tree a couple of shakes trying to dislodge one. Giving up, he was walking out of the yard when he heard one plop on the ground behind him. He bit into its thick skin with his teeth and again wished he had a knife. To hell with food; he figured his inch of money was enough to buy one.

Minutes later, he was licking sticky mango juice off his fingers and passing by the window of Auntie's Junk-it when he made a double-take. His knife was in the window! He went inside where Auntie was spread over her chair, Popeye preening on her shoulder.

Squaaawk!

"And good morning to you, too, Popeye."

Squaaawk!

"I think he likes me. Good morning, Auntie."

Auntie propped herself up enough to get a good look at his feet; he figured because she'd never seen him wear anything but his boots. "I don't have any more books today than I did yesterday," she said.

"I'm looking for a knife."

"I have a new one in the window. You go take a look-look, only don't make Auntie walk all that way. Her ankles hurten her this morning."

Cooper retrieved the knife and flicked open its blade. Of course it was his. He knew every nick and scratch on it. Taking it to the counter, he said, "This is mine."

Squaaawk!

"It will be, after you pay for it."

"It was stolen from me."

"I don't care how you lost it."

"I didn't say I lost it."

"And Auntie say she don't care."

Squaaawk!

Cooper knew he couldn't win and asked begrudgingly, "Okay, how much? And considering the circumstances, you better give me a discount."

"You might want these too." With a grunt, Auntie hoisted his boots onto the counter.

"What the frig!"

"I didn't put them out in the shop. Boots go fast-fast."

"Where did you get those?"

Auntie shook her head sadly. "Frankly, American, you are no match for our children."

"You knew they were my boots, and you still bought them from that little thief?"

"How else would you get them back?"

"Good point," Cooper had to admit, and absurdly found himself thinking maybe he should thank her for fencing his stolen goods. Heck, she probably recognized the vest and pants he was wearing! "All right, I'll take the knife and boots, but you better give me a package deal. And that's for *both* boots, let's make sure we agree on that first, and I might need some credit."

"No credit," Auntie said firmly.

"Whaddya mean, no credit? I see other customers getting credit."

"American credit no good. It's in the newspapers."

"So Uncle Sam might make me lose my boots after all," Cooper thought aloud.

Squaaawk! Popeye commented on the irony as well.

"I don't know your uncle," Auntie replied.

"Forget it. How much?"

Auntie held up her thumb and finger, and their bargaining began. Cooper compressed her fingers while Auntie widened them, until they squeezed out a price that he figured he could fluff up Sam Brown's bills enough to fill while holding back a couple for himself.

"For a cup of coffee," he explained when Auntie looked aggrieved. Then she tried for his plastic sandals—*Why did he need them now that he had his boots?*—but he explained they were borrowed.

"You see, Americans borrow too much-much!" she declared.

He left with his knife and boots, if not the four square meals under his belt that Sam Brown's money had once promised.

His head ached for caffeine, his stomach pleaded for food, and his couple of bills were only enough to satisfy one urge. So he made a tactical decision and aimed for the diamond arcade, figuring he'd wait for Sadiq to return from the hammam and finagle a cup of coffee from him. Depending on the success of that mission, he would then decide how to spend his last two cents, which was about all that his last two filthy bills were worth.

By the time he reached the port, the sun had burned a hot white hole in the sky, and sweat was dripping off everyone, soaking their shirts if they wore one. Cooper's own sweat had amply rehydrated the stains in his vest's armholes. He found his spot where he could look into al-Basma Diamonds, and expecting Mazen to be there, was pleasantly surprised to see Sadiq. He was about to cross to it when he realized that the boy was in a fierce argument with someone, and a moment later he recognized Munir when he took a lopsided step brandishing a newspaper. But no sooner had Cooper's danger radar clicked on than the argument ended abruptly. Sadiq, slump-shouldered, appeared defeated.

A moment later the two friends embraced too intimately for Cooper's comfort level, and he decided to go in. By the time he did, they'd resumed their excited conversation and failed to notice him when they embraced again, crying, "Ya Allah!"

They saw him at the same time and flew apart, looking like they'd been caught red-handed at something.

"Coopah?" Sadiq said.

Cooper held up the sandals. "I thought you might be going to the hammam."

Sadiq reached for them. "Sure, I can return them for you."

Cooper held on to them. "I thought we might go together."

"I won't be going today, my father is ill. Perhaps Munir can take them for you."

"I'm sure one more day won't matter." Cooper said, smiling feebly at Munir. "But thanks for the offer."

"I would not expect an American to like our Turkish baths," Munir remarked.

Cooper couldn't resist the chance to say, "I like your *Arab* ones. Are there Turkish baths in Langatown too?"

Sadiq burst into laughter. Obviously Cooper had heard his father's harangue, and they shared a moment of humor at Munir's expense, who grew quietly furious, clenching his jaw so hard that his ragged scar turned white. Sadiq made an effort to explain the joke, but Munir didn't find it amusing.

"It is your habit to mock me?" he asked Cooper.

"It's called having a sense of humor."

"We don't laugh at the same things."

"Apparently not."

"Your American laughter is insulting."

"You got that one turned back-assward," Cooper shot back. "As I recall, it was your country's insulting laughter that made my country invade yours. Saddam Hussein was thumbing his nose at the world until we stopped him."

"You were in my country?"

"I sure was. My job was to snuff out Iraqi ball-busters from a mile away, that or get my own balls blown off."

"Your job was to … *sniff balls?*" Munir asked incredulously, unable to keep up with Cooper's fast-paced English.

"Yeah, I did a lot of that in your country too," Cooper assured him. "It was a great way to pass the time."

"This is another American joke?"

"Trust me, it wasn't funny then or now. So what's in the news?" Cooper picked up the newspaper to read the headline:

U.S. SECRETARY OF STATE ADDS LALANGA TO AFRICA ITINERARY

And below that:

Credits Colonel's Democracy Initiatives for Revived Friendship

"That's unreal. Is she really coming to Lalanga?"

"Of course," Munir replied. "Now that Lalanga has oil."

Cooper pointedly tapped the newspaper. "The heck with that. It says right here that she's coming to bring democracy."

Munir's eyes narrowed. "It is funny for you to laugh always at people?"

"No, and I don't think it's funny to go around the world blowing people up, either."

Munir glanced at Sadiq. "Who has said such a thing?"

"No one," Cooper answered. "It was a comment on the state of the world in general."

The tinny call to prayer started, interrupting their conversation, and Munir, reverting to Arabic, asked Sadiq something. Cooper could pick out enough of the words to guess what they said to each other.

"You will come to the mosque for prayers?"

"I must stay in the shop while my father is away."

"He closes it for prayers."

"Only on Fridays."

While their conversation had been simple enough, Munir's asking Sadiq to accompany him to the mosque felt like an order on the scale of orders he'd received from Rick, testing his allegiance and testing his affection. Sadiq's refusal was no less an act of disobedience than Cooper's eventual refusal to go to Rick's tent, refusing to be seduced by the man keen on sending him to his death. He sensed Munir had some similar control over Sadiq that was more than the pull of simple friendship. Then it dawned on him. They were in love! Why hadn't he recognized it before? It explained why they were together so often, the evident tenderness between them, Sadiq's worried solicitousness for his wounded friend. Despite Mazen's fears of his sinister influence over his son, there was nothing more sinister in Munir's coming to Lalanga than an unfolding love story, though no doubt Mazen would regard their particular affair as singularly sinister. Cooper could imagine their dizzying affair in Beirut! He recalled the playful scene in the hammam when Munir fell across Sadiq's ankles and felt the sharp pangs of jealousy. He tried to recall every encounter between the three of them, what words had been used, and what their body language revealed, hoping he might debunk his own revelation, and he couldn't.

Lost in his own thoughts, Cooper almost missed Munir's saying that he was leaving, and then he was gone.

Observing Sadiq's worried frown, he said, "I didn't really mean to insult him."

"Munir is very emotional," Sadiq replied.

"I take it he doesn't like Americans very much."

"He hates Americans."

"That's rather black-or-white."

"It was Americans who wounded him."

"In Iraq?"

"Yes."

"He was an insurgent?"

"He was at his brother's wedding when it happened."

"A drone?" Cooper asked. He could easily imagine the whine of incoming fire, the thud of impact, the ripped apart wedding party. Or ripped apart worshipers. Or ripped apart shoppers on market day. He'd heard it, felt it, witnessed it enough times to be recorded in his bones.

"I guess a lot of people have a lot of reasons to hate Americans right now," he acknowledged, as much as he didn't want to. Cooper didn't like to sound unpatriotic because he wasn't, though he understood how it might appear otherwise.

Wanting to change the subject, he asked, "Was Munir a student in Beirut too? Is that how you met?"

Said laughed brightly. "You are asking a new question before I can answer the last one!"

He was being evasive, Cooper decided, concealing his affair with Munir.

"Do you want a coffee?" Sadiq offered.

"You said the magic word."

Sadiq lit the small burner. "It *is* an American addiction, isn't it?"

"I don't know about all Americans, but it's definitely my addiction. So I never asked, what did you study in Beirut?"

"How to be a playboy."

"A playboy?" Cooper laughed at his choice of words.

"That's what we call it, our Playboy Year. At eighteen, we used to be sent back to our villages for a year to learn our heritage, but now everyone goes to Beirut to have some fun before coming back here, marrying and dying."

"Wow!" Cooper exclaimed. "A whole year where the pressure is on to sow your wild oats? Who couldn't get into that?"

"You are funny, Coopah."

"I like the way you say my name. I guess I should be grateful to your nanny."

"Actually, I had several nannies," Sadiq confessed. "Once, two at the same time."

Cooper grinned. "That sounds kinky."

"Not for me, I was too young, but I've sometimes suspected that my father might know about that."

"Have you always been rich?"

"Not by American standards," Sadiq answered.

"Trust me," Cooper said, "I wasn't raised by overlapping nannies. So how did you meet Munir if he wasn't a student?"

Sadiq hadn't expected the abrupt question and stuttered, "He's ... he's become a colleague."

"In the diamond business? Doesn't he know it's dangerous?"

"I've told him." Sadiq clearly didn't want to talk about Munir, which made Cooper more jealous, but he sensed that he'd learned all Sadiq was willing to tell him about his rival.

Hiking up his safari vest, he asked, "How are my blueses?"

Sadiq ran his fingers over his back. "Did you pass blood this morning?"

"No."

"This one ..." he said, measuring a bruise, "is bigger than my hand and very black. You are lucky not to be passing blood." He had both hands on Cooper's back, who pressed his weight into them, and then abruptly turned around, setting the youth enough off-balance that he had to put a hand on Cooper's chest to steady himself. Their faces were close enough that their breaths mingled. They might have kissed were it not for the window to the street.

"Did I hurt you?" Sadiq asked.

Cooper laughed the moment off. "Naw, I'm tripping over my own feet! I'm not used to wearing these boots."

"They are not your boots?"

"Yeah, they're mine, they just went MIA for twenty-four hours. Though technically, I suppose, they're not mine but Uncle Sam's. I didn't stay around long enough to earn them."

"In Iraq?"

"That's right."

"How long before you earn your boots?"

"That was a growing problem," Cooper told him. "They could never tell anyone how long, except to always say 'longer.' I never made it to longer, only to long enough. I left on bad terms with my CO."

"CO?"

"Commanding Asshole."

"You didn't like him?"

"I didn't like his indiscriminate orders. 'Shoot anything and everybody that moves' was about as specific as he got. I'd've offed some hundred-year-old granny on a roof trying to grow a fucking tomato if she hadn't moved in that exact nanosecond. I plugged her watering can instead." Cooper held out his hand as if introducing himself for the first time. "Meet Sergeant Cooper Chance, first-class Sharpshooter First Class."

Warily, Sadiq accepted his hand. "Sharpshooter?"

"Try assassin with a paycheck from Uncle Sam."

"You assassinate people?"

"You'd have to ask Uncle Sam for the details. Most of the time, they weren't even names to me."

"You have a lot of business with Uncle Sam."

Cooper smiled. "Now you're learning. Only I quit working for him when his orders included suicide. My CO had me crawling through rat tunnels looking for insurgents and hoping the rats would get me first. He wanted me as gone as dead, and I finally obliged him. Gone, but not dead."

"I don't understand why your …"

"Commanding Asshole?"

"Would want you dead."

"It was hard for me to figure out too. I guess he didn't love me anymore."

"He loved you?" Sadiq asked, perplexed.

"He never said, or couldn't say, I'm not sure which," Cooper answered.

Until that moment, their attraction to each other had been so circumspect as to hardly have been acknowledged except by camouflaged touches. Cooper's use of the word 'love' instantly changed everything. He'd raised the possibility of love between two men. They had dreamt of such love but weren't sure how to take the next unfamiliar step. What mattered is that both had the same desires even though neither could describe them in decent terms, not knowing the lovers names for acts they could only conjure in the crude words they'd heard.

They had a reprieve from taking that next clumsy step when a very tall and very skinny African woman stepped into the doorway. She wore a bright yellow headdress that looked like a mile high pile of lemon meringue pie. Sadiq spoke to her in the local Creole, and she went outside to wait.

"I'll go," Cooper offered, "you have business-business."

"She'll wait a minute, she comes often," Sadiq said. "When will you bring more diamonds?"

"First I'm going to have to discover my own mine." Cooper fished out the two grungy notes that he'd held back from Auntie. "This is the only bankroll I've got left."

Sadiq, looking at the worthless notes, and then at Cooper's sorry cutoffs and vest, seemed to grasp for the first time how desperate his situation was. In fact, his worried look made Cooper wonder if he was underestimating the direness of his own straits.

"Wait a minute," Sadiq said, and went inside the cage.

When he opened the safe, Cooper glimpsed a gun he hadn't seen before. He couldn't identify its make except to know that it would set you back seriously if you took a direct hit. He wondered why Mazen suddenly felt a need for it, and asked, "Why the gun?"

"The rebels are gaining ground," Sadiq answered, "it makes it a more uncertain time."

"The rebels are always gaining ground," Cooper countered. "It's the political process here, isn't it?"

"It's the excuse I used with my father," Sadiq admitted. "I want him to have a gun for his protection. He is too trusting." Sadiq left the cage and handed Cooper a thick wad of money. "Here."

"What's this?"

Sadiq playfully measured the bills. "I'd say about three inches."

"I can see that. What's it for?"

"An advance."

"For diamonds? What will your father say?"

"It's the business-business."

Cooper stuffed the money into his cutoffs, saying, "Thanks."

The woman with the lemon meringue headdress peered in again.

"I guess I'm holding up traffic," Cooper said, "so I'm outta here."

They shook hands, and then touching their hearts, momentarily held each other's gaze. It couldn't be clearer. They wanted each other.

Cooper, elated, turned away, and was nearly out the door when Sadiq said, "Coopah."

He turned back. "Yes?"

"Don't trust the children. The police pay them."

The lemon meringue woman ducked in behind Cooper when he left. He had money in his pocket, his growling stomach reminded him, and he headed straight for a cluster of food stands to select something from among the local delicacies of crispy fried grasshoppers (bright orange and four inches long not counting their feelers); boiled goat heads, bloated and ready for finger picking; and spongy eyeball-ish orbs floating in watery milk that Cooper didn't dare try to identify. He tended to shy away from anything unrecognizable and bought two samosas from an emaciated Indian that were so stale they barely stained the square of newspaper folded around them. Staleness notwithstanding, Cooper scarfed them down, licking his fingers for their last flakes.

The *African Lady* had returned to its same dock and was closed up tight. The crewmen weren't to be seen, and Cooper heard no partying coming from belowdecks. It had been skillfully tied up, and the sophisticated sonar equipment suggested it ran long hauls. He wondered if it could be a drug runner. There was a lot of that business-business in Lalanga too.

Still hungry, he couldn't resist a vendor's offer of an ear of corn, grilled until lightly blackened the way he liked it, and squeezed a fresh lime over it. He ate it slowly, wandering along the waterfront, his thoughts on Sadiq. They had almost kissed. Cooper had almost pressed his lips to the boy's. He had never kissed Rick, nothing closer than rubbing faces, not so much as a peck good-bye when their crude lovemaking was over. Cooper hardly considered it lovemaking now. Perhaps that's why he came so close to kissing Sadiq. It felt more like love.

12

Where all the people hid during the day Cooper could never determine, but the broken concrete patches that passed as sidewalks were crowded at night with refugees who'd fled the ransacked countryside—though why they thought they'd be safer in Langatown was anyone's guess. The moonlight draining over them turned their black skins ashen, and the sky too seemed too white for night. Counterfeit white. Some people already slept while others, squatting in small circles or sprawled out lazily, kept up lively conversations. Mothers waved a hand over their babies' faces to chase off annoying flies while fathers fretfully dozed off, riddled by more acute worries. People cooked what they had managed to scrounge that day, and for sleeping, they spread out pieces of cardboard that they safeguarded as if royal beds. Youngsters tumbled and tussled about while their teenage brothers and sisters huddled together, separated by sexes and talking about each other.

Cooper was noticing how many kids there were when he saw her. Lulay. Walking off with a woman who must've been her mother. He'd never seen the girl outside The Mining Pan other than once chasing a john down the street who'd tried to sneak out without paying. He'd been a runty little guy who certainly didn't expect to be brought to heel by the strapping likes of Cooper, who'd chased after him too, on Lulay's behalf, and caught him first. Upon spinning around and seeing Cooper, he volunteered to pay double, and Cooper slapped the money into Lulay's hand, telling her to hide the tip from Juma. That was the only time he'd seen her in the great outdoors, if a mean street in Langatown qualified as great or outdoors.

She seemed so small, so ordinary, her hand so naturally in her mother's, who was tugging her along. In her stubborn Lulay way she was trying to yank her hand back and have things her way, and Cooper's eyes welled up with tears seeing her being a kid again. Then he realized that she might be leaving. She *was* leaving! Her mother had come for her, and he might never see her again!

He had to say good-bye and dashed after her. Startling people by coming up on them too quickly, they stepped out of his way and froze as prey does in the presence of a predator, making themselves as small and innocuous as possible hoping not to be selected.

"Lulay!" he called, but she didn't hear him. "Lulay! Lulay!"

Her mother, glancing back, saw him—a white man chasing after them! —and urged Lulay on. Of course they were afraid. They were running away themselves!

"Lulay! Lulay!" Cooper cried again.

They ran faster, scattering people as Cooper closed in on them, his hand reaching for the girl. "Lulay, wait! Lulay, it's Cooper!"

Her mother whirled around, panting, defiant and ready to take him on. Her daughter, sobbing fearfully, pressed her face to her mother's flat chest. She wasn't Lulay.

A sea of ashen faces surrounded them, waiting for Cooper's next move.

He stepped away from the woman mumbling an apology, and soon everyone was back to chatting or dozing off or stirring up fires. So many girls resembled Lulay, nut brown and beautiful and skinny and hungry, and he worried what life held for them. Would they end up working johns too? He hoped not. They might be sleeping on cardboard in the streets that night and for lots of nights to come, but they were safer than Lulay was. They weren't risking disappearing. Not yet.

He had to protect Lulay. He couldn't let her disappear, and Juma probably *was* trying to sell her, knowing it was only time before Little Ears would come back and take her for free. Cooper would buy her after he made his next diamond deal. That was his Lulay Plan. Then he worried, *What if Juma sells her, how will I find her?* He started running to The Mining Pan. He needed a backup plan, but what kind of plan? It wasn't like they had e-mail and cell phones.

When the power was on, the beer signs along Cowboy Mile cast a murky light at best, and for the moment there was no power at all. Instead, moonlight lit the familiar dusty stretch prowled by hookers and lookers on the ebb and flow of desire. When the electricity flickered on, the jukeboxes scratched out long, flat notes getting up to speed to play the inevitable cha-cha, and girls grabbed their prospective johns and pulled them into the middle of the street, jostling them in a semblance of dance-cum-foreplay. Cooper thought they never looked prettier than dancing in the moonlight. He would've liked to tell them, and maybe their johns had if they weren't too drunk to notice or speak.

"Why you running so fast-fast to see Little Sister?" one girl hollered out, and Cooper realized that he *was* almost running, and slowed down, supposing five minutes wasn't going to make a difference for Lulay. But as soon as he had that thought, he realized it might, that five minutes was all the time needed to sell her for a few inches of worthless money. He picked up his speed, not enough to attract attention except from all his wannabe girlfriends whose teases he endured, every one wishing he were running to her.

It was hot, and The Mining Pan's feeble fan didn't work any better with the power out, which it was again. Juma had stuck candles in the ashtrays, lighting up the place like a holy chapel. The candles flickered over the working girls' red-red lips and cheap glittery clothes. The men hanging on to the bar hadn't drunk enough to fall over, though a couple were teetering in that direction. Juma never missed a beat, and Cooper knew he saw him as soon as he entered.

Candlelight conceals as much as it illuminates—the shadows darker
for the brightness of the flame—and in that holied-up candle-bright bar,
the shadows were darker than midnight. Lucy could have been holed up
in any corner. Cooper didn't think so, not when his eyes started adjusting,
and he looked back at Juma, who was washing glasses in sudsy water
while taking a hit off a cigar-sized doobie held obligingly to his lips by a
customer. Was that big sprawling smile behind the perfumed smoke
mocking him? Cooper couldn't tell.

If Lulay wasn't in the bar, then she'd be behind the beaded curtain,
and Cooper began to get restless when she'd been behind it longer than
she needed to do her business. Like a lawyer, she sold herself by the
minute, and most guys didn't need more than the twenty-minute
minimum when the money clock was running, unless they wanted an
extra bit of lovey-dovey and cooed how they'd like to make her happy
again. Extra lovey-dovey part usually cost them an additional five minutes
and the second happy ending another ten. Lulay had never had a client
pay for a full hour. Except Cooper.

Where was she?

Sold?

To Little Ears?

Where was she?

Cooper, with an animal growl rising in his throat, pushed his way past
swaying couples unconcerned that the music had stopped again. Juma be
damned, he headed for the beaded curtain when Lulay emerged, the
sashaying beads sounding like a hard rain running off her shoulders. Her
john followed her out and aimed directly for a beer he'd left sweating on
the bar. Juma apparently had been worried about the girl too and gave the
john a stern look that sent him stepping away after he'd paid for his
overtime. Juma watched out for his girls; Cooper gave him credit for that.
He knew who they were with, and when they should be coming back out
front, and he didn't mind breaking something up if he thought anything

more than overtime might be going on. Juma watched for their safety like a horse breeder watches his colts. He didn't want sprains or breaks or horse thieves. He wanted his girls to have good teeth when prospective buyers forced open their lips.

Lulay didn't give her john a good-bye anything. She was done with him and needed her ice water, and Juma had a nice tall glass of it waiting for her. Crossing to the bar, she dodged come-ons from guys who knew she hadn't had time to spit out the last one, and she couldn't quite believe it, her expression said. She was still girl enough to have that look.

Handing her the water, Juma gave her a look that asked if everything was all right, and she said something that amused the barman and made him shake his head. Lulay took a mouthful of water, and leaning her head back, gargled it before swallowing. She took another sip, and swiveled on her heels, legs akimbo, zeroing in on Cooper. She always knew where to find him. She had Cooper radar, and she knew he'd seen her walk out with her john. She puckered her mouth like she was going to send him a big kiss with lips newly painted crimson, and instead squeezed out an ice cube like a turd into her palm.

The power came on and the jukebox flickered to life, spinning a seductive beat. Lulay's untrained body, still a girl's body, still a body remembering before her bleeding had started, and she could almost see womanhood but hadn't yet, that was the body that danced first, that found firm footing as she shook her glass at Cooper like a voodoo charm. Even the men slumped at the bar perked up for this dance of the Black Lolita. She rolled her chilled glass across her forehead, cooling that hot girl's body, cooling scenes seen by a woman, and that was the body that danced next—her woman's body. She swaggered into that woman's dance, moving her feet to a second beat, shutting her eyes in remembrance of every ass she'd grabbed and every night she'd swallowed.

When the lights flickered off again, Lulay rescued another cube from her glass and dabbed her neck with it like wet kisses washing away the johnny slobber. That cube melted fast, so hot was her little body; the next cube pressed to her face hardly touched her cheeks before turning into ersatz tears.

Again an animal cry threatened to escape Cooper's throat, so tormented was he by her wretchedness, and he pushed through the beery couples until he stood in front of her.

She held out her glass to him. "Do you want some ice water, Cooper?"

He shook his head no. What look Cooper had on his face, he couldn't say. Despair? He felt it. Fear? Impotence? Determination? He felt them all.

"Why did you start wearing lipstick?" he asked.

"Juma gave it to me."

"Did you have to put it on?"

"You don't think I'm pretty?"

"I think you're prettier without it."

"He didn't hurt me," she said, and when Cooper asked who, her eyes landed on her last john. He was swilling beer at the bar and exchanged no notice of recognition. "I talk-talk him into using one. That's why he takes too long. It slowed down his come-come."

"How did you convince him?"

"I told him it makes men bigger."

"That's good," Cooper said, chuckling appreciatively. "I hadn't thought of that strategy, and it's a good one. Men always want to be bigger."

"Men are big enough," she said, not having to look too hard to find several leering at her. Everything was emerging on Lulay all at once; hips, lips, tits all getting fuller and rounder and making her more and more desirable. "The next time he'll hurt me," she said. "It takes him too long and he has to pay more. It's too expensive not to hurt Lulay." She reached into her glass to retrieve the last ice cube and slipped it into one of his many pockets. "Free me, Cooper," she said, and left him to go back to work.

With her tears melting in his pocket, Cooper watched the girl push her way to the bar. She didn't need to try to seduce, she did so naturally, and she brought every man around when she slammed her glass of ice water on the long counter and said, "Make it a double" as if that African beauty knew a good time.

She brought Cooper to his knees, and on his soul he swore he'd set her free.

13

He strode up Cowboy Mile until he ducked into the neighborhoods where the Natives, restless under the hot waxing moon, sweated in droves along the broken sidewalks. Like a relay race, he passed from one outstretched hand to the next, somebody always begging for something. Money, gum, food—it didn't matter, whatever he had was more than they did. He didn't like the beggars touching him, and when somebody grasped his hand, he spun around ready to lay into his assailant, who turned out to be a granddaddy so white-bearded that Cooper was already reaching into his pocket for a couple of bills to give him before he noticed all the eyes watching his every movement. He shoved both hands deeper into his pockets and walked on.

The crowded streets eventually gave way to the narrow lanes creeping up the hillside. Occasionally a tin roof pinged or a board creaked from nothing more than the earth's rotation, putting Cooper on edge nevertheless. The innocent night sounds had been different in Iraq but equally nerve-wracking. The thud of an insurgent dropping over a wall. A whisper unsuccessfully concealed. The scratch of a grenade pin drawn. Every sound had been potentially fatal, and they were no less so in Langatown if for no other reason than every moment was potentially fatal there. Cooper pulled his knife from his boot. It was his second weapon of choice—the rifle his first—and if wars were fought with only those two weapons, he'd win them all.

Cooper had taught himself to shoot sitting on the steps of their trailer, taking out rattlesnakes from as far away as a hundred yards and earning ten bucks for every skin he took in to the local Elks Club. He learned to handle a knife by skinning the snakes. They'd been living outside Reno when a little girl died from a rattler's bite, and the Elks had sponsored a contest offering a hundred dollars to whomever brought in the most dead snakes in a week. Coops had brought in ten, more than twice the closest competition, and after that, the Elks offered him a ten-dollar booty for every rattler he killed. Luckily they'd hung around Reno for a while, and he managed to secretly build up a small nest egg that was still sitting in a bank. Reno was one of those places where his dad picked him up after school, and they were down the road without so much as a good-bye; certainly not a chance to withdraw his secret savings, which didn't amount to much but it was still something waiting for him.

Where Cooper rounded the corner expecting to see the bright steeple looming over the haphazard roofs, the charcoal sky was empty. The moon had set, and it took him some moments to make out the steeple's silhouette. The moment he entered No Man's Land, a chorus of cicadas stopped on a beat, silence suddenly blanketing the scabby hilltop. The barren land could have been the surface of the missing moon for its chalkiness. In the pitch dark, Cooper could barely see his own feet on the rough ground as he aimed for the church's faint silhouette.

A few cicadas restarted their chirping and then more joined in, the chorus growing louder and closer. Cooper glimpsed someone with a stick and realized that it wasn't cicadas at all but the *tap-tap tapping* of sticks on the ground. The noise surrounded him like a tightening noose, and he started to run, stumbling, glimpsing unfriendly faces leering at him, others trying to hit him with their sticks. When he finally burst through the white picket gate into the churchyard, it felt as if he had stepped into some living being's lung, the air was that soggy from the exhalations of so many people crammed within the garden walls. No one fussed with cook fires or chatted into the night; instead, they huddled as a single mass, arms and legs entwined, breathing a swampy breath that draped itself across his cheeks.

At the church's threshold he paused to peer into the interior ablaze with so many candles that it might have been on fire. He started up the center aisle, looking for Innocence, briefly wondering if the boy might have set him up to get arrested—Sadiq had warned him that the police paid the children—and in the next instant concluded that the boy had not. Cooper had seen too much honesty in those blind eyes.

An unfamiliar fury wracked the worshipers. They had pushed missionary benches into a circle at the altar, dragging into their center votives laden with candles stuck in sand. Around those holy flames men danced by scratching the ground while women encircled them, bleating like goats. When the men started to snuff out the flames, the women's voices rose in a tsunami of prayer. *Amen* they breathed in and *Amen* they breathed out in such thunderous unison that it was as rough as backwash and swept Cooper outside into the milky night.

He ended up in a corner of the churchyard that he had never been in. It was curiously deserted. A path ran a short few yards to disappear into a tall hedge, and Cooper followed it to a building that he guessed had been a stable at one time. The doors stood open to a dungeon's gaping hole that could have led into Hell, so tormented were the cries he heard coming from it.

As soon as he stepped inside, he smelled the abattoir.

Stalls ran along both sides of a long central aisle, some lit by bonfires illuminating their crazed inhabitants. The steady rockers, wailing Jesuses, writhing madwomen, irrepressible masturbators, the too daft and dumb. Few noticed Cooper, though two or three remembered to hold out a hand in an instinctive urge to beg from a white man. He stumbled along, stunned, fearful for his own mind when exposed to such lunacy, worried that sanity, like a button, could easily pop off.

Nearing the end of the aisle, several of the stalls had been removed to create an open space, and a dozen or so women, howling pitifully, were seated on the ground clutching young children to their chests. The children cried too, their wretched voices adding to the hellish anthem. Cooper, peering into the dim light, couldn't make out what was happening and stepped closer. A woman, her face awash with tears, lifted her son's frail arms up to him. His hands had been amputated! She wailed pitilessly, and unintentionally lessened her tourniquet grip on her son's wrists.

Blood spurted all over Cooper.

He reeled back, horrified, furiously wiping the blood off his cuts and scratches, and he tripped over a boy sitting cross-legged with a sleeping child in his lap.

The kid's T-shirt read Chicago Cubs.

"Innocence?" he asked. It was Janjay, Cooper could see, curled in his lap.

"Is that you, American?"

"Yeah," he replied haltingly, "it's me. Why aren't you in the church?"

"Did you come for diamonds?"

"Yeah … yeah," Cooper stammered, reminded of his business. "I got a special need … one last time … one last time and then it'll be adios, amigo. Comprendes?"

"No more diamonds, American," the boy told him flatly.

"I'm trying to help a friend. All I need is two good stones to help her, two really good stones like the last time." Cooper looked at the sweet girl in his lap. "My friend's not much older than Janjay. Can't you ask her, one more time?"

"No one more time." Innocence shifted his position and lifted his sister's lifeless arm to show her missing hand.

Only then did Cooper see the blackish blood pooled in the boy's lap. He could barely choke out, "Who did that to her?"

"The police."

The police! Cooper had led them there! He staggered under the weight of his certain complicity and fell against a wall, retching, adding his bile to that slaughterhouse stench.

14

The water seemed to run red forever swirling down the drain. Cooper grasped the showerhead with one hand while bracing himself on the wall with the other. So fatigued by the exhaustion of remorse, he could hardly stand on his tremulous legs. He wanted to open the top of his head and let the water flush away his memories of the children's slaughter, but he knew God wouldn't let him forgive himself that easily. Filling his mouth with water, he spat in a steady stream at a moldy patch on the ceiling as black as he imagined God's soul to be; for if man had been made in God's image—and Cooper had witnessed how black man's soul could be—then God's soul must be as black too. Had Cooper the courage of the ancients he would have chopped off his own hands in guilty sympathy for the mutilated girl, or ripped out his eyes to never see flesh so desecrated again; instead, he only had his tears that the shower washed away as soon as they sprang from his eyes. When he could finally trust his wobbly legs, he slipped off his clothes—vest, cutoffs, boxers: the sum of his wardrobe—and stomped on them like a winemaker to release their frothy red juice.

He'd have happily stayed submerged forever under the shower's spray, but the landlady had already banged twice on her ceiling, and now she was pounding on his door, shouting, "Too long shower, American!"

"Too long shower, American!" he called back, and twisted the faucet closed. "Too long fucking everything!"

Still wet, he went to the refrigerator and grabbed a beer when the knocking on his door started again. He stomped across the room shouting, "*I turned off the fucking shower!*" and flung open the door.

It was Sadiq.

Instantly Cooper dropped his hands at some attempt at modesty, but the long neck of the beer bottle mocked his effort. "Uhhh … what time is it?" was all he could think to say.

"It's early. My father thinks I'm at the hammam."

"You're not … you're … you're here!"

The boy had moussed his hair and was wearing jeans and a sleeveless shirt of stretchy material. "Yes, I'm here," he said. "May I come in?"

"Sure … sure …" Cooper stepped aside for him to enter. "Uh … I don't have any clothes. I mean I do but they're all wet. I was washing them. Let me get a towel." He ducked into the bathroom, calling out, "How'd you find out where I live?"

"It's easy to find a foreigner in Langatown," Sadiq informed him.

Cooper returned, tucking a towel at his waist. "That's not exactly reassuring. Why aren't you wearing your robe?"

"I'll change at the shop."

"You mean it's only a costume for work?"

"My father likes me to respect tradition."

"I know, he's a family man," Cooper said, "and he only drinks tea, which is more than I can offer. I don't have coffee, either, but I do have beer. Do you want one?"

"It's still the morning," Sadiq said, and declined.

"I've been up all night. It feels like no-time to me."

"I know that time," Sadiq admitted, his eyes crinkling with a mischievous smile.

"Exciting nights in Beirut?"

"Sometimes."

"Sounds like more than 'sometimes' to me. So you'll have a beer?"

"Why not?"

Cooper took two bottles from the refrigerator. "I'm surprised you drink at all. I thought it was against your religion."

"It is."

"Your father's worried that you've come home with some radical ideas," Cooper admitted.

"Like coffee?" the youth asked.

Cooper popped open the beers, handed him one. "Cheers," he said.

They clinked bottles and sipped from them.

"My father would kill me if he saw me drinking alcohol," Sadiq remarked.

"Boy, did we grow up in different neighborhoods." Cooper drank some more, and asked, "If I asked where you lived, could I find you too? I mean if I asked just anyone?"

"Of course, but I live here. I'm a citizen."

"Now there's a funny idea," Cooper replied, "Lalangoan citizenship."

Sadiq frowned. "It's only funny if you don't have it."

"Why not move to Beirut? You're Lebanese too, aren't you?"

"If I abandon my parents here," Sadiq explained, "my relatives in Lebanon would have nothing to do with me."

"It wouldn't exactly be abandonment," Cooper replied. "In my country, it's called doing your own thing. It's encouraged."

"Everything was predetermined the moment I was born because I had a penis," Sadiq elaborated. "If I had a sister, her life would be predetermined too, in a woman's way. Because I am an only child, I must be both a son and daughter to my parents. There's no room for me in my own life."

"So what will you do?" Cooper asked.

"Get married."

"Can't you refuse?"

"It doesn't matter what I want."

"That doesn't sound like a playboy's life," Cooper joked, trying to cajole a smile out of Sadiq, but he was too downcast.

They both pulled on their beers. "What do you do all day, Coopah?"

Think about you, he could have confessed, instead replying, "Worry if my visa is going to be extended."

"Why do you stay here?"

"Your friend Munir already asked me that."

"I know, and you didn't answer him."

"Every day there seems to be a new reason."

"What's today's reason?"

"I don't know, it's still early."

The boy's eyes twinkled when he suggested, "Maybe I can help you figure it out."

Cooper's heart leapt at the boy's obvious flirtation. "Maybe you can."

One of them needed to make the next move, but they were unsure both how to make it.

"You ready for another beer?" Cooper asked.

"Not yet."

"I can't get you drunk?"

"Do you want to?"

"If I have to."

"I'll take a glass of water."

"With ice?"

"You have ice?"

"I have a freezer, it's why I rented this palace." As if to prove it, Cooper pulled the dented tray out of the freezer and banged it a couple of time to free the cubes. He held one up. "You see? Ice!"

"It looks like a huge diamond!" Sadiq exclaimed.

"I wish." Cooper dropped several cubes into a glass, filled it, and handed it to him. "One glass of diamond water coming up."

"Thanks." Sadiq took a sip, and asked, "Why do you like the cold so much?"

"It's more that I hate to be hot. When I was growing up, we spent most of our time in a desert."

"You didn't like the desert?"

"It could've been Nirvana and I'd still be trying to forget it. The desert was cheap for living and that figured big in my father's calculations. No heat to pay for in the winter, and he didn't bother with AC in the summer. It's safe to say that I sweated most of my childhood."

Sadiq, draining his glass, reminded Cooper, "It's hot in Lalanga too."

"No shit. Though one thing's for sure, it's not as hot as Iraq. You want some more water?"

"No thanks."

"I agree, it ruins good ice. Another beer?"

Sadiq shook his head.

"You sure?" Cooper pressed him.

"I'm sure."

"Well I do. Talking about the desert makes me thirsty." Cooper's towel came loose when he stooped to reach into refrigerator, and he stood up to tuck it back in, his back to Sadiq. The boy fished ice cubes from his glass, and coming up behind Cooper, wrapped his arms around him and pressed the ice cubes to his nipples. Cooper reared back, clasping the boy's hands to his chest as the melting ice ran down his belly and followed the veins to his groin. He turned in Sadiq's arms and their mouths slipped together in a kiss of such longing that it could have been a complete act of love itself.

He drew off Sadiq's shirt, trapping his arms, tickling his underarms with his tongue as the boy squirmed pleasurably. Once freed of his shirt, Sadiq found Cooper's mouth again and tasted his own saltiness. They fell onto the bed, and when they were naked they paused, their hearts beating for each other.

"Are you sure?" Cooper asked.

Both were sure, and as morning became afternoon, they took each other more than once, occasionally slipping into the compact shower only to slip back into bed to lie side-by-side for the meager fan to cool them.

Holding him, Cooper fell deeper in love with Sadiq, who seemed so at ease with his body that Cooper finally asked, "Are you sure you've never done this before?"

"I'm sure."

"It didn't happen in Beirut?"

"Nothing like this."

"Wow. I can't imagine what you'll be like after some practice!"

"You're good too," Sadiq told him.

"I've never kissed a man before," Cooper confessed. "I haven't done any of it before, not really, and I've certainly never kissed anybody like that. Have you?"

"No."

"Did you know you *could* kiss somebody like that?"

Sadiq laughed softly. "I don't know. I hadn't thought about it until it happened."

"It all happened so naturally, didn't it?" Cooper remarked, truly astounded by the easiness of their lovemaking. "Let's kiss again," he suggested.

They did, but their desires had temporarily flagged, and their kiss was more tender for it.

When they rolled apart, Cooper asked, "Does Munir love you?"

Sadiq answered guardedly, "I told you, he has business here."

"I know, you said the diamond business. It's a long way to come to talk business. Couldn't you have used e-mail?"

"You know there is no e-mail in Lalanga. Why do you want to know about Munir?"

"I don't really, except to know if you ever kissed him."

"I haven't."

"Don't sound so unhappy about it!"

"I wasn't sounding—"

"I'm kidding." Cooper stopped him, and maybe doing a little checking out of the competition at the same time. It suddenly dawned on him that perhaps it was Sadiq who was in love with Munir; but no, Munir would not come so far—diamonds or not—if he didn't love Sadiq. Or need him. With his injuries, maybe he couldn't get a wife, and suddenly Munir seemed especially lecherous for chasing Sadiq all the way back to Langatown.

"Do you love him?" Cooper couldn't help himself from asking.

"I feel sorry for him."

"Is that all?"

"We are only friends," Sadiq emphasized.

"Like us? Aren't we friends too?"

"You are different, Coopah."

"Different how?"

Sadiq touched his cock. "Different like this."

"So you didn't ... in Beirut ..."—Cooper touched Sadiq in turn—"... do this with him?"

"No," he replied, and they made love for the last time that day, and showered again, lazily soaping each other up. So little age separated them, yet Cooper had seen a soldier's world. He'd lived nightmares that he'd carry to his grave, but that day, the memory he'd take away was the trail of soap running down the crack of Sadiq's ass.

"How will you explain to your father that you are so late coming back from the hammam?" he asked.

"He already accuses me of being unreliable."

"Are you?"

"I was always daydreaming as a child."

"That doesn't necessarily make you unreliable."

"It did me," Sadiq confessed.

"Are you finished?"

"Yes."

Cooper turned off the water and turned back around to embrace the youth one more time, their bodies already memories to be savored.

Sadiq trailed water into the room to retrieve his clothes while Cooper pondered the soggy mess resembling roadkill on his bathroom floor. "So what did you daydream about as a kid? Beirut?"

"In fact I did," Sadiq answered, "although now that I know Beirut, I can't claim that I really daydreamed about it because I couldn't have. I didn't know some things existed until I got there!"

Cooper wrung out his boxers over the sink. "You make your playboy days sound pretty exciting for someone who didn't do anything."

"All I did was come up with increasingly preposterous excuses for not sleeping with a prostitute," Sadiq elaborated, "which got me into some pretty interesting situations nevertheless."

Cooper stepped into the doorway to slip on his boxers. "So does spreading your wild oats include men?"

"It's never talked about."

"I thought, with the hammam and all, maybe it was more okay here."

"What happens in the hammam stays in the hammam."

Pink runnels dribbled onto the floor when Cooper picked up his vest and he dropped it back on the pile. He joined Sadiq in the room, and from his closet pulled out his jungle-rotted T-shirt. A large spider ran off when he shook it out. "I guess I'm not dressing for dinner," he remarked.

"You don't have another shirt?" Sadiq asked.

"I'm not much of a clothes horse."

"A clothes horse?"

"A fancy dresser," Cooper translated. "It's an American expression."

"Sometimes I think Americans need subtitles."

"Now there's a scary thought," Cooper replied, bemused. "Do you really want to know what we're thinking?"

"Here, take mine," Sadiq said, and pulled off his shirt.

He handed it to Cooper, who didn't want to take it. "What are you going to wear?"

"I have plenty more at home. Come on, take it." Sadiq pressed it on him.

Cooper slipped it on. What had made the youth look merely skinny clung to him revealing his strong chest. Sadiq pinched his nipples and used them to pull him into a kiss. It was sweet, a foretaste of the next time, and then it was over. They didn't cling to love for the display of it.

The boy was out the door.

Cooper followed him a minute later.

15

He had never seen Langatown so festive. An amnesty must have been called because an army of street cleaners, including Stubby men of all ages, was stirring up dust clouds using twig brooms to sweep trash out of sight. Others were busy hanging long streamers of triangular flags interweaving America's red-white-and-blue with Lalanga's black-and-blood-red. Full-sized flags were paired too, mounted high on utility poles so no one could easily steal them before the secretary of state's visit the following day. Colonel Diamond intended to put on a show for her, that was clear.

Cooper was swept along by the good cheer, passing normally taciturn shopkeepers who were greeting everyone; even the typically frazzled drivers seemed to aim less intentionally for pedestrians. Cheap souvenirs had already gone on sale, and he had to fend off vendors hawking T-shirts with caricatures of the Secretary puckering up to kiss Colonel Diamond over *Let the good times R-oil!*

Near the port, Cooper followed the sounds of steady hammering to discover a speaker's platform under construction on the wharf at the opposite end of a square from the Parliament building. He could imagine the whole hokey show they were planning to put on, complete with lighting up the Parliament if there wasn't a power outage, as if it were lit up every night when Cooper knew it hadn't been since he arrived, certainly not during the nights when his platoon had camped in it. Not a single window remained unbroken, and graffiti reached all the way to the top floor.

Not that the secretary of state would give a hoot whether or not the Parliament building had been abandoned. There was no pretense about her coming in anyone's mind least of all her own. She was coming for the business-business of oil, and Cooper would've bet that he had heard her speech before. He'd heard enough of them: the bullshitting Iraqi politicians saying exactly what the Americans wanted to hear, and the American politicians dishing it right back, all meant to mislead the public by denying exactly what they were really doing. Cooper knew the bullshit so well he could have prepared both their bootlick remarks.

A team of construction workers swarmed the platform while children played in the sawdust gathering beneath it. They scrambled for any piece of wood tossed down, collecting little kindling piles and using the longer pieces to bat cans, cheering gleefully whether or not they scored. More than anything else, it was the children at play that made Langatown so festive that morning. Normally hidden from a treasure trove of risks, suddenly there they were, making toys from carpentry ends and squealing just to hear their own voices. With a loud *smack!* a can came flying at Cooper, and he ducked in the nick of time to miss being hit. The children jumped up and down high-fiving each other, and Cooper, suspecting correctly that he'd been intentionally targeted, played along, pretending he'd been hit and taking a couple of stunned steps. The kids went wild.

It was astonishing to hear the children's laughter, but everything that morning seemed astonishing. With Sadiq it had been the perfect consummation of a dream, and Cooper might have convinced himself that it had been a dream were it not for the fact that he was wearing the youth's shirt. He sniffed it for faint traces of him and wondered if Sadiq had worn his Western clothes with the premeditated intention of seducing him. Was he truly as inexperienced as he claimed?

A wave of anxiety swept through Cooper. They hadn't used protection! Despite his lectures to his sister, to Lulay, to himself, he hadn't used protection. What did he really know about Sadiq? The boy went to the hammam. He had had a playboy year in Beirut. He was handsome—how could he not have done things? How often unprotected things? What did he really know about Sadiq's relationship with Munir? Wasn't Munir buying condoms at the pharmacy for God knew-what? And who had Munir been with before Sadiq? The questions and recriminations were endless, drowning the morning's pleasure in a widening circle of anxiety until Cooper remembered the honesty in the boy's face and the innocence behind his mischievous smile. However naturally their lovemaking had come, for both of them it had had its first-time anxieties too. He could trust the boy, he decided, and calming down, again marveled at their astonishing morning.

He felt the wad of Sadiq's advance jammed into his pocket and hoped it was enough to buy Lulay. It would have to be enough. He couldn't ask Sadiq for more, and he had no idea where else to get cash. Contemplating a future subsisting wholly on wind-felled mangos, he was realizing how precarious his situation had become when he turned a corner and it instantly became more so.

Only steps ahead of him, a rebel squad executed a man and woman against a wall. They slid down leaving twin bloody trails. It took Cooper a moment to react to what he had witnessed; it was too out of context with the rest of the day.

In that moment, the commander saw him. They locked eyes, or as best as Josef Nimwe could from behind his sunglasses. He snapped an order as Cooper started to run, and the first shots rang out behind him as the rebels gave chase. Cooper whipped around a corner, but they kept coming, led by a kid wearing a green cap backward while the others fired indiscriminately.

Cooper knew that web of streets, and like a spider's web they ran in long narrow lanes with short cut-throughs. Nimwe's kid lieutenant knew them too, and he forced Cooper to shift from lane to lane, taxing his knowledge of which cut-throughs lined up and which ones didn't. He mentally thanked every tout he'd ever hired to show him shortcuts. At least he was an even match for the kid, who clearly knew that street, shouting orders to the others while ably second-guessing Cooper's moves and gradually closing down his options. In fact, Cooper figured his only hope was to get to Cowboy Mile where the rebels were likely to encounter government soldiers who used it as a spare bedroom.

He had miscalculated.

The rebels sensed victory. Nimwe's lieutenant had commanded them well. He was a good field commander, if "field" applied to urban warriors. With rebels poring into the lane behind him, Cooper ran as hard as he could, headed for the drunks staggering past at the far end of the longest block he'd ever known. Only a few more strides!

The kid jumped out right where the road intersected Cowboy Mile, and Cooper literally tripped himself trying to stop too fast. He hit the ground just as the kid's chest exploded outward, so hard that his cap was knocked off before his body hit the ground. A second later, an army truck roared into view, running over the kid and his cap, rifles blasting as soldiers standing in the back engaged the fleeing rebels. Cooper rolled out of the way and stayed down until the battle had moved out of sight.

Picking himself up, Cooper sauntered down the Mile, brushing the dust off Sadiq's shirt. He hadn't worn such a nice shirt for a long time, and it didn't go unnoticed.

"You going to show off your new shirt-shirt to Little Sister, American Cooper?" one girl called out, and a second one cried, "Oo-la-la, next thing American Cooper will be getting new shoes!"

He pointed to his boots and held out his palms—*So what's wrong with these?*—and they laughed, sending him on his way, and calling after him that if Little Sister didn't like his new shirt-shirt, to come back. They wouldn't complain.

It never took much to turn Cowboy Mile into one long street party, and that afternoon, the precelebration celebration of the secretary's arrival had the jukeboxes cranked up full blast. Johns twirled their ten-minute dates in the street stealing free kisses whenever they could. Even Cooper, a shy though surefooted dancer, spun a girl or two before pushing his way through The Mining Pan's saloon doors. The crowd was louder than usual, the smoke cloud thicker, Juma's neon beer signs more lurid for it still being daylight.

Cooper looked for her. No Lulay. That didn't mean she wasn't hidden out of sight, blocked by all the men competing drunkenly for the next girl freed up. That's when he realized how many men there were waiting for a turn behind the beaded curtain. All those impatient johns, rarely out-and-about during the day, didn't care if what walked out next was pretty—moneyed sex almost never was—she just needed to walk out. Obviously Cooper hadn't kept Lulay supplied with enough condoms to keep up with demand, and he dispiritedly hoped that her recycling method was working.

He shouldered his way through the crowd, fending off gropes that hoped he might be available, and Cooper supposed he looked the part wearing such short shorts and Sadiq's skintight shirt. Indifferently pushing away the exploratory hands, he wormed his way to the bar and signaled to Juma, who, eyes bloodshot and lost in a purple haze, smiled back not in any hurry to serve anyone. Cooper glanced in the direction of some raucous laughter, thinking he'd recognized the moustached oilman's lurid laugh, and instead saw four Thick Necks he'd never seen before sitting together in a booth. New arrivals. Cooper knew the whole whoring scene well enough that he could have advised them: *Sit two to a booth max, or you'll have no room for the girls, and don't keep buying them drinks when it's not whiskey but whiskied water that Juma's charging you for. Stick to beer, and make sure he opens it in front of you.*

Suddenly Cooper was ready to explode with anger, thinking about the stuff he'd learned that he happily could have gone through life not knowing. The stained mattresses behind the beaded curtain, or the girls sold by their mothers, or the lipsticked boys who sold themselves. And it wasn't happening only in The Mining Pan but at The Deep Shaft and The Slurry Hole and every other wretched bar on the street. The more he thought about the indecency that it was happening at all, let alone on such a scale, the more he needed a drink and signaled Juma again.

The barman had been watching Cooper warily and stepped down to inform him, "The ice machine is broken."

"Fortunately I don't like ice in my beer," answered Cooper, "and I know you've got beer. You haven't stopped pissing, have you?"

Juma gave him a bottle from the cooler. "Americans don't know beer," he said.

"But we do know piss, and this"—Cooper took a swallow—"tastes straight from the tap."

"I don't know a crazier white man." Shaking his head, the barman stepped away to refill a customer's drink.

The beer was a long way from cold, but it still felt good to roll the bottle on his forehead as Cooper swung around to take in the room. Oil had lubricated the afternoon inside The Mining Pan too, and for all the chatter and good cheer, it could have been a drunken Saturday night. Some of the women—for there were some women too, not only girls— seemed to have taken on an unwonted languidness, and he watched one sultry dancer who soon disappeared behind the beaded curtain clutching a fistful of bills with her highest bidder in tow. Lipsticked boys, trawling for their minority clientele, were as made-up and sometimes prettier than the girls. Cooper's upbringing had exposed him to his father's perverted sexuality that he'd gratefully never discovered in himself, just as when the lipsticked boys pranced past him he couldn't recognize his homosexuality in them either. It was the love of a man he longed for, not those girly boys, and his thoughts naturally returned to Sadiq. He couldn't imagine him in that bar. It was too tawdry, and there was nothing tawdry about their love.

Sipping from his bottle, Cooper took in the fanny-slapping courtships and two-drink drunks in a room filled with dancers jostling for space to gyrate their hips to a popular bebop beat. In a party mood himself, Cooper rocked a little on his barstool and might have danced if he hadn't felt so helplessly white in a room of black abandon. He drank off his beer, and setting the bottle noisily on the bar, asked, "Who do you have to fuck to get another drink around here?"

Juma stirred himself enough to reply, "You pay to fuck."

"And all this time, I thought that was free. Now how about that second beer?"

"You got money?"

"Enough."

"You still owe me for a coffee."

"I thought that was on the house."

"I don't give something free to a white man making trouble," Juma said, nevertheless setting up his beer. "That's two beers and a coffee."

"Run a tab."

"Can't. You used up all my ink."

"Fuck it," Cooper complained half-heartedly, and reached into his pocket to pull out a couple of bills as discreetly as he could. For his part, Juma watched what he was doing, hoping to glimpse what Cooper was trying so hard to conceal. Slapping the money on the counter, he asked, "Has my buddy Little Ears been back?"

"You see him in here?"

"Let me be more specific. Is he in the back?"

"Not yet," the barman replied just as evasively. Juma made it sound like Little Ears was fast becoming a regular customer, which didn't make Cooper very happy, but at least it wasn't him in the back with Lulay at that moment.

He resigned himself to waiting out her john to have a chance to tell her what he was there for, and to tell her to be ready to leave quick-quick.

He didn't know how the negotiations with Juma would go, but the more he observed the crowd, with the painted up girls and leering johns, the more he grew determined, one way or another, to break Lulay out of that bar that afternoon. He had dwindling resources, and she had dwindling time. He'd make Juma see the light and take what money he had for her; otherwise, he had his knife. But first he needed to see Lulay, tell her his plan, let her know he was making good on his Cooper promise.

"Where's Lulay?" he asked when Juma delivered a new beer.

The barman made the point of looking around and shrugged. "She must be busy in the back."

His nonchalance instantly made Cooper suspicious. Juma never treated his girls so offhandedly. "She's not been out for water for more than a half hour," Cooper reminded him.

Juma picked up a rag and started swabbing down the bar. "Maybe she's not thirsty."

"She always comes out between johns."

"Maybe she has a long john."

"More than a half hour?"

"Maybe she's not johning."

"You want to stop with the roundabout funny talk and tell me, where is Lulay?"

Juma stopped working his rag. "Why is she so important to you?"

Cooper told him, "I want to buy her."

"Lucy?"

"Yeah, but her name's Lulay. So where is she?"

"You couldn't buy coffee two days ago."

"I robbed a bank. Do you care?"

"If it's my money you robbed, I do."

"It'll be your money again if you sell me Lulay."

"How much you got?"

"Over three inches."

"That's short."

"How much did you pay her mother?" Cooper asked, making it sound like the accusation he intended it to be.

Juma went back to wiping down the counter.

"So do we have a deal?"

"No deal."

"Why no deal?"

"You're short."

"Okay, I'll come up with more." Cooper pretended to cave. He never really expected Juma to take his offer, but he still wasn't leaving without Lulay. "I want to tell her."

"She's not here."

"Not here? She's always here."

"Not today."

"Why not today?"

"She takes the day off."

"*Off?* Since when does Lulay get a day off? Especially when it's packed in here like Times Square on New Year's Eve and she's your most popular 'virgin.'" Cooper nailed Juma with a hard look. "Where is she?"

"Ask her when she comes back."

"I'm asking you."

The barman shrugged. "Maybe she visits her mother, I don't ask."

"Her mother lives three days' walk away."

"Then she better walk-walk fast."

Cooper threatened, "I'm going in the back to find her."

Juma took a step closer to his gun. Cooper didn't miss his move and had half-expected it when the barman said, "I sold her."

"Then you can buy her right back."

Juma picked up the gun from on top of his cash box. "You go away. I don't want your trouble."

"You already have my trouble. Now tell me, *where is Lulay?*"

COOPER'S PROMISE

A hush swept the room.

"Who did you fucking sell her to?"

The wheezing ice machine made the only sound in the room as the customers eagerly awaited their next move, some hoping for blood, when a lipsticked boy splashed his way out through the beaded curtain. The long strands of glass beads tinkled brightly as everyone glanced at him, but it was Cooper's eye he caught, and the boy instinctively threw him a glossy kiss with a bit of tongue. Immediately the crowd broke into laughter in the same instant that Munir followed the boy through the curtain. He was easily recognizable by his ruinous scar, and he scowled at the laughter, thinking it was for him.

Cooper pushed his way through the crowd, but once on the street, he had no idea what to do. How to find Lulay? He debated going back inside to cut the truth out of the barman, but he couldn't imagine jumping Juma before Juma got to his gun.

Who would know where Lulay was?

What *did* he know? Cooper took a rough inventory of everything the girl had said, and Little Ears ended up as the star suspect in her disappearance. It was when Little Ears had come onto the scene that Lulay became really scared. Could Cooper retrace his way to the police station where he'd been jailed? Probably not, there were too many turns on that journey through miles of indistinguishable slums when his mind had been concentrating on escaping a fatal situation, not returning to it.

Who could help?

For something as simple as an ant bite, Cooper didn't know a doctor he could go to, let alone someone who could help track down a disappeared girl. A disappeared slave. Sold and resold. They might have already changed her name again. To Lily. To Linda. To Lost, because she was lost unless he found her. No one else was searching for her. She'd been right. She was at risk of disappearing if she hadn't already.

Cooper had to find her.

But where?

It wasn't ad hoc, the slave business; there had to be a network with routes, traders, people, and money exchanging hands. Someone had to know how it worked and where the girls were taken. Someone who kept tabs on those sorts of things.

Then it dawned on him, and he started running as fast as he could, knowing every minute was vital.

He ran as hard as he'd run when he came home before deploying to Iraq. He'd wanted to surprise Becky and waited outside her school until the other students had gone home. When Becky didn't show up Cooper went to find her teacher. "Your father said there was an emergency at home," she told him, "and he picked her up about an hour ago." Cooper fled the school and ran down the road against a wind blowing so hard it sandblasted his cheeks. They had moved up in the world from their small green trailer to a double-wide when Cooper's father had decided they needed to stay put for a while—probably, Coops had grown up enough to realize, because they had run out of towns to be run out of. His father had married a woman as fat as her trailer was wide to get his hands on the trailer—with a pretty little girl thrown in as a bonus: Becky. The first time Coops saw her, he was scared for her, and he made it his enterprise to protect her from his father, keeping his "Uncle Roy" radar always on and making sure Uncle Roy never got his chance. And Uncle Roy went mad. He attacked Cooper and physically threw him out of the house. It was a big scene, with everybody shouting out everything, but at least Becky's mother finally knew what to watch out for. It was Cooper's eighteenth birthday, and he'd never outed his dad before. He'd never dared. His temper was too lethal, and that night it would have been if Cooper hadn't gotten to the rifle first.

Becky chased him down the dirt track leading from their trailer, assuring him she'd be okay, that she'd known all along what his dad was about, it didn't matter if her mother was clueless. Cooper shouldn't come back 'cause one of them was going to kill the other, that was evident from the murderous scene that had just happened. "I promised I'd protect you!" he cried, and she assured him that he'd protected her long enough—and now she was old enough to protect herself.

He made himself believe her because that was the only way he could leave. He'd enlisted in the army and headed straight to Pendleton and didn't go back home until he was shipping out. That's when he'd found himself running to that behemoth of a double-wide on his first rescue mission to save Becky.

Now he was racing to another behemoth on a second rescue mission.

In all of Langatown, nothing inspired so much awe as the American embassy. Standing atop the town's second highest hill—God had appropriated the highest for His own house—it had been recently refitted to add a guard tower to each of its four corners at double the height of the security wall. Creating a clear zone around it had required leveling shanties, and the cleared encirclement was now peppered with uneven concrete blocks resembling tombstones. As added defense, an open-bed army truck sported enough antiaircraft equipment to bring down a small air force. The entire hulking complex of walls and towers, recently painted camouflage green, shined brilliantly in the afternoon light. Its nickname was Oz.

Cooper looked for its welcome mat, and missing that, knew from his drill in Baghdad to approach with arms slightly extended, no quick movements, and stop when told. He stopped before he was told, wanting them to see that he couldn't possibly have a weapon; his shorts were too short, his shirt too tight, his hands too empty. He waited for the sense that they'd relaxed some, but it wasn't forthcoming, and that's when he realized they were all marines, not sprinkled with the usual handful of friendly Natives on some pretense of bilateral cooperation. These were serious soldiers. Some real security had arrived.

Cooper approached a green Plexiglas window and spoke to the marine on duty through a patch of tiny holes. "I'm here to see Sam Brown," he said.

"Are you an American citizen?" the soldier drawled. He was tall, blond, and all Texan.

Cooper crisply saluted, barking into the pinholes, "Sergeant Cooper Chance, Twentieth Infantry Regiment, first-class Sharpshooter First Class. I was taking out insurgents in Fallujah before getting transferred to Lalanga."

"Yes, sir! Sounds like you drew two short sticks, sir."

"Special Ops," Cooper told him, "we go where we're told."

"Is Mr. Brown expecting you?"

"He's always expecting me. We have that kind of relationship."

"You don't have an appointment?"

"Roger that."

The marine hesitated. "We're on a high security status until—"

"Until the secretary of state leaves, no one's permitted inside, I know, I know," Cooper said. "I've been briefed. If I have to wait to see Sam Brown until the secretary is gone, she might not make it out of the country."

The marine heard the threat and its urgency. "Do you have your passport?"

Like I said, "Special Ops," Cooper replied. "We don't carry passports in case we're compromised."

"Do you have any ID?"

"I'd have the same problem, wouldn't I?" He could sense that the marine was growing suspicious, and with his boxers drooping below his cutoffs and no ID, Cooper could understand why. But he needed to see Sam Brown. He'd convinced himself that the CIA man was his only chance for finding Lulay. "What's your name, Marine?" he asked.

"Porter."

"*Private* Porter?"

"I wouldn't be in this plastic box if I had stripes."

"Then, Private Porter, this is an order. You get Sam Brown on your telephone, and you say exactly this to him. 'Sergeant Cooper Chance wants your fucking black ass out here so he can step foot on American soil one more time before he dies.' Do you roger that?"

The marine hesitated. "I can't say to him—"

"I outrank you, Private, and that was an order. Do I need to repeat it?"

"No, sir."

He watched the marine pick up a handset. "That bit about his fucking black ass is code between us. Don't fuck it up."

"No, sir. I mean, yes, sir."

He watched as the marine spoke with someone on the other end of a line, glancing at Cooper a couple of times before hanging up. When he did, he said, "You can come in," and a buzzer sounded.

Cooper pulled open the heavy metal door and stepped into a small rectangular room with a plaster wall to his left and a second Plexiglas window revealing Private Porter to his right. He reached for the exit door and pressed on its metal bar. Locked. He whirled around and tried to catch the first door from shutting, but it closed a moment too soon. Cooper threw himself against it. In the same instant the Plexiglas window went opaque.

He'd been trapped.

"Someone will come to escort you in a minute," Private Porter said through the intercom, his voice too big for the tiny space.

Cooper strained to hear anyone coming to rescue him. The more he listened the more silence he heard. He had to talk himself into staying calm, fighting back the urge to try both doors again, which would accomplish nothing more than to reveal his mounting anxiety, and Cooper didn't want to show Sam Brown any weakness—the CIA man would simply hold him in that claustrophobic room longer.

"It's been more than a minute," he directed at the opaque Plexiglas, his own voice dull between those heavy walls. He shivered. Was it really cold? He decided it was. He wasn't used to air conditioning and longed to be back outside, in the hot sun he generally detested. He shivered again. "Hey man, it's freezing-ass cold in here. I'll wait outside." He pushed on the metal exit bar but the door didn't budge, and he shivered again. "I outrank you, Private, so I'm ordering you to open this door." He pushed on it again, growing increasingly frustrated. "You've got no fucking right to keep me in here." He started kicking the exit bar repeatedly. "*Open this fucking door!*"

Sam Brown swung open the door behind him and said, "I hear you want to fuck my black ass."

Cooper roared as he leapt for him, and the CIA man deftly stepped aside. He bounded into the embassy's lobby, where two marines had their weapons drawn. "So what, am I under arrest?" he asked.

"Only a welcoming party."

"Well, you can tell them to put away their weapons."

"Search him," Sam Brown ordered. "He has a knife in one of his boots."

"How do you know about that?" Cooper wondered.

One of the marines stepped forward to frisk him, and Cooper told him, "It's in my left boot."

"I didn't know you were left-handed, Chance," Sam Brown remarked.

"I'm not, but anyone trained to frisk footwear is trained to look in the right shoe first. It can make a split-second difference." .

"They were right when they said you were smart." The CIA man took the knife and dismissed the marines.

"So what was keeping me in your holding tank all about?" Cooper demanded.

"It was to make a point."

"I guess I missed it."

"You've got to get smart, soldier, because otherwise you're going to end up in a cell a lot smaller than that and for a lot longer."

"Unless I do what you want? Is that your threat?"

To ask the CIA man for a favor was the last thing Cooper wanted to do. He knew the price he'd have to pay. In war, he had no objections to assassinations; they were strikes against the enemy. In Iraq, Cooper had only needed to know that he was pointing his rifle at an enemy to pull the trigger. But he saw no duty to his country in shooting Colonel Diamond, who, though a buffoon with many reasons to hate him, wasn't at war with America; in fact, he was about to throw one helluva welcoming party for her secretary of state. But there would be no arguing with Sam Brown. His terms were nonnegotiable.

"Lulay's disappeared," Cooper told him, "and I'm looking for her."

"Lulay?" Sam Brown pondered her name. "Oh, you mean Lucy, the girl from the bar?"

"Yeah, I mean Lucy, the girl from the bar, and you know who I mean. Quit fucking with me. You know her real name is Lulay."

"I remember she's sweet."

"She needs help."

"There's a girl everywhere who needs help."

"She's a special girl."

"How's that?"

"She reminds me of my kid sister."

Sam Brown snorted. "That would make her special all right, since you don't have a kid sister."

"I have Becky."

"She's a stepsister."

"That doesn't matter," Cooper answered. "I'm a brother to her. Now can you help me find Lulay?"

16

Cooper stumbled drunkenly around a corner and slouched against a building. The heavy moon floating on the horizon cast a wide golden band across the water that silhouetted boats rolling in the bay. On shore the night was thick with shadows; only the swaying lamps tied to the *African Lady*'s rigging illuminated that stretch of the wharf. The rising wind carried sounds to him—ropes creaking, tin roofs popping, a window breaking seemingly so close he expected glass shards to lash him—and each one made him jump.

He staggered closer to the boat, gripping a grimy cloth slung over his shoulders that he'd snitched from a bum who'd wandered off to take a piss. From the smell of it he'd pissed the blanket a few times too. The whiskey bottle he'd picked up behind a bar on Cowboy Mile, choosing one with enough dregs in it to flavor his breath should anyone doubt his state of inebriation. Along the way he had picked charcoal out of dead fires to paint every inch of his visible skin black.

The *African Lady*'s only visible crewman—Cooper's man—barely noticed him, except for being amused by an especially successful belch that Cooper managed to produce. He watched Cooper stagger a few steps for their entertainment value before becoming distracted by someone opening the cabin door, emitting a burst of light and throbbing music. A man climbed the couple of steps to the deck, checking his zipper and grumbling good-bye at the crewman before crossing the short gangplank to shore.

Feigning to trip over a line, Cooper landed on a pile of nets, where he made sure that his stolen bedding concealed his army boots. He squirmed around until he had a good view of the *African Lady*'s comings-and-goings, and though he couldn't see into her cabin, he didn't have to guess very hard at what was going on. Frequently men arrived, handing money to the crewman before going below, and then leaving a few minutes later. To a man, they checked their zippers on their way ashore.

He assumed the second crewman was belowdecks and tried to ascertain the existence or not of a lookout on the bridge, but the black tinted windows made it impossible. Then the crewmen changed places, with Cooper's man going belowdecks and the second crewman coming topside carrying two beers. He started up the laddered steps to the bridge and found it difficult moving on the rolling boat. Close to the top, he barked out a name, and a man reached down to save the beers. A minute later, the crewman and lookout were sharing a joint on the landing and moved inside when they found it too difficult to keep it lit in the stiff wind.

When a john approached on the gangplank, the crewman climbed back down to the deck and stayed there collecting the money as more johns came along to do their business, leaving some fraction of an hour later. Periodically the crewman would throw his empty bottle over the rail and go belowdecks to fetch more beers, each time delivering a fresh one to the lookout on the bridge, each time passing a joint between them. It grew from late to very late, and eventually the johns petered out until they stopped coming altogether.

Cooper, sprawled on the nets, waited for his chance to strike, and when the crewman emerged another time carrying the usual two beers, he eased the grimy cloth off his legs ready to dash aboard. The crewman shouted for help; the lookout predictably came out and crouched down to reach for the bottles. Cooper slipped his knife from his boot and rose on his elbow, ready to leap as soon as both their backs were turned, when a car shot out of a side street, its headlights spotlighting the crewman midway up the ladder. Cooper pretended to pass out again as he nudged the cloth back over his boots.

The car bounced to a stop next to the yacht and cut off its lights, and two men got out.

One was rail thin, the other obese.

Cooper recognized them instantly.

Little Ears and the chief of police.

"Fuck," the crewman on the ladder mumbled as he started back down. The lookout followed him down, and the men shook hands all around. The police chief looked fuller than the moon in his starched whites, and by the way the others deferred to him, he was clearly the head honcho. It was his slaving operation. The crewman handed the cops the two beers he'd been carrying and went belowdecks, returning a short minute later with Cooper's man and more beers. Little Ears shook his bottle hard, and holding it at his crotch, spewed foam on the deck. The men laughed appreciatively, but none as hard as Little Ears himself, who kept heehawing until the police chief finally snapped at him to shut up.

Two crewmen lit cigarettes and strolled off, leaving only Cooper's man behind. Little Ears looked about ready to slip belowdecks when the police chief upbraided him, holding him back to go first himself. He pinched his collar points and brushed off his coat before squeezing his way down the steps, barely managing to wedge himself through the cabin door. Cooper felt sickened imagining him sprawled atop Lulay.

Little Ears tried to keep up a conversation with the remaining crewman, his laughter vacillating from lewd to a jackass's, and apparently the man thought he *was* a jackass because he preferred to spin the chamber in his pistol rather than talk to him. He aimed it at a couple of seagulls perched on a halyard and pulled the trigger.

Plunk!

An empty chamber.

Little Ears heehawed.

The guard spun the cylinder again and pulled the trigger.

Plunk!

Another empty chamber.

Heehaw! Heehaw!

Again a spin.

Plunk!

Heehaw! Heehaw!

Spin.

Plunk!

Heehaw! Heehaw!

Spin.

The crewman suddenly swung the gun on Little Ears and that stopped his annoying laugh.

Shoot him! Cooper urged silently.

Slowly the crewman raised his aim from Little Ears' chest to smack dab between his eyes. Even from his disadvantageous position, Cooper could see Little Ears's fearful expression.

Pull the trigger!

In a flash the crewman swung on the birds.

BANG!

Feathers showered them, and Little Ears swore obscenely at the laughing crewman. The cabin door flung open and the police chief, in a fix because of the gunshot, furiously attempted to button up his pants while squeezing himself up the narrow stairs. There was an audible sound of something tearing, and the crewman and Little Ears instantly shut up. They stared at each other wondering who was in for the worse. The police chief, reaching the deck, examined the damage done to his pants pocket by the handrail. He kicked the dead bird, which landed at Little Ears's feet, who was making squeaky sounds trying to appease his boss. The fat man thunderously ordered him to shut the fuck up, get belowdecks, and get done with his business!

Little Ears didn't hesitate to disappear.

The police chief tucked in his shirt and squared his epaulettes. By the time he replaced his dark glasses, his fury had abated somewhat, though he continued to look at his torn pants with the same concern he would a flesh wound.

The crewman, taking no chances, said, "I'll check on things" and followed the skinny cop below decks.

Now was Cooper's chance.

In one stride he was across the gangplank and on the deck, leaning against the bridge's housing. Knife in hand, he crept toward the police chief, who was standing unsteadily on the rolling deck, one hand grasping the rail while the other grappled below the overhang of his belly, searching for his zipper so he could take a piss. Cooper inched forward. The big man finally managed to pull himself out and started to relieve himself when a gust of wind blew his piss right back onto his starched whites. He lumbered around and surprised himself by ending up peeing on someone's shoes. He looked up and was astonished to see Cooper, who was equally astonished to have the police chief pissing on *him*.

He plunged his knife into the policeman's yielding gut, and with all his strength wrenched it up and out, trailing intestines with it. The police chief pressed his hands to his ruptured stomach as Cooper plucked off his sunglasses. "Is that how it feels to be hungry like a rock?" he asked, and with a single clean sweep, slit the fat man's throat, cutting short a cry before it became more than a gurgle. Spurting blood, he fell onto Cooper, who, for all his strength, staggered under the dead weight as he tried to prevent his body from crashing noisily onto the deck.

Cooper cleaned his knife on the policeman's white lapel before darting down the steps and pressing his ear to the cabin door.

All he could hear was a throbbing disco beat.

He slipped inside.

The music was so loud he could feel it, and the room was dark, lit only by cartoons flickering across a large flat screen. The crewman, bare-chested, sat in front of it. Mistaking Cooper for a john, he muted the sound only long enough to say, "Take the one on the left" and waved him down the hall. With another click of the remote, he reamped the deafening music.

Cooper headed confidently for the hallway until he reached the crewman's blind spot, and in a couple of strides came up behind him and tapped his shoulder.

The startled crewman spun around.

Cooper pointed to his army boots.

The man looked down and instantly recognized them. He glanced back up wide-eyed, giving Cooper an easy target for cutting his throat. The man sagged in his chair and Cooper retrieved the remote, turning the music down enough to give him some cover while still letting him hear danger.

In another couple of steps he was at the start of the narrow hallway, paneled in light-brown veneer and lined with cupboards fastened with brass latches. A couple of dim lamps gently rocked in cradled sockets, and for a moment, Cooper was back in the double-wide with the same cheap wood paneling and brass latches; even the yacht's creaking in the water sounded like their trailer buffeted by the wind. The cupboards loomed at him; he could almost imagine their doors flapping open and closed like big gaping mouths wanting to swallow him. He experienced the same slackening fear that he had felt as a child each time his father imprisoned him, calling it a game; torturing him with his games until he'd been old enough to flee.

He wanted to flee now, away from that narrow hallway and out of that waterborne trap; but then he heard a girl crying, barely a whisper of sound under the music. Measuring his steps to roll with the boat, he approached the two doors at the end of the hall.

The left door was open, and he heard whimpering sounds coming from it. Cautiously peeking into it, he saw Lulay on the bed frantically biting her wrist. The instant the girl saw him, she yelped and pulled in her arms and legs to make herself into as tiny a ball as she could. One arm wouldn't cooperate no matter how hard she jerked it, and Cooper saw that she was tied to the bed; she'd been plucking at the knots with her teeth.

He crouched beside her, whispering, "Lulay, it's okay, it's Cooper … it's me, Cooper …" but she still kept her face hidden after he cut the nylon cord and her arm sprang free. "It's Cooper, Lulay, it's really me, this is only charcoal …" He tried to wipe enough charcoal off his face for her to glimpse his white skin, and when she did look up and saw that it *was* Cooper, both her arms shot out and clung to him.

"You stay here," he told her, and held her back when she tried to spring up. He kissed his fingers and pressed them to her forehead, and mouthed *You're going to be okay* before scuttling to the second cabin's door.

The music had cut itself off, making it easy for him to hear the recognizable sounds of forced lovemaking, sounds Coops couldn't've drowned out if he had counted to eternity inside his father's cupboards. They'd insinuated themselves into the pauses between his numbers. Trying to count faster never helped; it only made him have to pause longer for breath, and the insinuating sounds were always there waiting for him, waiting to ambush him. When Coops had pressed his ear to his father's bedroom door that fateful afternoon, he'd heard Becky whimper like the girl Cooper was hearing whimper now. He turned the doorknob.

Locked.

With a single kick he broke through the flimsy door half-expecting to see his father's white buttocks poised over his stepsister. But the buttocks he saw were black not white, and so were the girl's little hands trying to push Little Ears off her. The skinny cop glanced around at the sound of the splintering door but couldn't disengage himself before Cooper was across the room with a roar, tossing aside his knife to hold down Little

Ears's head with one hand while grabbing his balls from behind with his other. He squeezed them hard, harder, as hard as he could while Little Ears bucked and screamed just like his dad had bucked and screamed when he'd caught him on top of Becky. Neither man was a match for his strength, and Cooper squeezed them both until one testicle popped and then the other, turning into mash in his powerful fist. The cop, as pale as Cooper imagined an African could look, passed out, and he picked him up off the girl and dropped him on the floor.

It was the first chance that Cooper had to see the girl's face. He recognized her terrified eyes. She was Ayana, the girl from the jail. Only she wasn't looking scared at him but at something over his shoulder.

Cooper glanced around to see Sam Brown in the doorway holding a gun on him.

17

Quickly assessing the situation, the CIA man lowered his pistol. "I caught this one running out," he said, and pulled Lulay into sight by the cord still dangling from her wrist.

"I told her to stay put," Cooper said.

No one had told Ayana to stay put, and the instant she saw Lulay she jumped up and walked right across Little Ears's unconscious body to get to her. The two girls clasped each other hard. They were both naked except for a scruffy little blouse that rode up Ayana's ribs. Apparently Little Ears hadn't felt the need to get entirely undressed either because he was still wearing his holey socks. Sam Brown kicked apart the policeman's legs to see evidence of what he likely suspected to be damage inflicted by Cooper, and there it was—the bruised, swollen flesh. "You ever think of working on a pig farm?" he asked. "I hear they need people with your skills."

"How the fuck is it that you show up every place I am?" Cooper wanted to know.

Suddenly the yacht tipped sharply, and there was a loud splash before it righted itself again. *The police chief's body going overboard*, Cooper guessed, and asked, "Who's up there?"

"Patriots." Indicating the unconscious cop, Sam Brown added, "Let's go before his friends come back."

Lulay grabbed Cooper's arm. "You take us with you!"

"Of course I take you with me. Go get your clothes. Hurry!"

Lulay dashed off and Ayana jumped back atop Little Ears to pluck her skirt from the bed. Digging in her heels harder than she needed to, she slipped it on while the cop mumbled incoherently and drooled betel nut slobber. Lulay ran back, tripping over her dress as she scrambled to put it on. She was ready to dart out ahead of them all when Sam Brown again snared her by the nylon cord.

"You better let me go out first," he cautioned her, and led them down the paneled hallway.

Cooper, retrieving his knife, followed the girls, who were fussing with buttons and zippers. Both wore flip-flops and looked innocent enough to be going to a sock-hop instead of escaping slavery. But the dead crewman, splayed in his chair with cartoons flickering across his bare chest, was an instant reminder of their sinister circumstances.

"I told you Juma was going to sell me," Lulay complained. "I told you they want to make Lulay disappear!"

"I promised I would find you, didn't I?" Cooper defended himself, knowing that he'd promised that she wouldn't be sold in the first place, so it broke his heart to hear her add, "You wait too long, Cooper. Too many men hurt me."

"Now that'll stop," he barely managed to choke out, unwilling to contemplate how many men *had* hurt her. His plan had been to rescue Lulay. He hoped that he had saved her at the same time. But what were the odds of Lulay or Cooper being saved? Or all three of them? Because now there was Ayana, who was indeed prettier than the prettiest flower. What resources they had amounted to nothing. But the girls had him, and he had a room where they could be safe, and he'd figure out what to do with them once he got them there. That was as far as the next installment went in his Lulay Plan.

Sam Brown cautiously stepped onto the heaving deck checking for any trouble. The others followed him topside all struggling to keep their balance. The moon had disappeared behind swollen clouds blacker than the night itself; only patches of lightening illuminated the choppy bay.

Cooper looked around for the so-called patriots and saw a white jeep parked a short distance down the wharf. At Sam Brown's signal, the driver flashed his lights once and started his engine.

Lulay held out her arm. "Cut me free, Cooper."

Someone had wrapped the nylon cord around her frail wrist three times, knotting it until it had become a thick gnarled braid. Cooper knelt in front of her, cautiously trying to insert the point of his knife under it, but the tipsy sea thwarted him every time.

"Be careful!" Lulay cautioned.

"I am being careful," he replied. "Why didn't they tie up Ayana?"

"Because only I try to run away."

"Not surprised," Cooper said. "Good for you." He finally managed to snip the thick cord and her knotty shackles fell to the deck. They both stared at them. No matter that they were nylon, they both saw the slave shackles for what they were, and Cooper hurled them down the wharf as far as he could. The wind took them after that.

Ayana hadn't moved more than an arm's length from Lulay's side. She clearly had no intention of letting Lulay try to run off again, certainly not without her.

"Do you know this girl?" Cooper asked.

"She is Ayana," Lulay informed him.

"Did you know her before coming to this boat?"

"No, but she is my Little Sister now."

The jeep pulled up. On its side Cooper could make out GlobOil's logo. The pockmarked and dandified oilman was behind the steering wheel. His stubby cigar glowed in the dark. Two Thick Necks got out to stand at the end of the gangplank. They both carried high-powered rifles and looked so menacing that Ayana immediately burst into tears.

"What's going on?" Cooper demanded of Sam Brown.

The CIA man ignored his question, saying instead, "The girls are coming with me."

196

"No!" Lulay cried out. "Don't let him take us!"

Cooper might not have had any real plan for the girls but he wasn't ready to relinquish them, especially not knowing why the CIA man had shown up at all. They hadn't planned a joint rescue. Sam Brown had made an "educated guess" as he put it where Cooper might find Lulay, and now he'd shown up with a couple of Thick Necks to kidnap her.

"What the fuck for?" Cooper asked.

"They're my insurance."

"You already have my promise."

"That's the problem with deserters—you learn not to trust them."

Lulay grabbed Ayana's hand and tried to make a run for it, but one Thick Neck caught a girl in each hand while the second managed to snap handcuffs on Ayana. Wiggling with all her strength, Lulay broke free and bolted down the wharf. The pockmarked oilman turned on the jeep's headlights to spotlight her, and then a second jeep and a third turned on theirs. The girl looked every which way frantic for an escape. She was trapped. The only way open to her was the sea.

She ran to the edge of the wharf and peered into the rough, black water, looking back and forth as if measuring her odds against it versus the men stalking her. She must have decided her odds were better with the sea, and she took a step closer, ready to leap.

"*No! Lulay, no!*" Cooper hollered.

She spread her scrawny arms and leaned into the wind. It was the only thing keeping her from toppling over.

"*No, Lulay, stop! You're going to be okay! That's a Cooper promise!*"

"*You're too late!*"

"*I'm not too late!*"

"*The men already hurt me!*"

There was a wind pocket, and Lulay fell through it, falling into the treacherous water.

Cooper pushed past the Thick Necks and ran to the spot where the girl had fallen in. There was no trace of her. Diving in, he blindly felt for her, touching debris and globs of seaweed, but no Lulay. He came up for a gulp of air and immediately dived back under, paddling deeper, circling as he went, throwing out his arms and legs in every direction trying to make contact with her body.

Suddenly he was caught by a renegade current. He didn't fight it, saving his strength for when he hoped it would slam him into the seawall, and it did. He pressed his feet against it to propel himself to the surface, and instead pushed straight into Lulay's limp body. He lost his momentum and the current caught him again, and he grabbed on to the girl as it sucked them both back against the wall. Again he braced his feet against it and pushed off with all the strength he had left, dragging her to the surface.

The choppy waves broke over them, filling Cooper's mouth. Choking, he struggled to keep the girl's head above the water, but Lulay clung so hard to his neck that she threatened to sink them both. The harder it became for him, the more desperately she clung to him, and he was sure they would both drown when she was plucked from his arms. Cooper looked up to see a Thick Neck lifting her up, and a moment later a second pair of strong hands hoisted him onto the wharf and stood him on his feet next to her.

They were still puking up vile water when a jeep pulled up carrying Sam Brown. In the back, handcuffed to the roll bar sat Ayana, so stunned her mouth was open in a long silent scream.

"Get the girl in the vehicle, Sergeant," Sam Brown ordered.

"No, Cooper ..." Lulay barely had the strength to whimper.

Cooper knew he didn't have a choice. "Come on, you gotta go," he said, and helped Lulay into the back. "If anyone touches her," he directed to the oilman, "he's the next man I'm coming for." The man snorted contemptuously and sucked on his cigar. Cooper wanted to take him on right then, but he wanted to get the girls to safety even more.

In a flash a Thick Neck handcuffed Lulay to the roll bar as well, and she wailed, "*Cooper!*"

"That's not necessary!" he protested.

"I can't keep her safe if she runs off," Sam Brown answered.

"*Cooper!*"

"You're going to be okay." Kissing his fingers, he pressed them to her forehead. "I have his promise," he added, indicating Sam Brown.

"Men promise lies!"

"He won't. Not this time. I won't let him."

"Get rid of that shirt, Sergeant, you look like shark bait," Sam Brown told him, "and move your ass out of here *now*. That's an order. You still have a mission to accomplish before you get this girl back."

He signaled the oilman to drive off and the other two jeeps fell in line. Traveling without lights, they were a stealthy convoy sneaking off with stolen goods. Hostages! Cooper pulled off Sadiq's shirt, and balling it up, threw it at the receding taillights. "*Fuck!*" he shouted, angry at the situation, angry at being blackmailed by Sam Brown, angry at allowing himself to be set up. Angry that he'd freed Lulay from slavery only to have her kidnapped by the CIA.

Cooper knew he needed to get away from the incriminating yacht and started walking along the wharf. Lightening cracked ominously overhead as the first heavy drops of rain landed on his shoulders. The wind seemed to cease with a deep intake of breath, and then, with an audible sigh, it let loose a drenching downpour. Cooper raised his arms, watching as blood and charcoal ran off his elbows. His chest too was a delta of blood-red tributaries flowing to his belly. A shower couldn't have been more cleansing, and Cooper suddenly felt more ecstatic than ever before. He wanted to celebrate! He had rescued Lulay! He hadn't failed her! He ran a few steps, twirling and jumping and landing face-to-face with the crewmen on their way back to the yacht, still smoking and wearing their cool sunglasses. They were laughing until they saw Cooper and gave him wide berth as he continued his madman antics, frolicking and jumping about while putting distance between them.

He ducked into a side street as they boarded the *African Lady*. Though safely away, he started to run anyway, feeling the need to move, to feel his heart pounding and his lungs working and the blood coursing through his veins. Everyone else had sought shelter from the downpour, leaving the muddy streets to him, and Cooper bounded down them leaping over potholes and skirting bums too drunk to get out of the rain. The clouds moved out as fast as they'd come in and silver moonlight soon washed over the streets, sparkling on everything wet. The storm had knocked out the power and the night seemed brighter without it.

People drifted sleepily back onto the streets, and by the time he reached his neighborhood Cooper was forced to stop running. He wound his way through the families curled up in restless clusters, recognizing some of the regular nighttime denizens. A couple of times he heard "American" murmured, but the children who frequently dogged his heels begging for a pen or bubblegum were too drowsy to dog him with more that night than a silently cupped hand. It seemed an ordinary end to an extraordinary day, and it was with relief and exhaustion that Cooper slipped into the small yard behind his building.

He didn't need the mango tree glistening in the moonlight to remind him that he was hungry; his stomach hurt so much that he worried that it might be snacking on itself. He expected there'd be several mangos felled by the storm and searched the ground for their blackish lumps. There wasn't a single one! True, there were only so many mangos on the tree and he'd eaten plenty of them, but for not *one* to have fallen? It was impossible. Someone had run off with them already. Trying not to think about how many hours it had been since he'd last eaten, Cooper was ready to abandon his foraging when …

Plonk!

A mango hit the ground next to him, falling close enough that, any closer, it would've raised a lump on his head. Cooper pressed it with his fingers to test its ripeness. It was perfect. He could smell its perfumed flesh before slicing into it and devouring it. The juice ran through his fingers, and he greedily licked them, not wanting to miss a drop.

As he started up the steps, he saw someone hiding beneath them. He gripped his knife, ready to confront the culprit when he heard, "Is that you, Coopah?"

Cooper's heart leapt. "Sadiq?"

The youth stepped out where he could be seen. Caught by the moonlight, his robes fell like spilled cream from his shoulders. Cooper had never experienced passion that made him so instantly giddy. Every part of him tingled, every worry disappeared. Merely seeing Sadiq in his yard made that long, endless day, which had started with their lovemaking, worth its treacherous journey if it ended with their being together again.

"Did I frighten you?" Sadiq asked.

"Almost everything frightens me," Cooper answered truthfully.

"You're still braver than I am."

"How's that?" Cooper glimpsed the boy's anguished expression and took hold of his arm. "What's wrong?"

Sadiq jerked his arm free. "I can't tell you."

"Tell me," Cooper insisted.

"I can't!"

"Do you want to come upstairs?"

"No."

"Tell me," Cooper coaxed him. "How can I help you if I don't know what's wrong?"

"It's everything!" Sadiq said, his body sagging under the weight of his distress. "Coming back to Langatown … meeting you.… You can't imagine what my life is going to be here! Beirut was supposed to cure me, not make me worse. It was supposed to make me want a wife, not make me want you! That's why—" He stopped himself before he said too much.

"That's why what?" Cooper demanded.

"But I can't be cured!"

"That's why *what?*"

"That's why I decided."

"You decided *what?*"

"That I didn't want to live!" Sadiq blurted out.

"What do you mean, you didn't want to live?" Cooper tried to touch him but Sadiq slapped his hand away.

"He made me feel dirty and that's why I did it! I've sworn by Allah!"

"Then 'unswear' by Him!" Cooper cried.

"I can't!" Sadiq moaned. "I can't unswear by Him or I'm doomed. I'm already a dead man, that's what I'm trying to tell you!" He pushed past Cooper and fled the yard.

Cooper started to chase after him and stopped, watching his pale robe disappear in the dark. What Sadiq was struggling with he had to struggle with alone.

What had he sworn?

Walking back into the yard awash with the silver moonlight, he noticed something blackish under the steps. It was a pile of mangos. Sadiq had collected them for him. Cooper gathered them in his arms and carried them up the steps wondering what the new day would bring.

18

Celebration! The word seemed incongruous with distraught Lalanga, and yet the festivities had been going on since dawn, the crowds occasionally waking Cooper with their rousing cheers. He'd stumble out to the landing and lean out far enough to glimpse the road where most of the welcoming American flags had been torn into long red-white-and-blue streamers that virtually everyone carried, creating an hallucinatory swirl of patriotic color. Not quite ready for so much celebration, Cooper kept going back to bed, sleeping fitfully as the street noise invaded his dreams: joyful cries turning into barked orders, the cheering crowd sounding like an angry mob, firecrackers an ambush of enemy fire that jolted him upright in bed, sweating as if he'd never left those shifting deserts. By the next round of firecrackers, Cooper had sorted out that he wasn't back in Iraq, and it was equally clear that he wasn't going back to sleep that morning.

He showered but passed on his usual exercises. His body ached from the prior day's overexertion while his somersaulting stomach reminded him he was famished. He rifled cupboards and the refrigerator to discover that everything had sprouted enough mold to look extraterrestrial. Before going to bed he'd eaten three of the mangos rescued by Sadiq, the effects of which he was used to, but nevertheless he couldn't bring himself to eat a fourth: it seemed pointless to try to fill up on something that made him crap every ten minutes. He needed something more nourishing, more stick-to-the-ribs, and he briefly let himself fantasize eating a breakfast of eggs over easy and crispy bacon. It was dangerous, a stomach cramp reminded him, to fantasize about food.

He pulled on his cutoffs, and that's when he remembered Sadiq's advance that he had never spent, neither on diamonds nor Lulay. Taking out the wads of wet, pinkish bills, he saw that there was no point trying to dry them, so he stuffed them back into his pockets and looked for his shirt before remembering he didn't have one, having balled up Sadiq's and thrown it after Sam Brown's disappearing ass the night before. Again his stomach demanded attention, and Cooper left the room on a mission to find food.

His street was thick with people, and when he turned onto the main road, he began to wonder if the country's entire population had descended on Langatown to celebrate the secretary of state's visit. Anyone who owned a red, white, or blue garment was wearing it, and frequently he was greeted jubilantly with cries of *"American! American!"*

The usual number of food stands had doubled overnight, some featuring American-style hot dogs, and Cooper bought four and devoured them on the spot. Picking gristle from his teeth a minute later, he considered the real possibility that they *had* been made from dogs. T-shirt vendors had sprung up too, offering a range of honorific designs, including the secretary shaking Colonel Diamond's hand over the caption *Got Oil?*, which was the first shirt shoved in Cooper's face. He bought it and slipped it on.

The previous night's torrential rains had left a sweltering day in their wake, and Cooper, desperate for a cold beer, found himself almost walking into The Mining Pan before remembering his welcome had been revoked at the end of Juma's gun. Cowboy Mile had plenty of other drinking holes, and he ducked into one where he thought none of the girls would know him. He didn't want to be fending off questions about Little Sister; he had enough questions of his own, like, *Where the hell is Sam Brown holding Lulay?*

His thoughts suddenly turned so black that he must have scowled fiercely because at least two comers-on gave him wide berth as he elbowed his way to the bar to order his first beer, which he downed in less time than it took to order two backups. He tried to ignore the basic business going on around him, the same basic business going on in all the bars, the business of all the Lulays and lipsticked boys whom Cooper had once thought were nothing more than poor kids turning tricks for a few coins. Now he knew they'd been bought and sold for those coins. By the time he'd finished his third beer, he was ready to do battle for all of them.

Leaving a mound of soggy bills on the counter, he returned to the streets where he was soon swept along by the festive crowd. Magically, carnival rides had popped up, miniature merry-go-rounds and bucking stallions that made nasally neighing sounds. On almost every corner there was another curious attraction. Flamethrowers eliciting predictable *Ahhh*s of admiration. Shills attracting the gullible to their sleights of hand. *Maribouts* wearing little more than ashes while spinning poetic prophecies. Cooper wanted to stop and watch, but he'd already been slowed down by the crowds and knew he couldn't be late for that night's date.

Ducking onto side streets, he thought to avoid the worst of the crowds by following the docks, but the wharf was mobbed as he approached Parliament Square. He struggled through the crowd, the only white man in a raging African sea. The nearby *rat-a-tat-tats* of firecrackers had him swinging this way and that way, almost tripping over his feet when he'd suddenly hear the rapid fire coming from another direction. He felt caught in the crowd with no escape. He'd never been in such a sea of people before and started pushing his way to an edge of it that he couldn't see, he only knew he had to get there; and like a sea's currents, the people pushed and pulled him until finally tossing him into the ring of soldiers guarding the speaker's platform.

Instinctively, a soldier reacted and cracked Cooper's forehead with his rifle.

Cooper landed on his butt in the narrow security zone that the soldiers had established around the platform. The soldiers, clutching their rifles like battering rams, were scared shitless knowing they'd be helpless against the crowd. Cooper wondered if they even had bullets to defend themselves.

Where are the marines?

Picking himself up, Cooper fingered the knot already forming on his forehead, looking at the soldier who'd knocked him down for some explanation. The man's expression, hidden behind another pair of omnipresent sunglasses, gave away nothing. Except for berets, little differentiated these soldiers from Josef Nimwe's ragtag rebels. And why not? They'd been ragtag rebels themselves until a year ago and were probably carrying the same rifles they'd slogged through the jungles subduing *their* detractors one brutality at a time. Now they were the legitimate elite. The Elongated. They weren't sure how to respond to one of them having flattened a white man, so they didn't respond at all and stayed standing at very tall attention facing the turbulent crowd.

Suddenly brilliant floodlights illuminated the Parliament building. The building's Greek revival columns and peaked portico—obviously some colonialist's idea of a proper structure to house a proper government—prompted a moment of awe before the crowd let out a huge cheer. People whooped and shouted, cheered and cried, and chants rose up and faded until the crowd found a common rhythm, and as one they danced, celebrating the promise embodied by those columns and in that portico and in the secretary's visit. Cooper recognized the revolutionary moment for what the people hoped it was.

With Parliament Square transformed into one enormous dance floor, the crowd seemed friendly, not threatening, and Cooper wormed his way through it by exchanging high-fives and twirling girls and doing a bit of cha-cha-cha-ing. He forgot the panic that had sent him reeling only minutes earlier and was laughing at the end of his dance spree when he wheeled around the back corner of the Parliament building to find himself on an inexplicably deserted street.

Then he saw why. White jeeps blocked both ends of the road; in the deepening twilight, Cooper could just make out their oil-drenched logos. From off to one side he heard, "You're late, Sergeant Chance."

Sam Brown stepped out of the shadows.

"I hadn't anticipated the crowds," Cooper told him.

"Apparently you had time to stop for a beer. I can smell it on your breath."

"Make that three beers." Cooper was an inch from walking away, not liking the mission or the CIA man, but across that inch he could feel Lulay's fingers pulling hard on him.

"You're lucky the secretary is late too."

"I'm glad we could coordinate our schedules."

"You listen to me, Sergeant, and you listen good. I couldn't give a fuck if your ass rots in this country or in a stinking jail for the rest of your life. But a lot of people are counting on you tonight. Your country is counting you."

"I'll try not to disappoint Uncle Sam."

"You get one shot."

Sam Brown turned on his heel, obviously expecting Cooper to follow.

Cooper had no choice.

Two Thick Necks flanked the building's back entrance, and across the street, in a lone jeep, the moustached oilman sat in darkness. Cooper smelled the cigar before he saw its burning tip.

"What the hell is he doing here?" Cooper demanded.

"Protecting your ass," Sam Brown told him.

He swung Sam Brown around by his arm. "Who the fuck are these guys?" Then it dawned on Cooper. They weren't oilmen, they were mercenaries. All in fighting shape and uniformly well-equipped, he should have recognized them before.

"I told you I was a recruiter," Sam Brown answered.

"You said you worked for the CIA."

"They aren't necessarily exclusive careers."

"Why use South Africans?"

"Do you think we could send Americans in here without CNN reporting it before they landed?"

"So they're keeping the seats warm for the marines, or something like that?"

"You're asking too many questions, soldier." Sam Brown started to walk off, and when Cooper grabbed his arm to swing him around again, the CIA man belted him, knocking him to the ground. "That's the answer to the rest of your questions," he said. "Now get off your ass."

Rubbing his jaw, Cooper followed Brown into the building. Inside, they had to pause to let their eyes adjust to the dimmer light. "Do you know where you are, Sergeant?"

"This is the service area, there's the mess, and the main stairway is through here."

"You lead the way, Sergeant. Top floor."

Well before Cooper had arrived in the country, Colonel Diamond had abandoned the Parliament building, preferring to govern from the main military garrison where he was closer to his big guns. He had first turned the building over to his elite guards, which proved a mistake when they orchestrated a failed coup against him. Since then every mercenary and rebel force had occupied it, sometimes only long enough to take a dump in it, but in that victory-less country that counted as something.

So much debris covered the stairs that Cooper had to clear a trail as they climbed them. When they reached the top floor, it was Sam Brown's turn to lead, and he guided them down a hall past offices as looted as the democracy the building had once hoped to represent. Doors, fixtures, plugs, switches—all gone—and sledgehammers had dug trails into the walls following the path of pipes in trenches that might have been made by super earthworms. Without a window intact, the monsoons had regularly swamped the rooms replenishing stagnant pools, and the air was thick with mosquitoes.

"In here," Sam Brown said, and stopped at a gaping doorway to let Cooper enter ahead of him. "Welcome to the presidential suite."

Cooper, walking on an inch of soggy papers, immediately crossed to the middle of three windows. It was eight floors up and dead center opposite the speaker's platform. A perfect shooting position except for the floodlights, which blinded him.

"Try this on for size." Sam Brown tossed him a high-powered rifle leaning against a wall.

Cooper caught it handily and gave it a quick inspection. It was oiled and ammoed and ready for action. He put it to his shoulder and aimed at the speaker's platform, squinting into the spotlights to make out the men attaching a bulletproof screen to the podium. "I didn't think they had this much juice in the whole country," he said.

"They don't," Sam Brown confirmed. "We lent the colonel a couple _

The moment that followed was long enough for both men to wonder if he might actually shoot the CIA man before Cooper lowered his rifle and said, "You should've brought sunglasses."

"I brought these." Sam Brown tossed him a pair of night vision goggles.

Cooper, inspecting them, asked, "Are you and Langley planning a blackout?"

"Even Uncle Sam can't guarantee they won't blow the national fuse."

Cooper slipped on the goggles and glanced out the floodlit window, reeling back and ripping them off. He opened and closed his eyes with a stunned expression. "Fuck, I think I'm blind!"

"I hope not …"

"Me too!"

"Because she's here."

An army truck with heavily armed soldiers in the back led a line of limos to the speaker's platform. A second army truck took up the rear, and behind them all, half a dozen white jeeps tagged along.

Cooper, stumbling around, cried, "My optic nerves are fucking fried! All I'm seeing is green!"

Sam Brown watched the motorcade's doors start to open. "Blink!" he advised him. "It'll go away."

"I *am* fucking blinking and all I see are green blinks!"

The soldiers remained in the trucks, but from the lead and rear limousines a phalanx of bodyguards jumped out to converge on the middle two cars. Colonel Diamond unfolded himself getting out of his limousine, and his diamond-encrusted coat flashed with a million rainbow prisms before the tallest of the tall bodyguards enveloped him.

Cooper, groping around, found the rifle. "Point me in the right direction so I'll be ready."

"You're shitting me, aren't you?" Sam Brown asked hopefully.

"*Fucking point me!*"

The CIA man pivoted him to face the window, and Cooper put his eye against the rifle's scope, swerving it around in search of his target.

The secretary got out of her limo, a permanent smile plastered across her face, and the crowd started cheering. Colonel Diamond, completely shielded by his guards, stepped over to her, and they shook hands.

"You can see now, right?" Sam Brown asked anxiously.

"I'm trying!" Cooper continued to wave the rifle around, finally settling his aim in the dignitaries' direction. "Is the secretary the one in the blue suit with a run in her right stocking shaking hands with Liberace?" he asked.

"You sonofabitch," Sam Brown said. "You owe me."

Referring to the white jeeps, Cooper asked, "What's with your South African recruits?"

"Extra security," Sam Brown answered. "Colonel Diamond wasn't quite up to the state department's requirements."

"Why not call in the marines?"

"They're in the jeeps."

As the dignitaries ascended the platform, the firecrackers went on a holiday exploding all around—cherry bombs, Roman candles, belts of firecrackers sounding enough like automatic weapons to make Cooper duck a couple of times. Bodyguards flanked both sides of the secretary and colonel and marched them to two rows of chairs. The dignitaries slipped into the back row while the tallest bodyguards sat in the front, and the remaining bodyguards formed a protective shield by standing behind everyone. Cooper only caught glimpses of the colonel's diamond-studded coat.

"The secretary will be introduced by their minister of foreign affairs," Sam Brown informed him. "She'll make her remarks, ten minutes max, and then Colonel Diamond will join her. That might be your best shot, when he's moving to the podium."

"I'll know my best shot," Cooper let him know.

The foreign affairs minister launched into his lengthy introduction, lauding the renewed ties with America and the promise of American aid with no strings attached despite Colonel Diamond's commitment to nationalizing the oil industry "for the people." He spoke of a new morning in the country where oil suddenly made their dreams possible. He might have been running for office if Lalanga had elections, but she didn't, she only had rebellions and coups, and the people weren't buying any of it. They'd heard the rhetoric before and were still bereft, broken of any dreams except for the phantom dream of America; and there, personified in a beautiful woman, America had come to them. She was the Statue of Liberty herself! So at the foreign affairs minister's frequent mention of "America" or "Madame Secretary," the crowd cheered deliriously.

"So," the foreign affairs minister finally concluded, "let us welcome my counterpart from our good and generous friend, the United States of

America!"

As the secretary made her way to the podium encircled by bodyguards, the foreign affairs minister left the protection of the bulletproof shield. Instantly, other bodyguards tried to shield him, but he brushed them aside and moved to the edge of the stage, whipping up the crowd's enthusiasm, which was already boisterous enough to be intimidating. There was a loud bang and everyone froze, expecting someone to keel over. It turned out to be nothing more than a fireworks rocketing skyward, and instantly the crowd cheered again and the foreign affairs minister, wiping his brow, took his seat.

The secretary of state stood at the podium. Custom-built for the Elongated Colonel Diamond, she could barely see over it. She took a deep breath, composed her smile, and stuck her short arms out like a pitiable dodo bird flapping its useless wings, ostensibly to greet the crowd, but the gesture could as easily have been construed as a futile effort to fly away. From what Cooper could make of her face, the secretary definitely wanted to be outta there. When she dropped her stubby wings, the crowd immediately quieted, and then she raised them part-way and the people cheered part-way. Playing with the crowd, she raised and lowered her arms and the people adjusted their volume up and down, and soon the whole world seemed to be laughing. Certainly all of Langatown was, and that, Cooper realized, was undoubtedly an unparalleled achievement.

"Thank you," the secretary effused, "thank you, thank you, and thank you, Colonel Diamond, for your invitation to come to your beautiful country," which she unfortunately wouldn't see, explaining she had a busy global schedule. She'd seen their intriguing capital, and that was enough for her "to know how much—and how little—Americans and Lalalanders have in common, and I've seen a lot!" Except for misspeaking Lalalanders for Lalangoans, she proceeded to give a fine speech, promising US aid, foreign investment, and the political reforms that would bring Lalanga back into the community of nations. To Cooper, it was clear that oil lubricated her words; he had heard the same promises in oily Iraq.

"So tonight, what I promise you is America's partnership in developing your tomorrow," the secretary of state concluded, "and with your oil resources, it should be a very bright tomorrow. But let me reassure you, it is only because of your commitment to democracy that I am here today. I can report to you tonight that, in my meeting with Colonel Diamond, he has promised elections as soon as the people are ready." She paused, scanning the crowd awed into silence to hear such a great woman speak, making each person feel like she was speaking to him or her alone. "Are you ready?" she asked.

The crowd erupted. If ten years of the New Year's Eve celebrations in Times Square could be packed into one, Cooper estimated it would be about half of what he was witnessing. The fireworks grew from a battle to a firestorm. The secretary, beaming, turned to the colonel and cried, "I think they're ready!"

The foreign affairs minister caught the contagious enthusiasm and jumped up, applauding rhythmically, and the secretary joined him, clapping roundly with her little flapper arms. Soon the whole enormous crowd was clapping in unison so thunderously that Cooper felt the building vibrate; all, that is, except Colonel Diamond, who applauded tepidly behind his wall of bodyguards. That wouldn't do, or so the excitable foreign affairs minister apparently thought, and in a daring act he grabbed Colonel Diamond's hand and dragged him to the podium, where he took hold of the secretary's hand and lifted their hands over their heads as if they'd won some sporting event.

"Now!" Sam Brown said, seeing an opening that evaporated as a flank of bodyguards rushed to shield Colonel Diamond.

The foreign affairs minister, giddy from the crowd's cheers, dragged his hostages from behind the podium. The secretary looked horror-stricken as the bodyguards, ignoring her, scrambled instead to keep Colonel Diamond surrounded.

"You've got the shot! Now!" Sam Brown shouted.

But Cooper knew he didn't have the shot. Not the perfect shot. Not quite yet.

The foreign affairs minister, himself a tall, powerful man, held up the secretary and colonel as if proudly displaying prized hams, and strode so close to the front of the stage that the bodyguards had to jump out of the way or be pushed off into the crowd.

Sam Brown put a gun to Cooper's head. "Shoot him now, Sergeant Chance, or you won't have another one."

How long does it take to pass judgment—fair judgment, Cooper prayed—when the penalty is death? Up until that moment he'd functioned as a soldier with an order to carry out as the price for rescuing Lulay. But in fact he wasn't a soldier, and Sam Brown couldn't order him, and Lulay was somewhere temporarily out of harm's way. He knew he had to decide personally whether Colonel Diamond deserved to die.

He remembered Janjay and how she'd been butchered. He remembered the mutilated children—the silent witnesses—he'd seen behind the chain link fence. He thought of Lulay and how that man in his crosshairs had created the conditions of her desperate life. How he had made it all possible so he could wear his diamond-encrusted jacket and look like a pimp's pimp. In that nanosecond, when all these thoughts flashed through his brain, Colonel Diamond offered Cooper the perfect head shot, and he took it.

BANG!

Probably no one heard the shot above the general din, but its results could not have been more visible. The top of Colonel Diamond's skull exploded, splattering the foreign affairs minister and secretary, and he crumpled onto the stage. In the length of the gasp that it took to realize that something momentous had happened, there was another shot, and the secretary went down.

There was a second assassin!

The foreign affairs minister, his hands still aloft, looked bewildered at the two bodies now at his feet.

The people's outrage was instantaneous. The pandemonium universal. With a fierce roar, they rushed the speaker's platform, easily stampeding the soldiers guarding it. In seconds, they had dislodged the structure from its flimsy footings, and as dignitaries were still jumping off, toppled it into the bay.

The floodlights popped and sizzled and everything went dark.

"Holy fucking Jesus," the CIA man muttered.

There were gunshots in the far corner of the square, and Cooper sensed more than saw the wave of panic ripple through the crowd. Grabbing the night vision goggles, he slipped them on and was suddenly plunged into a surreal world of green ghostly figures. The square before him pulsated as a single scrambling living beast except for one corner, where people were fleeing in an ever-widening circle from two figures in its center. One of them turned slowly with his arms outstretched, holding a gun.

It was the second assassin!

Then the two figures began to run. The one with the gun had a pronounced limp. Cooper's heart sank. It had to be Munir, and the other figure with him was certain to be Sadiq.

Ripping off the goggles, he knocked Sam Brown down with the rifle and then flung it at him, fleeing down the hall. He descended the steps two at a time, bursting onto the street. The white jeeps at the corners had disappeared, and the street was mobbed with panicked people. The moustached oilman—or not an oilman but a mercenary, Cooper now knew—sat stoically in his jeep across from the back entrance, looking puzzled when Cooper bolted out alone and ran down the street.

As he rounded the building's corner, Cooper heard the rat-a-tat of small-arms fire, and before disappearing down a side street saw a pitched battle unfold between the GlobOil mercenaries and Colonel Diamond's soldiers. He fought his way through the narrow lanes with elbows punching him as hard as fists, but by the time he reached the waterfront, it was all but deserted by the fleeing mobs who'd ducked for cover anywhere they could. Nobody wanted to be caught in the crossfire of the battle Cooper could still hear behind him.

He sprinted past the *African Lady*'s now empty berth and over the stretch of paving stones slippery with fish scales, slowing down only when he could see the pastel colors of the arcade awash in moonlight. There were no lights. The power had blown everywhere. As he approached al-Basma Diamonds, he saw candlelight flickering through the shop's cracked open door.

The two youths were inside the cage in front of the safe. "Don't take everything!" Sadiq cried, and Munir, stuffing diamonds into his pockets, shoved him aside so forcefully that he almost lost his own crippled balance. When Sadiq lunged back, Munir pistol-whipped him, and Sadiq yelped in pain.

Cooper stepped into the shop. "Don't hurt him," he said.

"Coopah! Watch out! He has a gun!"

Munir swung around. "Your American is here," he sneered.

"What's happening, Sadiq?"

"Go away, Coopah!"

"Why did you do it?"

"Is she dead?" Munir asked.

Cooper figured she had to be, either from a gunshot or drowning, and replied, "Yes."

"Humdililah."

"Why did you shoot her?"

"For Allah!"

"I doubt Allah has it in for an innocent woman."

"What does your God think about all the innocent women and children you have killed?" Munir wanted to know. "What does He think about the Americans who killed my brother at his wedding?"

"I don't know what he thinks about them, but that wasn't me," Cooper assured him. "I've never flown an airplane. Why did you help him, Sadiq?"

"I wanted him to love me!"

"Silence!" Munir ordered.

"I swore jihad to Allah because I wanted us to die together," Sadiq said pleadingly to Munir.

"Silence!" Munir commanded again, and Sadiq fell to his knees with a sharp cry, weeping in his distress.

Cooper rushed toward the cage's door, but Munir waved him back with his gun.

"You know it's true, Munir!" Sadiq cried.

"You can have your filthy love with your American queer."

"Get out of the cage, Sadiq," Cooper urged, retreating to the center of the small shop, away from the cage's door, hoping to draw Munir's attention away from Sadiq.

"It's not filth!" Sadiq protested.

"Allah wants your filth destroyed!"

"Are you trying to pretend, Munir, that you don't like getting your cock sucked by boys?" Cooper asked. "Because I know you do. Or do you only like to get fucked by them?"

It took Munir a moment to understand what Cooper had said, and then he couldn't believe it had been said at all. His face contorted in a mask of hate and he roared, "*You are filth!*"

Stunned, Sadiq asked, "Is it true, Munir?"

"He goes with boys in the bars," Cooper continued. "He likes the lipsticked ones. Or did he tell you he was buying condoms for women?"

"*Silence!*"

Munir swung his gun on Cooper and pulled the trigger.

BANG!

The cage deflected the bullet in a burst of sparks.

"Get out of there, Sadiq! Two nights ago," Cooper continued to taunt Munir, "your lipsticked boyfriend was wearing a nice shade of pink, remember? You got some on your cheek—"

BANG!

Another burst of sparks.

"—that nicely matched that ugly fucking scar on your face. People mistook it for one big lipstick smear from one big wet kiss. Get out of there, Sadiq!"

BANG! Sparks!

"Run, Sadiq!"

Sadiq, still on his knees, was too distraught to run.

BANG! Sparks!

Munir started for the cage door to get a clear shot of Cooper. When Sadiq realized what was happening, he lunged at his friend crying, "*Nooooo!*"

They struggled, and the gun went off, and Sadiq sagged to the floor.

Cooper ran to the cage door, but Munir blocked him, holding out the gun and forcing him to step back. "You will not be the first American soldier I kill," he said, a satisfied smile crossing his wretched face as he savored the moment.

BANG!

He had savored it too long.

Blood trickled from a clean black hole that appeared in his forehead a moment before he toppled over.

Cooper whirled around.

For the second time in twenty-four hours Sam Brown stood in a doorway holding a gun on him.

Cooper ran into the cage and knelt beside his fallen friend. "No, Sadiq, no … no …" He pulled him onto his lap, clutching him, his tears falling on the café latte boy's face, wishing him to be alive and beautiful again.

"No, Sadiq, no …"

He pressed his cheek against Sadiq's and wept.

19

Cooper heard the handfuls of heavy earth thud on the coffin.

Then it was over, and Mazen brushed the soil from his hands as his wife clung to his arm, clearly needing his support. Relatives and friends came to their rescue, perched over a grave they'd sooner wish were theirs. Sadiq's grief-stricken mother appeared close to throwing herself into the hole after him, preferring to be buried alive than endure a life without her son. Mazen wrapped an arm around her and shuffled her off, and the rest of the funeral party followed. Filling in the grave would take place later, out of sight of the mourners.

Unsure of his welcome, Cooper had hung back during the brief ceremony, and only when the last stragglers had left did he walk over to peer into the grave. The earth was so soft from the daily torrential rains that already its muddy sides were crumbling onto the coffin. He didn't want to imagine Sadiq in that long box. He almost couldn't. He'd seen too many comrades sent home in long boxes. Guts spilled out, systems shut down, the animal self-extinguished—that was death as Cooper knew it, the stinking death of the battlefield, not the civilized death of cemeteries.

He tossed a handful of dirt on the coffin. Its dull thud was hardly the exclamation point Sadiq deserved. But he hadn't deserved death either. He had unsworn to Allah. He had not shot the secretary of state. He had decided to live. Cooper was sure of it all. They had opened each other's eyes to the possibility of something other than Munir's filthy love or Rick's self-hatred. They had glimpsed the possibility of a love they had hardly dared imagine, and then the boy had been robbed of it. That was the biggest tragedy of his death.

Mazen approached him, and Cooper could see that in only a few hours the lines on his face had deepened. Had it only been hours ago that Mazen had been summoned to the diamond shop to discover the unbearable scene? His beloved son dead? Sam Brown had taken charge of everything, assisted by a couple of Thick Necks who took Sadiq's body home and then disappeared with Munir's. About the time that the crocodiles finished chewing the last fat off the chief of police, Cooper liked to imagine Munir's scrawny body floating into the mangrove swamps, but more likely it would be the missing secretary of state who was served up next.

Cooper hadn't expected Mazen's embrace. He'd expected questions, recriminations, grief, but not an embrace. Kissing him on both cheeks, the older man said, "You tried to save my son's life."

"I wish I could have."

"They say the other one was a terrorist."

"He shot the American secretary of state. I guess that makes him one."

"Did Sadiq ever say anything to you?"

"I hardly knew him," Cooper replied honestly, "but he wouldn't have been involved in something like that. I would've sensed something."

"I don't know why Sadiq had to bring that one home," Mazen said.

"He followed him home. Sadiq didn't bring him."

"Yes, I suppose he did. There were always rumors," Mazen continued thoughtfully, "and they started again as soon as Sadiq came back. People gossip about what parents already know about their children. I knew everything about my son. None of the gossip mattered."

Mazen stared longingly at the coffin. He obviously wanted to embrace his son, tell him that none of it mattered, that he loved him unconditionally. Cooper wasn't surprised when Mazen spoke directly to the grave. "There were other ways to manage what you needed to manage, to have what you wanted," he told him. "You didn't have to bring that one home.

"He was always so impressionable," he said to Cooper. "That's why his mother and I didn't want him to go to Beirut. We knew the dangers, but we couldn't stop him. He had the right to go. It's our tradition—did he tell you?"

"He said you were a traditional man," Cooper replied. "He respected you for it."

"He said you had become friends."

"We had."

"It's too bad you knew him for such a short time." The older man's voice cracked when he added, "Things would have turned out differently."

Cooper put his hand on Mazen's shoulder. As much as he too wished he had known Sadiq long enough to have changed his fate, there was nothing he could say that would alter what had happened or lessen his father's grief.

He took a last look into that muddy hole—that maw of eternal tears—before returning to the car. From the backseat, Lulay and Ayana, clasping hands, solemnly watched him with their big brown eyes as he slipped into the front. Sam Brown started the engine and drove off. No one said a word, and that was fine by Cooper.

The CIA man kept to the wharf as long as he could. It was easier driving, and the Natives were still restless after a night of looting that left the streets littered with debris and bodies. The battle that had broken out in Parliament Square had turned into a rout as soon as the Thick Necks joined forces with Josef Nimwe's rebels to battle soldiers loyal to Colonel Diamond. The new order had been confirmed by now President Nimwe's soldiers driving drunkenly through the neighborhoods, firing their rifles and intimidating anyone on the streets.

At Parliament Square, Sam Brown braked to maneuver the car past a makeshift checkpoint manned by Thick Necks who waved them through.

"Must be nice having your own private army," Cooper remarked.

"Are you looking for a job?" Sam Brown asked.

"I told you, I'm retired."

When they passed the spot where the speaker's platform had stood, Cooper thought that, if they ever found the podium, they would need to resize it for their new Stubby president, a huge portrait of whom had been draped from the roof of the Parliament building. *That was quick work*, he thought, in the same instant realizing that it hadn't necessarily been quick at all. It had been a coup long in the planning; that would explain how Nimwe's men had American weapons, and Cooper had been an unwitting pawn in it. Only briefly did he fret over his role in the beleaguered country's grinding history. He'd assassinated Colonel Diamond for a reason.

He glanced at the girls in the backseat, solemnly holding hands and anxious about what comes next. It was for them that he had done it, and for every girl in their situation. It was for the hope he heard when their girlish laughter sometimes surfaced.

No one could doubt that the Americans were behind Colonel Diamond's assassination, and oil was behind that. The luckless secretary of state had been unfortunate collateral damage in a mission otherwise successfully carried out. The US ambassador to Lalanga, while demanding an inquiry into the assassinations, in the same statement extended his government's recognition of the legitimacy of the newly self-installed President Nimwe, who conveniently was not planning to nationalize the oil industry.

"If Nimwe's picture on the Parliament building is supposed to send some kind of message to the people," Cooper commented, "the people expected more." He recalled the crowd's exuberance when the lights suddenly illuminated the Parliament building, and added, "They certainly were hoping for more."

"People usually get the government they deserve," Sam Brown replied flatly.

"What if they don't have a choice?"

"They create those circumstances for themselves too."

Cooper wondered if the CIA man thought Sadiq got what he deserved, or did he think in personal terms? Did people matter in his geopolitical wagers? Could he ever admit that the boy made a mistake too common for him to have died for it? He'd fallen in love, and infatuated with Munir had come under his misguided influence. It was no more a mistake than Cooper's falling in love with his CO. They'd both been taken advantage of, and he saw that now.

"You're lucky the foreign affairs minister pulled the colonel out front," he remarked. "I wouldn't have had a shot otherwise."

"We weren't sure if he'd be able to pull it off."

"It was planned?" Though not much would have surprised Cooper, that did.

"It was an active contingency," the CIA man informed him.

"What's he get out of it if his tribe's out of power?"

"A green card and a job at the UN in New York."

"So in comes Nimwe, who declares no nationalization of the oil industry and lets in the Americans. Is that the idea?"

"Something like that."

"He has American rifles, and that's not coincidental."

"That's right."

"And the secretary? Was that planned? Or no," Cooper realized, "it couldn't have been, unless you were in cahoots with Munir as well." Suddenly anything seemed possible, and he asked, "Were you?"

"No. Catching him was a lucky break."

"You didn't exactly catch him."

"You're right," Sam Brown agreed, "we got luckier. We killed him."

Sam Brown explained how Munir had been on a watch-list for some time, and like Cooper, he'd conveniently dropped into Lalanga's—and more specifically the CIA man's—lucky lap. Munir recruited Sadiq into his terrorist network in Beirut, preying on his naivety and confused sexuality, and convincing him that for men like them with deviant desires, their only salvation was through martyrdom, and while Sadiq himself wasn't on a suicide mission, his task was to support those who were by using diamonds to launder terrorist funds. He'd returned to Langatown to put their scheme into play, and Munir had come with him to ensure that Sadiq's commitment didn't flag. He'd wanted Sadiq to become too ensnared in the plot to quit. The beauty of the plan was its simplicity. It could be scaled up gradually in a business that was secretive to start with, everybody along the way would get rich, and it could be done right under Mazen's unsuspicious nose.

"And you learned all of that by eavesdropping at the hammam?" Cooper asked.

"It's where I filled in a lot of the details."

"Are you running the country now?"

"Me? No. Nimwe is."

"I meant 'you' Langley."

"We're advisors."

"I'll bet you are."

Sam Brown eventually had to abandon the waterfront for Langatown's narrow lanes. Broken crates, empty boxes, and shattered glass added to the challenge of navigating the already pockmarked streets. Coming around a bend, they nearly had a head-on collision with a pickup truck careening down the road. The soldiers in its back were still celebrating their victory by firing their rifles into the air. For everyone else they passed, the celebration was clearly over. No one was dancing in the streets. As their embassy car approached, the women who dared be outside doing their endless chores still glanced protectively for their menfolk and children, and occasionally a man could be seen loping off on his Elongated legs. It was their turn to hide.

Cooper had never been in a car on Cowboy Mile, and it felt odd to be insulated from the girls in their doorways shamelessly coming onto johns. He missed their banter. He wanted them to be kidding him about his Little Sister instead of imagining what they were really saying. Lulay and Ayana too were staring at the working girls in the doorways, no doubt picturing themselves there and hoping they'd escaped that life but probably expecting a double-cross.

Cooper turned and asked Lulay, "Are you sure you want to do this?"

"It's my picture!" she responded defiantly.

Sam Brown pulled up to The Mining Pan, and they all got out and gathered outside the saloon doors.

"I'm not letting you go in there alone," Cooper said.

"Juma don't want me no more," Lulay replied, "I'm too full of ideas now."

Over the top of the swinging doors, Cooper could see Juma wiping down the counter. Except for a cluster of working girls at the bar, the place was nearly deserted; so quiet, in fact, that Cooper could hear the wheezing ice machine on the street.

Lulay shoved a small cardboard box into Cooper's hands. "You hold on to this," she ordered, and unclasping Ayana's hands from her arm, stuck them to Cooper's thigh. "Don't you lose my Little Sister."

Then Lulay sent the saloon doors flapping and crossed the bar headed straight for the beaded curtain. Juma stopped wiping down the bar when she disappeared behind it. Keeping an eye on the barman, Cooper examined the cardboard box. On its side Lulay had written *Makes men bigger,* and inside were some four dozen condoms slipping around in their slick little packets. She was taking them back to her village, where she planned to teach some lessons. Earlier that day, at her insistence they'd stopped at the pharmacy, where she cajoled Sam Brown into buying every condom in stock. The missus nearly fainted as her pharmacist husband counted them out while grinning ear-to-ear.

"It's something, huh?" Cooper remarked, and proudly showed Sam Brown the box again.

"How's she going to get refills?"

"Lulay'll find a way, if there is one."

"She's a cute kid," the CIA man acknowledged. "They're both cute kids. I hope they come out of this okay. The medic said they would need to wait three months to be tested for—"

"I know." Cooper stopped him. He didn't want to hear the word.

The ice machine was definitely working. Cooper could still hear it, and Juma certainly wasn't scrimping on the ice, filling a very tall glass with it. "Why don't you arrest him if you know he's trafficking in people?"

"It's not my jurisdiction," Sam Brown answered.

"How about talking to your buddies in the new government?"

"They would need to pass a law first, and that's not likely to happen any time soon." Sam Brown indicated the man to whom Juma was serving the tall cocktail. "That's one of their top officials over there, enjoying his spoils of war."

Definitely a member of the Stubby Tribe, the man was barely the height of the bar and hidden by a couple of very tall girls, which is why Cooper hadn't noticed him.

Lulay reappeared in a splash of beads and aimed straight for the door. Juma had a glass of ice water ready and held it out for her as if she'd been johning. He rattled the ice, smirking and drawing attention to her.

She ignored him, but Cooper couldn't. "Hold this," he said, and pushed the cardboard box into Sam Brown's hands, in the same instant snatching his gun from his shoulder holster.

"Hey!" the CIA man protested, but Cooper was already through the saloon doors.

Juma made a move for his gun, and Cooper warned him, "Don't even think about it."

"What are you doing, Cooper?" Lulay asked, scared for him, and fearful that he might ruin her chance to escape.

"Get outside!" he ordered the girl while motioning for Juma to move farther away from his gun. Cooper would've been glad to blow his fucking head off, but he didn't want to ruin Lulay's chance to escape.

The ice machine was the only sound to be heard, and Cooper swung on it, pumping several rounds into it before it died with a fatal rattle. "The ice machine is broken," he announced, and walked back outside, sending those saloon doors flapping for the last time.

Lulay immediately accosted him. "Why you do such a crazy thing?"

He spun around, wanting to make sure no one was following him out. The Stubby official was back speaking into the working girls' navels, and Juma was crossing to the jukebox.

Sam Brown was none too happy when Cooper came back out and handed him his gun. "Are you done making your point?" he asked.

The music started up. It was a cha-cha-cha.

Cooper asked Lulay, "Are you ready to go home-home now?" Her smile was so big that he said to Ayana, "I bet you can hear *that* smile."

That made the little girl grin, and she said, "You can't hear a smile."

Cooper told Lulay, "With all your teaching, don't forget to teach your Little Sister about smiles."

"I don't want you to forget me, Cooper," Lulay said.

"It's not even remotely possible."

She pressed the photograph of her mother into his hand. "I'm planning to look like my mother, so when you look at her, you'll be looking at me too."

"I can't take your only picture," Cooper protested.

"It's already in your hand."

"Are you going to come visit Lulay, Mr. Cooper?" Ayana asked.

"Someday. I hope someday."

"Is that a Cooper promise?" Lulay wondered.

"I hope so."

When she looked so disappointed, he said, "Yes. Yes, it's a Cooper promise."

Lulay started to cry, which made Cooper tear up, and Ayana held out her little arms and embraced them both. His open palm almost covered the littler one's back, and he gave her an extra-hard hug, wondering when she would get another hug from a kind man. He had no idea what the future held for either girl, or for himself for that matter, but for them it would be better than their immediate past. How could it not be?

When they pulled apart, Lulay kissed her fingers and pressed them to his forehead. "You're going to be okay," she said.

Cooper snorted. He figured he just might be.

She took Ayana's hand. "Come on, Little Sister, we're going home-home."

"At least let me drive you to the edge of town," Sam Brown offered half-heartedly.

Lulay fixed them both with her eye. "I'm taking back every step they stole from me, and when I get home, I'm taking back what the maribout stole from me too. That way, nobody's got a part of me and nobody can try to make Lulay disappear again." She retrieved the box from Cooper. "I don't know if I got the skinny-skinny, but you protected me. I'm still here."

The girls, holding hands, started down the street.

"I guess she told us," Sam Brown remarked.

"She's tough."

"Are they really sisters? I never asked."

Cooper didn't have to think about it. He knew a real sister when he saw one, and replied, "Yeah, they're really sisters."

The girls came to a corner where they were going to turn and be out of sight. Lulay looked back, and with her biggest voice she let him know,

"That was a Cooper promise!"

And then they were gone.

A man followed them around the corner, and Cooper asked, "Is that your man?"

"Yep."

"You sure you've got someone following them all the way?"

"Until they get home-home. For the next three days, there are no safer two girls in Africa."

Cooper thought about the girls' journey home and what home meant as best as he could envision it. Whatever it meant, he was glad he'd helped them get there.

"What about you, Sergeant Chance?" Sam Brown asked, breaking into his thoughts. "Are you ready to go home-home?"

Cooper had only one question. "No brig time?"

"No brig time."

He didn't have to think about it again. "Yeah," Cooper Chance said, "I'm ready to go home-home."

Author's Note

The United Nations estimates that there are between twenty-four and twenty-six million slaves in the world today. An estimated seven-hundred fifty thousand young women, men, and children are trafficked cross-border each year, and an equal number are trafficked within their own countries. While some become forced laborers, most are sex slaves who have either been sold by unwitting parents into servitude or have been tricked with the promise of a job only to find themselves as indentured prostitutes, held against their will by threats of retribution against their families should they attempt to escape.

The grisly civil wars that have brought to ruin many African countries—Sierra Leone, Liberia, Angola, and the Democratic Republic of the Congo, to name only a few—have been financed by "blood diamonds." Rebels and governments fight for control of diamond mines to sell the rough stones to buy weapons. More recently, blood diamonds, which represent some 5 percent of the world's diamond trade, have been linked to money laundering by al-Qaeda and other international terrorists. The control of the diamond mines is achieved and maintained by some of the most brutal actions possible—slaughter, amputations, and rape. Children are frequently the victims.

Cooper's Promise takes place in the fictitious African country of Lalanga, but the conditions that prevail are not fictitious. Sadly, they are all too real in too many places.

TJS

Acknowledgments

Every book draws on the experiences of a lifetime. It would be impossible to recount all the many people, places, and events that contributed in big and small ways to *Cooper's Promise*. Some date to my childhood.

My research for the novel took me from the brothels of West Africa to the diamond district in Antwerp. Along the way I met the many characters who people Cooper's world: diamond cops and dealers, trafficked women, pirate barmen, mercenaries, arms smugglers, and CIA agents. My thanks to everyone who contributed in any manner.

I would especially like to thank the many friends who have read and reread my manuscripts over the years and encouraged me to continue writing.

Of course, I am especially thankful to my partner, Michael Honegger, for his encouragement, patience, insights, and inspiration.

About the Author

Raised crisscrossing America pulling a small green trailer behind the family car, Timothy Jay Smith developed a ceaseless wanderlust that has taken him around the world many times. En route he's found the characters who people his work, including Polish cops and Greek fishermen, mercenaries and arms dealers, child prostitutes and wannabe terrorists. He's hung with them all in an unparalleled international career that's seen him smuggle banned plays from behind the Iron Curtain, maneuver through war zones and Occupied Territories, represent the United States at the highest levels of foreign governments, and stowed away aboard a "devil's barge" for a three-day ocean crossing that landed him in an African jail.

Tim's first novel won the 2008 Paris Prize for Fiction, and his first play, staged successfully in New York City, won the prestigious Stanley Drama Award. He's won numerous screenwriting awards, including taking the grand prize in several international competitions for his screenplay adaptation of *Cooper's Promise*. He is the founder of the entertainment company Kosmos Films and the executive producer of an award-winning web-based comedy series.

Tim and his partner split their time between Paris, Greece, and Miami Beach. Learn more about Tim's writing at www.timothyjaysmith.com.